DIRTY MONEY

PRAISE FOR THE MCKAY THRILLERS

"Soak it up! I love a taut plot, meaty details, and stone-scary heavies, all of which Hughes delivers express. But most of all I feed on language—crisp, alive, and juicy. From a kicked knee that pings like the last kernel in a hot-air popper, to the hero's *haute cuisine,* an Italian beef sandwich, doughy, soaked, slathered, with bright, deadly-hot peppers, Dirty Money is scrumptious crime fiction *au jus*!"

> —Arthur Plotnik, author of *The Elements of Expression* and other language bestsellers

"Bone Mountain is a damn good book!"

> —Doug Peacock, author of *Grizzly Years: In Search of the American Wilderness*

"Big sky, big bones, and big story—Robert D. Hughes' fast-paced debut mystery has it all."

> —Michael Bracken, author of *All White Girls*

"Bone Mountain is a hella fast-paced high plains thriller."

> —Elwood Reid, Executive Producer of the hit Showtime series, *The Chi*

DIRTY MONEY

A Brian and Darcy McKay Novel

Robert D. Hughes

C J KEENAN Publishing

For Mary Jane Corrigan and Dave Hayes, fellow writers and friends who make my writing better

Thieves respect property. They merely wish the property to become their property that they may more perfectly respect it.

—G.K. Chesterton, *The Man Who was Thursday*

1

Matthew Growney had only a few minutes to live, but he didn't know it yet. In the darkness of the luxurious 47th floor office, the lanky twenty-five year old accountant tapped keys and gazed at the computer monitor providing the only light in the room. He was tense, focused. Hunched over the keyboard with his thin shoulders nearly level with his ears, he cast a nervous glance at the doorway. Had he heard a noise from the hall? Who else would be in the office at three on a Sunday morning?

A sudden creak from the outside wall startled him. He twitched and swung his head around. There wouldn't be window washers on a precarious platform hanging on tracks outside the building at this ungodly hour. He listened intently for another moment. Nothing. He shrugged. Must have been the massive high-rise swaying in the Chicago wind—he knew these buildings were designed to flex several inches near the top when the winds blew strong. You noticed it on the upper floors.

He'd better hustle it up though, find the data and get the hell out. If the office's rightful occupant caught him in there, he could kiss his job goodbye. It had been a long trial and error process figuring out the password. He'd accessed dozens of folders on the hard drive and finally hit on a tantalizing file about invoicing special sales, when one of the uniformed guards had strolled through an hour ago. He'd fed the guy a bullshit story about going to New York the next day and needing to get some reports off the boss's computer before he left town. The older man had asked for ID and still seemed skeptical as he departed. No way the guy believed he was there with the knowledge of the person assigned to that office, an individual a lot older and a few levels up the chain of command. Would the guard call the guy? Nah, he wouldn't want to take heat for waking him up.

Matthew had been in this particular office only once before, a two-minute welcome-to-the-company chat the day he'd started work at Belcoe Inc. He knew the night guards patrolled every three hours, give or take, and he wanted to be gone when the uniformed man returned. He'd taken enough chances already. The keycard system down in the lobby would have a record of when he checked in and out of the building, if anyone wanted to investigate. Plus the lobby guard might remember him. And the program he was now using without permission would indicate the date and time files were last accessed. But then, how likely was it that the authorized user of the machine would notice? He clicked the mouse to print the current doc and three pages began to hiss from the printer on the rosewood credenza behind him. Then he saved the Excel file to a tiny flash drive and tucked it into a front jeans pocket.

He glanced at the framed photograph on the desktop to the left of the monitor: the man, his pretty wife and a couple of smiling kids, a boy and a girl. A sleek Lexus sedan from the early 2000s was in the background. So the picture must have been taken fifteen years or so in the past.

Matthew's thoughts drifted to his girlfriend, Darcy. He was supposed to meet her for brunch in a few hours. She'd be asleep now, unless she was in night owl mode, studying physics or some other heavy-duty course she was taking at U of I. She'd confided that she planned to go on to paleontology in grad school. He considered giving her a call, thought better of it.

As Matthew was retrieving the pages from the printer, the door squeaked open behind him. He felt his heart quicken as he swiveled around in the heavily padded chair. A person barely visible in the gloom entered and regarded him silently in the glow of the monitor screen. An arm came up, holding a stubby object in a gloved hand. At first, he thought he was being offered something and, by reflex, he started to raise a hand to accept it. The individual took a step closer. Now, Matthew could make out a familiar face and the thing in the extended hand, something square, dark—a handgun.

The person pointed the gun at Matthew's forehead. The young accountant thought back to countless scenes of close-range shootings he'd seen in movies. He imagined his head snapping back as it exploded in a red mist. How could this be happening? Sure, he shouldn't be spying on someone else's computer files, but why would—

"Out of the chair. Lie face-down on the floor mat."

"Hey, wait a minute. I'm not—"

"Shut the fuck up. Get down there. Now!"

Matthew's legs felt rubbery as he slowly rose from the desk chair. He went to a pushup position, and then eased himself down until his chin rested on the hard plastic mat beneath the chair's casters. He was between the chair and the desk. He considered moving further under the desk, but what would that buy him?

The gunman stepped closer. Matthew's eyes were only inches from new-looking dark-rinse jeans over brown leather loafers. For an instant, he considered striking like a rattlesnake, taking a bite out of the nearest leg. The thought fled when a hard object pressed against the side of his head above his right ear. Instinctively, Matthew jerked his head sideways and brought up his right arm, as if he might slap the gun away. He thought he heard a click, but couldn't be certain. Then a sharp cracking noise and a sudden burst of excruciating pain. The world exploded into white, then pitch black, and finally, nothing.

The man approached Matthew, stripped off his latex gloves, and grasped a wrist between thumb and finger. Satisfied there was no pulse, the shooter stood and regarded the motionless body. He noted with satisfaction that there was no blood spatter on the protective floor mat or on the surrounding soft gray carpet. That meant the small-caliber bullet was still inside the cranium. He picked up the fan of freshly printed pages from the floor, where they'd ended up when they slipped from Growney's hand, and scanned them quickly. He walked down the hall to the nearest shredder and ran the pages through. Then he returned to the office to take care of the dead body on the floor.

2

Darcy McKay lounged on the couch in her North Side apartment, her MacBook propped against her thighs, a cup of chai tea on the small coffee table within easy reach of her right hand. She read from dense text on the laptop screen, a digital textbook on organic chemistry. Working on her junior year coursework in Biological Sciences at the University of Illinois Chicago campus. Final exams would be coming up soon. She had to be ready. A straight A student, she knew that now was no time to let up. Thoughts of graduate school admission hurdles were always in the back of her mind.

Her thoughts strayed to the previous summer, when she'd worked on a dinosaur dig in Montana, assisting on the excavation of the world's first intact *T. rex* skeleton. A brutal thug had unleashed a campaign of lethal violence aimed at people on the dig, including Darcy, who'd been shot and kidnapped. She and her uncle, former FBI agent Brian McKay, had outsmarted the thug and his co-conspirators, solving the crimes and helping to launch a new world class dinosaur museum dedicated to supporting the people of the impoverished local Crow Nation.

College biology seemed tame by comparison. Yet, the BS degree she was pursuing would be a necessary step toward her goal of becoming a topflight paleontologist. All her life, she'd been a keen student of all things dinosaur. In her reverie, she could picture the headline in the New York Times: "Noted paleontologist Darcy McKay discovers world's largest known predatory dinosaur, *McKayus Giganticus*." She had recently been considering a Masters program in organismal biology with research in vertebrate paleontology, at the University of Chicago. She was considering another option as well. Possibly a life in the Rockies? Montana State University in Bozeman seemed like a good possibility. MSU had a Masters curriculum in earth sciences, with possible concentration in vertebrate paleontology. Darcy knew that most recent discoveries of *T. rex* specimens had been in the Mesozoic bone beds of Montana. For an ambitious paleontologist, being close to the action would be an advantage. In any case, grad school applications would be due next January, so she had a few months to decide.

Since returning from Montana, Darcy had kept in touch with her tent-mate on the Bone Mountain dig, a young woman named Becky Stanton. Becky was now in her junior year at Montana State. Like Darcy, she planned on a career in paleontology. Becky had decided to apply for that earth sciences graduate program at MSU. She raved about the courses she was taking as an undergrad, things like Macroevolution & the Fossil Record. This got Darcy thinking more intensely about studying in Montana, where the dinosaur country was within day-trip distance…

Darcy was on a full scholarship to the U of I as a varsity softball player. The current season would end soon, shortly after finals. She enjoyed the camaraderie with her teammates and the physical rush of making a good play in front of cheering fans, but, as she'd confided to Becky, she planned to leave the team after her junior year to free up more time for her studies. Being a jock required a huge time commitment. Her skills with a bat had come in handy though, last summer, when she'd belted a kidnapper with a steel closet rod, knocking him senseless.

She needed to get through the chapter in front of her to be ready for her genetics lab early tomorrow morning. She returned to her reading, occasionally highlighting a passage with her track pad for later review. Her thoughts strayed away from the text again. She would be meeting her boyfriend Matthew Growney for brunch in a little while. This had become a Sunday morning custom for them. Today should be a special treat, dining at the Art Institute's Museum Café, followed by a stroll through the new *Impressionists of France* exhibit. She'd been dating Matthew off and on since the previous summer. As she'd confided to her friend Natalie Katz, they weren't exactly a serious couple, but it could be going in that direction. She glanced down at her frayed jeans and bare feet. She'd better get dressed up a little. She didn't want to give the impression of taking anything for granted with the developing relationship. But a little studied carelessness might be good. As with everything else going on in her life, striking a balance was always the challenge.

3

Brian McKay sipped from a mug of powerful black coffee as he paged through the front section of the bulky Sunday edition of the Chicago Tribune. The old school hard copy version was a weekly indulgence; he normally perused the daily Trib on his iPad. He'd already read the sports and business sections and discarded the countless pages of real estate ads. It was quiet in his North Side apartment, while outside, the wind squalled, sweeping the barren elm and honey locust limbs back and forth near the living room window. He'd slept in, caught part of the local news on TV, drunk nearly a carafe of coffee and still felt slightly hung over.

He and his girlfriend, Michelle Emerson, had been out until the wee hours and he'd not gotten home until nearly dawn. Michelle was a partner in a major Chicago law firm. She worked galley slave hours for top-tier compensation. At the same time, Brian had his own rigorous work schedule since breaking free of the FBI and starting his investigative practice the year before. He'd recently obtained his Illinois Private Detective license. His investigations business had taken off since he'd returned from the Bone Mountain dinosaur dig case in Montana five months ago, and he was working nearly fulltime. He was now making almost as much income as he had as a veteran Special Agent with the FBI. Lately, his and

Michelle's conflicting schedules meant they got together less and less frequently. Maybe not a good sign for their relationship, he thought.

He considered fixing himself a fried egg sandwich, but that would mean leaving the couch. Maybe later. It was a perfect day for unwinding. Maybe the Bulls game would be on TV.

He wanted to get out to Montana sometime that spring, before the tourist season started. The inviting little western town of Clarkville beckoned. Nearby, the snowy peaks of the Absaroka and Crazy mountain ranges towered over the local river valleys. Trout fishing would soon be starting up in the high country as rivers and lakes de-iced after a long frigid winter. Plus, he'd promised to visit Jerry, the thirteen-year-old son of Laura Jensen, the sheriff's deputy who'd been slain as she worked with Brian and Darcy on the murders at the dinosaur dig. He wondered how the boy was holding up.

His phone sounded off with his ringtone: CCR's "Bad Moon Rising." He considered letting it go, sighed and glanced at the display before picking up.

"Brian. Jesus, I'm glad you're there." His niece, Darcy, sounding wired.

"What's happening, kiddo?"

"Look, I hate to hassle you, but I need help."

"Sure, long as we're not talking dinosaurs."

"Actually, this involves Matthew," she said. "We were on for brunch this morning at the Art Institute, then the Impressionists exhibit. Kind of a big deal—we planned it last week. Anyway, I chilled on the front steps 'til noon, but he didn't show."

"Hey, I've been stood up, myself."

"But listen, I keep getting his voicemail when I call, and he's not answering my texts, which is totally bananas."

"Maybe he's not feeling well and he—"

"No way. Look, I, uh, have a key to his place, so I went over there a little while ago, and he wasn't around. The bed was made and his briefcase was missing, which means he must have gone to the office. I called his work phone. No answer."

"So *you* went to the office?"

"Yeah. Just got back. Here's the weird thing. I asked the guard at the desk when Matthew checked out of the building. He looked it up in the system and then eyed me real funny and said he came in last night but still hadn't signed out. Then he tried to like brush me off. Of course, he wouldn't let me in without a company ID."

"Was the guard wearing a uniform?"

"Yes. Gray with red stripes around the jacket cuffs. And it had those epaulet things on the shoulders."

"Sounds like Sekurit. I know a guy there I could call."

"Can we like just go over there? I know you could finesse your way in. I could pick you up."

Brian sighed. "Okay. See you in a few minutes."

A short while later, the petulant bleep of a high-pitched car horn sounded outside. Brian glanced out the front window. Darcy's bright blue Ford Focus was double-parked below. He drained the last of his coffee and headed out.

As they approached One Belcoe Plaza, the quiet of the Sunday afternoon Loop was shattered. A WGN News helicopter thundered by a hundred feet above them. Sirens ululated, the shriek rising steadily in volume as they got closer to Belcoe. A Chicago Police car screamed by the Focus and took the turn onto Wabash on two wheels. They followed in its wake.

There were police vehicles on the windswept plaza surrounding the Belcoe tower, unmarked sedans and squads with blue roof lights flashing. A thin layer of snow covered the plaza. They could see uniforms standing outside the sleek green glass-clad skyscraper, others milling around in the two-story marble lobby. They left the car in a NO PARKING zone across the street and trotted to the high-rise. They noticed the garish company symbol as they neared the main entrance—the sixty-foot-high, green and gold revolving block letter "B" was about as subtle as a rhinoceros at a ballet recital. After dark, it became a neon-lit landmark.

They were met inside the revolving door by a grim-faced Chicago Police Department patrolman.

"Hold it right there, folks." The cop held up a fleshy paw like a bouncer on the red carpet stopping the unwashed from even thinking about getting in.

Brian extracted his wallet and showed his Illinois Private Detective license to the man. "We've got business here."

"That and a Ventra Card'll getcha a ride on the CTA," the cop said.

A *basso profundo* split the air. "It's okay. Let them in."

Brian spotted the Central Area Violent Crimes Section Chief strutting their way. He knew Dick Cissel—also known as the Bird Man, or just plain Bird—well. They'd grown up together in the Wrigley Field neighborhood, home of the Chicago Cubs. After high school, they'd both gotten athletic scholarships to the University of Michigan—Brian's baseball, Dick's football. They'd shared a dorm room freshman year, ended up in law enforcement careers in Chicago and bumped into each other occasionally.

"What are you doing here?"

"Fine thanks. How about yourself, Bird?"

"Cut the shit. I'm kinda busy." The big cop made a show of consulting a chunky chromed watch on his wrist.

"Look, we're interested in a young guy works for Belcoe, name of Growney."

"Why?"

"He's Darcy's friend."

The big cop looked uncomfortable. "Darcy? Oh hi, Darcy. Didn't recognize you at first. You're all grown up. Well, that friendship deal makes it different."

"We'd like to find out if Growney's still checked in here," Brian said.

Cissel regarded them soberly. "He uh, checked out."

"You mean he signed out of the building?" Darcy asked.

"No, I mean he checked out permanently. He's deceased. Sorry"

Brian glanced at Darcy. She'd gone pale as chalk. Wordlessly, she turned and walked to an angular polished granite bench just inside the building entrance. She dropped to the seat and covered her face in her hands.

There was an awkward silence as the two men regarded her for a moment.

Brian said, "What happened?"

"The kid took a small caliber slug in the head. We found him up on the roof in the HVAC room. Looks like a do-it-yourself on the surface, but..."

"But what?"

"Well, looks like the body mighta been moved after death."

"Why do you say that?"

"Pattern of the rigor. Lack of disturbance where they found him."

"What kind of wound?"

"Near-contact with stippling. Bullet lodged in the head, which is typical for the caliber."

"Shell?"

"Yeah, .25 on the ground. Matched the piece next to the kid's hand."

"They bag the hands?"

Cissel frowned. "Hey, this ain't our first rodeo."

Brian knew they'd covered the victim's hands with plastic bags to protect them from contamination until police crime lab technicians could test them. They'd attach adhesive strips to the hands and lift them off for further analysis. If they found certain metallic substances, like antimony or lead, it would indicate Growney had fired a gun recently. "Was there a note?"

"Nope."

"How about letting me have a look."

"No way."

"Well, at least tell me what went down. And I'd like your opinion as to whether it's a suicide or not."

"You know the drill. The ETs'll do their thing, we'll work up the evidence, talk to everybody in the building, all that stuff. For now, there's not a hell of a lot more I can tell ya."

"Hey, come on, Dick. How about letting me take a peek?"

"Negative. Tell you what. Maybe you could stop by and eyeball the file once this's cooled down a little. We can take it from there. Best I can do."

A pair of men wearing the white-shirted, dark pants uniform of Chicago Fire Department paramedics emerged from an elevator behind Cissel pushing a wheeled scissor-legged gurney between them. A human-sized form lay on it, wrapped in a big black plastic bag—a body bag.

They watched silently as the paramedics worked their way over to an emergency door held open by a police officer. The litter-bearers moved deliberately to a waiting fire department ambulance that had been backed up close to the door. The wheels of the gurney skidded a little in the light snow, but the men bulled ahead, hoisted the gurney and slid it inside the back of the vehicle, with the folding legs snapping upward. The doors slammed with a THUNK. One of the paramedics pulled out a cigarette and lit up. A couple of uniformed cops walked over to join them, and the four men chatted casually. No rush, plenty of time for a little break.

Darcy stood and approached Brian and Cissel, tears running down her face, a tissue held to her nostrils. She blew her nose noisily.

Cissel turned to her and said in a low voice, "Awful sorry about this, Darcy. We'll get to the bottom of it." Then, to Brian, "Look, there's not much more for you right now. Call me tomorrow afternoon. Best I can do." He shrugged his big shoulders, raised a hand in farewell and turned toward the nearby elevators.

Darcy shook her head and said, "Why? Why the hell does damn near everyone I care about have to die? What is it—a curse?"

No way to answer that one. The memory of Darcy's parents' deaths in a two-car accident on the Kennedy Expressway two years earlier was fresh in Brian's mind. He'd lost his older sister, Darcy's mom, in the crash. Some drunk had driven onto an exit ramp in the Loop, blasted into traffic going the wrong direction and plowed into the couple's sedan while doing sixty. At least it had been quick. Damn thing must still be a bleeding wound to Darcy. Everybody's afraid of death, he reflected. When someone you love dies young, it's the worst. His own parents had gone early, too. Darcy and he shared a strong bond, as they had no other living relatives. Plus, in his twelve years as an FBI agent, he'd seen it with survivors—a sense of guilt at enduring while the loved one is taken. What could make a person feel more helpless?

"I'm really sorry you had to see all this." He gestured toward the ambulance, which was now rolling slowly across the plaza toward the corner of Wabash and Wacker for the trip to the nearby city morgue.

"Don't be sorry. You didn't kill him." She pulled out a tissue and dabbed her eyes dry.

"Come on, I'll buy you a cup of coffee," he said.

They walked a block to the nearest Starbucks. After they'd picked up oversized paper cups of steaming coffee concoctions and found seats in a corner, Brian said, "Matthew was in finance, right?"

Darcy sighed. "Yeah. He worked in corporate accounting. They put together the financial statements, prepared for the audit, worked on buyouts of other companies, stuff like that."

"Must've had his hands full. Belcoe's been hot on the mergers and acquisitions trail."

She wiped at the corner of an eye, tucked the Kleenex in a jeans pocket and sighed. "Right. He told me they added seven new companies in the last quarter alone. His group's had a hard time keeping up, so he's been putting in major OT. And he said some of the stuff going on there was a little strange."

"Strange how?"

"Like what you hear about on the news. Companies stretching the truth 'til it snaps, trying to make their numbers look good. He mentioned something about offshore financing sources. I didn't understand it all, but they were apparently trying to make the balance sheet look good for the stock analysts and still keep the auditors happy."

"Was Matthew okay with this stuff?"

"Not really. He said he didn't agree with all of it, but they had to push the envelope to compete. And he said everybody else did it, too, I guess meaning other companies. Makes you wonder if business reports are worth diddly. Anyway, the auditors had to sign off. Plus, his bonus and options were tied to the stock price."

"From what I was reading in the paper this morning, Belcoe had been around forever, doing okay, nothing spectacular," Brian said. "But with this latest Chief Operating Officer, what's his name, Spurgeon, they blasted into the fast lane. Used to be mostly a metal fabrication company, now they're into electronics, defense contracts, God knows what all."

"Which is why it seemed like such a great opportunity for Matthew. I absolutely cannot believe he killed himself. No way." Her lower lip trembled. Brian expected more tears, but she regained her outward cool, staring into space.

4

At nine o'clock Monday morning, the quarterly meeting of the Belcoe Incorporated Finance Department staff was about to begin. The sliding walls on the east side of the massive Boardroom had been opened and the huge teak wood table pushed to the rear of the vast space. A theater-scale movie screen took up most of one wall. A banner hung above the screen: BELCOE: LEADING THE WORLD. Rows of chairs had been set up starting a few feet from the smoke-colored dais, at which A. Hamilton Massey, a slightly built man about six feet tall, stood eyeing the assembled group of about thirty men and women with humorless gray eyes. The Chief Financial Officer ran a hand through his helmet of close-cropped salt-and-pepper hair and arranged a smile on his narrow face.

"Welcome. We're about to get started," he said. He had a vaguely European accent, though he'd been born and raised in Indianapolis. "Today, we have a special treat: Belcoe's Chief Operating Officer, Doug Spurgeon, is going to chat with us a bit and give us his vision as to where the company's going, near-term. And I understand he's got some interesting words about stock options."

There was a low-pitched murmur of approval, which caused Massey's face to brighten a millimeter, although it didn't reach his eyes. He continued, "Meanwhile, I've got some comments—"

"Holy shit, what a crew!" A wide, barrel-chested man in a beautifully tailored gray suit had burst into the room and now race-walked to the dais, where he nearly knocked Massey over as he shouldered himself into place behind the microphone.

"Thanks, A.H. I'll take it from here," Spurgeon said. There were a few scattered chuckles at the "A.H." Massey was known to hate that nickname using the initials of his first and middle names—it was too close to "asshole," another appellation his detractors employed.

"Jesus Christ. I haven't seen this many bean-counters in one place since the IRS building caught fire." There was polite laughter. Doug Spurgeon surveyed the group, basking in their undivided attention.

"All bullshit aside, thanks for your hard work and creativity. As you all know, Belcoe's achieving its goals. We're slated to hit number twelve on the Fortune 500 list this year, up from number twenty. We've eclipsed the 150 billion dollar mark in sales. We're a phenomenal growth machine. Stock's above ninety and rising fast in a challenging market. The analysts continue to recommend us as a strong buy.

"Belcoe prides itself on being one of America's most innovative companies. And I don't just mean R & D or marketing. No sir, I mean finance as well. In fact, you guys are on the bleeding edge of innovation. Hell, you've gotta be. I don't need to tell you we've taken on a dozen acquisitions during the last six months. Yeah, I know it's been a pain in the ass, but it's Belcoe's lifeblood. And each of you benefits big-time, as do the shareholders at large, as we grow earnings." He tapped sausage-like fingers on the dais for emphasis. "M & A transactions are among the most complicated and least understood by the investing public." He paused for effect and then said, "Let's keep it that way."

The audience was silent for a beat, not sure whether Spurgeon was joking. Then Massey brayed a loud laugh, a bright smile forced onto his tanned visage. Gradually, the others joined in.

Spurgeon acknowledged the display of appreciation with a quick grin. He continued, "Like a lot of things, it's a good news-bad news deal. What do you want first? The good or the bad?"

Someone in the back piped up, "The good."

"Tough shit. I'm giving you the bad first. We anticipate another couple dozen acquisitions in the coming year. We're gonna keep on keeping on with the due diligences, the appraisals of value, the purchase accountings, the integrations of assets into our systems, all the happy horseshit that keeps you guys and gals off the streets and at your computer screens. But, here's the good news—the Board has approved my plan to haircut the strike price on all currently outstanding share options to ninety bucks. And we're not changing the vesting schedules one damn bit, so...you do the math."

Everyone in the room at that moment was well aware that the lower the strike—or "exercise"—price for a stock option, the better the chance of profit to the recipient. By lowering the strike price from a hundred a share to ninety, Spurgeon had, in effect, accelerated the timeframe for cashing out stock options and allowing current profits to be taken by the people in the room. Many thousands of dollars were at stake.

Spontaneous applause and cheers erupted. Someone yelled, "Woo woo!" Another voice cried out, "You da man!"

Spurgeon shot a cuff and peeked at his $20,000 Patek Philippe Calatrava watch. "Gotta run in a few minutes. But I've got time for some quick questions. Anyone?"

A diminutive blonde woman in a white blouse and black slacks rose. "Yes, Mr. Spurgeon. Can you tell us what happened to Matthew Growney? I worked with him a lot...and, well...did he really uh, do himself in?"

Dead silence. Then Spurgeon rubbed his temples, as if being attacked by the mother of all migraines. "You know as much as I do about that, what's been on TV and in the papers. The police said it's a suicide, so that's it. In any case, we'll miss Michael Growney, but hey, life goes on. Anything else?"

A few of the staff looked at each other in disbelief. Had the COO really referred to Matthew Growney as "Michael?"

A young man wearing a purple tie over a striped shirt stood and said, "Is it true the SEC's conducting an investigation of the company's accounting practices?"

"Yeah, that *is* true. But they won't find anything out of whack. They've got quotas, though, just like traffic cops. So, don't be surprised if you hear about some findings against us, maybe some assessment of fines. But, in the grand scheme of things, it won't amount to jack shit. Keep up the good work. I'm outta here."

Spurgeon raised a hand in farewell and exited stage left, like a guest on the Colbert show hurrying to the next interview.

Massey regained his position at the dais. "Okay, here's the planning matrix for the year-end closing and audit, subject to change, of course, as we get financials from the latest acquisitions. We'll start with U.S. entities and then go on to international." He clicked a mouse and a computer image projected onto the screen behind him as the lights dimmed. The heading on top was BELCOE FINANCIAL ORGANIZATION. An organization chart below portrayed a mind-numbingly complex multicolored spider web of interconnected companies. Massey led them through each color-coded geographic region of Belcoe's American empire: Northeast, Southeast, Midwest, Great Plains, Southwest, Mountain, Pacific. Next were the European and Middle East locations. The CFO then moved on to the timeline for the year-end closing of the books by region, and within region, by line of business—Chemicals, Telecommunications, Agribusiness, Electronics, Defense and Metal Fabrication.

Massey had an assistant hand out a loose-leaf book to each management employee, detailing assignments and deadlines for the various teams within the department. Each team leader would delegate the work to their six to ten subordinates. This was understood to be an opening salvo. The evolving plan would be updated frequently and shared on the company financial computer network.

In the rear of the room, two team leaders began a quiet conversation. Jack Wilson, the young man who'd asked about the SEC investigation, turned to the dark-haired young woman next to him, Natalie Katz. "Hey Nat," he murmured. "What say we swap a few entities? How about I give you Chemicals in trade for Electronics?"

"Not an option, Jackster. We go messing around with the assignments, I'd get creamed in the next rank and yank, and so would you." This was a reference to Belcoe's semi-annual ranking of all employees, in which the bottom ten percent were summarily fired. No one wanted to end up anywhere near the terrible ten, so competition to look good in the eyes of management was cutthroat.

"Well, anyway, think about it. What A.H. doesn't know, won't hurt him."

Massey heard the low-pitched voices and peered toward the back of the room, frowning. "Is there a question or comment?"

"Yeah," a studious-looking man wearing black-framed glasses said. "Have we shared this planning info with Kimmelman? And if not, should we?" He was referring to the independent accounting firm responsible for auditing the books—Kimmelman and Elder.

"Absolutely not," Massey responded. "I'll see that they get the information they need separately. Anything else? If not, we're adjourned."

As they filtered back to their cubes, Jack and Natalie resumed their discussion.

"What did you think of Spurgeon's remarks about Matthew?" Natalie asked.

Jack raised an eyebrow. "First of all, he didn't even get the poor guy's name right. Second, he didn't seem to give a shit."

"My take, exactly. You know, I've got a friend who was dating Matthew. I'm gonna get in touch with her and compare notes."

5

Brian wheeled his Grand Cherokee into the parking garage at One Belcoe Plaza. It was Tuesday morning, two days since he and Darcy had been in the building, when they'd observed the body of Matthew Growney being rolled out on a gurney. He was there at the urging of his friend at Sekurit Corporate Services, Rod Hamelburg, who'd let him know that Belcoe was seeking help in beefing up security in the wake of Growney's murder. Rod had arranged an interview for Brian with a high-level Belcoe exec. Although Brian's fledgling private investigation business was busy, he welcomed the opportunity to pick up a potentially high-paying contract gig with a booming Chicago business.

The Jeep's tires squealed on the rubbery surface of the ramp winding down through the employee and visitor parking. Each section sported a slogan on a billboard: The first one had foot-high letters forming the word INTELLIGENT, followed, in slightly smaller script, by: ENOUGH TO JUDGE A SOLUTION ON IT'S MERITS. But apparently not intelligent enough to realize that "its" *without* an apostrophe is the possessive form of the pronoun "it," Brian mused. Proceeding forward, he saw signs reading INNOVATIVE, RESOURCEFUL, PERSISTENT, ENTHUSIASTIC and, his personal favorite, IMPACTFUL.

Why was he really here? The Growney killing kept gnawing at him and this was a chance to look into it. Darcy had let him know she'd appreciate his help finding Matthew's killer. And Belcoe had dough to spare. A fifteen million dollar golden parachute had softened the landing for the former CEO who'd committed the sin of presiding over an unexpected quarterly operating loss two years earlier, resulting in the regime change that swept in Douglas Spurgeon.

The parking spaces were crammed with luxury cars and SUVs. Brian finally found a space and tucked the Grand Cherokee in between an Escalade and a Jaguar convertible.

He took an elevator up to the lobby. Even this leg of the journey wasn't free of corporate propaganda. A mammoth wide-screen TV above the door featured a fresh-faced young man in a tan suit who breathlessly plied the captive audience in the lift with "Belcoe Briefings." In the lower right-hand corner of the screen was the current quote for Belcoe common stock, $93.25 per share.

"Did you know that Belcoe is the world's largest provider of fabricated structural metal products to the construction industry?" Fresh Face inquired.

"Thanks for sharing," Brian said. He knew that the elevator interior was probably camera-monitored. A little insouciance never hurt.

He stepped into the main floor lobby of pale granite floors, soaring marble walls and a half dozen matte-silver steel elevator banks. Revolving doors punctuated the outer glass walls of the first level at intervals but, as he'd learned on Sunday, all were locked except the one directly in front of the security desk. Visitors coming in from either the street or the parking garage elevator were automatically funneled through a guard station with a steel gate before they could get into the building proper.

When he spotted Brian approaching, the uniformed guard at the desk put down his phone and pretended to scan an array of small TV screens mounted at an angle in front of him.

"Help you?" Pained expression.

"Yes. Brian McKay here to see Lou DeRosa."

At the mention of Belcoe's Executive Vice President, the guard's demeanor sharpened up considerably. Brian thought he might have heard the man's heels click under the counter separating them.

"Yes sir. One moment, please."

After consulting a computer screen and engaging in a brief telephone exchange, the guard said, "Cheryl Janis will be with you shortly."

"Who?"

"The assistant to the Human Resources lady, what's-her-name, Liz Wheaton."

"Whoa. I've got an appointment with DeRosa."

The guard shrugged. "Hey, I'm just passing on the word. Here, put this on." He handed Brian a laminated ID card attached to a light chain necklace. Brian looped it over his head with the ID hanging in front at chest level. The guard shot a surreptitious glance at the sports section of the newspaper at his elbow.

Brian sighed. Just then, a young woman in a short skirt came out of the nearest elevator.

The guard pressed a button and the security gate opened. Brian passed through toward the woman.

"Mr. McKay, how very nice to meet you," she gushed.

"Same here."

"Please follow me."

She turned and made her way to the furthest elevator bank.

As they rode up to the 47th floor, the annoyingly enthusiastic spokesman on the video screen welcomed them with, "Say, Belcoe's on the move. The company just opened its newest defense products plant in Norwich, England. The 200,000-square foot facility will provide state-of-the-art munitions to European allies while employing 350 U.K. nationals."

"Do you ever get tired of that stuff?" Brian said.

"Oh no," she said. "The Information Guy makes my day." But she rolled her eyes.

On 47, they went to a private office on the south side of the building. Brian's escort knocked on the open door, waved at the occupant and departed. Brian entered a nicely furnished office with a pair of south facing windows overlooking the Chicago River and the skyscrapers of the Loop.

She was a hard-eyed, tight-mouthed blonde wearing a pale gray suit. Her nails gleamed with transparent polish. Angular cobalt earrings rotated and caught the light as she stood and offered a hand. Brian noticed a large poster on the wall behind her desk, a mist-shrouded, impossibly green forest scene, with the word ATTITUDE at the bottom. He wondered what the picture had to do with the caption. Maybe Wheaton was proud of her own attitude.

"Liz Wheaton."

"Brian McKay."

She offered coffee and he accepted. She buzzed Cheryl, who came in immediately with a couple of black javas and left.

"So you're interested in coming on board, Brian?"

"Actually, I work as an independent contractor. Excuse me, but I thought I'd be meeting with Lou DeRosa."

Her eyes went flat. "Everyone goes through me."

"What exactly is your role?"

"Vice President of Human Resources." She eyed him over the edge of her cup as she sipped. "Look, Brian, let's not play games. I'm a necessary evil. Some might say just plain evil." She shrugged as if such opinions weren't worthy of further comment. "Thing is, I've got to vet you before you talk to Lou. No way around it for either of us."

Brian sighed. "Okay, what do you want to know?"

"Do you have a current resume?"

"No."

Liz Wheaton looked at him as if she'd caught a whiff of dog excrement. "You joined the FBI right out of college—right?"

They *had* been checking up on him. "Yes, right after I got my MBA. Four years in Violent Crimes and Major Thefts, then eight with the White Collar Crime unit, until last year."

"Why'd you leave?"

"Boredom. And I wanted to be on my own."

"Doing?"

"Private investigations, security consulting."

"How about a couple of references."

He gave her names and phone numbers for James St. Claire at the FBI's Chicago Field Office and Christine Pellas, a lawyer who'd been a client of Brian's the year before. James was a young agent Brian had taken under his wing. They'd worked well together, most notably, on Brian's last case with the FBI, involving black market sales of human organs, dubbed OPERATION ORGAN GRINDER. And James had helped Brian on the kidnapping of Darcy and the murders in Montana the previous year.

An assertive baritone voice from the doorway behind Brian interrupted them. "Aha! This must be Brian 'Crimestopper' McKay."

Crimestopper? Brian turned to see a tall and stout Armani-clad specimen looking like a sybaritic Mafia don from a movie enter the room. Brian rose and took the outstretched hand. As he did so, he studied the executive's face: wrinkles around the eyes, downward sloping lines flanking the nose and mouth, a slight pouch under the chin all betrayed the initial youthful impression—the guy must have been in his mid sixties, at least.

The man squeezed Brian's right hand in the standard macho bone-crusher grip. Brian squeezed back with emphasis on the soft, fleshy area between the thumb and forefinger. The aggressor tried to suppress a slight flinch and gave it up.

"Lou DeRosa. C'mon, let's go talk."

"Lou, you'll want this." Liz Wheaton handed a piece of paper with hand-written notes to DeRosa. The summary dossier on himself, Brian guessed.

As they walked through a hallway carpeted in a thick gray weave, Brian caught glimpses through doorways of people at computers or on the phone, and one iconoclast standing and staring out the window. DeRosa's corner office was commodious enough to house a racquetball court.

DeRosa shut the door behind them and headed to a corner. "Come over and check this out."

Brian joined him at a massive window facing east. Forty-seven stories below, tiny matchbox cars clogged Michigan Avenue. Ant-like pedestrians scurried between the cars. Honking horns could be heard faintly. The verdant carpet of Grant Park buffered Lake Michigan from the hard concrete city. In the distance, the eternal tranquility of the lake was a cerulean blue bowl dotted with sailboats cutting the air like fish teeth.

"Best god-damned view in the city, you ask me."

"Impressive."

"Let's take a load off over here." DeRosa gestured to the side of the aircraft carrier desk at a group of brown leather chairs, expensive ones with brass tack-heads in the edges of the upholstery. DeRosa dropped into a chair and crossed an ankle over a knee. He smoothed imaginary wrinkles from the topmost charcoal worsted pant leg as he glanced at Liz Wheaton's notes on Brian, then tossed the paper in the general direction of his desktop. It missed and settled on the floor.

"Sorry you had to endure the inquisition with the Dragon Lady. Human resources, what a turn of phrase. Company policy is everyone's gotta go through the humans. I don't agree with that crap. You're here because we've got a hell of a problem and Barry Webb wants it solved. You're also here because you're recommended. Anyway, let's get to it. We're all devastated, of course. This Growney kid—nothing like this's ever happened at Belcoe. Not even in the field." He shook his head as if contemplating the proportions of the tragedy. "Can't let this kinda thing happen and not resolve it. Blows the hell out of morale. Affects efficiency."

"I'll bet."

"You got some questions?"

"Any word from the police?"

DeRosa shrugged. "Not much. Said it looked like suicide to them."

"What about Sekurit?"

"Can't really blame those guys. They do a competent job. Probably nothing they coulda done to prevent it." He sighed.

"Any other in-house security?"

"At some of the plants and distribution facilities, sure. But not here. "

"What actually happened, as you understand it?"

DeRosa patted his shirt pocket. "I could sure use a smoke," he said. "Not allowed in the building. Funny, people kill each other in here, but we can't light up."

Brian wondered if he was stalling.

"But here's what I think," DeRosa continued. "Just my deductions, mind you. The kid was in over his head. Happens all the time in a pressure cooker like this." He gestured vaguely toward the closed door.

"Anyway, I checked the kid's file. Looked OK, but then, even here, some guys don't want to pull the plug on a marginal performer. I heard some rumors to the effect the kid didn't fit in. Worked a lot of hours, maybe just trying to keep his head out of the soup. Hey, it might have been compounded by personal problems—girl trouble, whatever." He shrugged again, causing the shoulders of his immaculately tailored suit to bunch up. He seemed to realize this, dropped his shoulders and smoothed first one side, then the other.

"So," he continued, "the cops are probably right—it's suicide. But even that's not good for our reputation."

"A man who commits suicide is like a man who longs for a gate to be opened and who cuts his throat before he reaches the gate."

"Come again?"

"Dylan Thomas." Brian had majored in English before going over to the dark side of finance. "What about the records of people who signed in and out over the weekend?"

"Just a sec." DeRosa went to his desk, opened a drawer and extracted a sheaf of pages, which he handed to Brian.

"Building uses electronic ID cards. This is a print of access over the weekend. As you can see, there were around fifty people came into the Belcoe space between five Friday afternoon and eight Monday morning. They all signed out. All employees, no visitors. Nothing ah, suggestive. You can keep that."

"Any way to bypass the sign-in process?"

"I'd think so. Lots of folks smart enough to keep their name off that list if they wanted to. But actually, being here on the weekend's kind of a badge of honor. They say Spurgeon goes over the building log to see who's been working his ass off."

"But how could you beat the login system?"

"Don't know," DeRosa said. "But it's been my experience that, whenever you've got a system to prevent something, somebody with the proper incentive's gonna find a way to beat it."

"Mine too. Is there video of the people going through security?"

DeRosa seemed startled by the question. "Don't know. Hadn't thought about that. Anyway, let's get you to work. What do you need?"

"A retainer of ten thousand dollars. I'll ask for more if I need it. I want complete access to all employees and facilities—you could provide me with a letter and put out a broadcast e-mail to that effect. I'll contact you as necessary. If

I could have a small office here to hang my hat, that'd help. I'll be in and out. And I want to see Growney's personnel file, his office and the HVAC area on the roof where they found him."

"Done. Liz's assistant can get you the file and show you around. I'll get a check, a letter and an email in the meantime." DeRosa speared a four-digit extension on his phone and murmured brief instructions.

A few minutes later, Cheryl Janis's voice came from the doorway. "Hello, Mr. McKay."

DeRosa was picking up the phone as they left.

6

Here's Matthew's associate file," Cheryl said. She handed Brian a slim manila folder.

"Thanks."

"I'll show you your office. It's on 46, next to Finance."

They took carpeted spiral stairs down a level and walked through an open area of cubicles occupied by casually dressed men and women ranging in age from twenties through gray-haired. Most were working at computer screens. The few engaged in conversation fell silent as Brian and Cheryl passed through.

He followed her to a small windowless office containing a desk with swivel chair and phone, a new pad of lined paper, a personal computer and a putty-colored four-drawer metal file cabinet.

"Kind of basic. I hope it's okay."

"Yeah, yeah, it's fine. Thanks."

After Cheryl left, Brian tossed the Matthew Growney folder onto the desk, slumped into the swivel chair and propped his elbows on the barren desktop, cupped hands supporting his jaw. What had he gotten himself into? He'd chafed at desk jockey duty with the Bureau, impatient with the bureaucratic bullshit but well enough versed in realpolitik to survive, if not thrive, in the rigid hierarchy of the nation's second-largest FBI operation. He'd always been at his best as a field agent. His specialty had been white-collar crime. He'd become expert at peeling back the layers of subterfuge cloaking illegitimate activities in large organizations.

Brian grabbed the small corporate phone book. He placed his list of the 50 office visitors over the weekend on the desk next to the phone book and began to methodically look up each visitor's name in the directory. The Controller, Dan Nitrick, had been in and out on Saturday. The Director of Corporate Audit, a woman named Karen Sexton, spent a couple of hours in the office. Most of them were from the Finance department. Not unusual for March—they'd be working on the year-end P & L results. Belcoe was on a February 28th fiscal year-end. Brian noted the titles and phone extensions of the various visitors next to their names on the Saturday check-in list.

He then looked up a few people by department and title in the phone book. Next, Brian breezed through the slim personnel file on Growney, wondering whether it had been edited before being turned over. There was a job application indicating Growney had graduated from the highly regarded University of Chicago MBA program with high honors three years earlier, and then had taken a Financial Analyst position at Belcoe. The only other items in the file were annual Performance Evaluation forms which all rated Growney "outstanding." He'd already been promoted twice and held the title Senior Financial Services Coordinator when he'd died at the age of twenty-five.

Brian picked up the phone and called his friend James St. Claire at the FBI's Chicago Field Office.

"Special Agent St. Claire."

"I'm glad you finally learned how to answer the phone. Got time for dinner after work?"

"Sure."

"How about that new Brazilian steak place on Rush around six?"

"See ya there."

Brian grinned as he hung up. James had grown up at the now-demolished Cabrini Green, one of the most crime-ridden subsidized housing developments in the United States. He had been guided by the firm hand of an education-conscious grandmother who'd refused to let him settle for anything less than the honor roll. The young agent was the first in his family to graduate from college. His job with the FBI made him the pride of the St. Claire clan.

Brian examined his surroundings. No artwork on the off-white walls. Nothing in the desk except office supplies. Empty file cabinet drawers. A hard plastic carpet shield under the swivel chair extended beneath the desk to the spot where one's feet extended while sitting.

He switched on the computer. The start screen displayed the usual assortment of Windows programs—WORD, Excel, Outlook, PowerPoint, and Publisher. He set up an ID and password. There were no e-mail messages for him. He scanned the directories of the hard drive for data files and found none.

The freight car in the elevator for the HVAC room atop the office tower was a far cry from the posh one Brian had been in earlier. Soiled pale green quilted blankets protected the walls. The floor was a mess of dark stains and the air smelled oily. But it wasn't all bad—no on-screen Information Guy.

The car lurched to a stop. He stepped out into a huge room full of stout concrete pillars supporting a low ceiling, fabricated metal boxes, fan housings, ductwork and, in the center, an open office area. A short, stocky man in a gray work uniform occupied the steel desk. A fringe of dark hair encircled his head like a laurel wreath. He was the sole visible occupant of the floor. The whoosh of air conditioning compressors reminded Brian of the unceasing din of jets taking off at O'Hare International Airport.

A dozen small computer monitors were arrayed in front of the man. He had a headset clamped over his ears and he bopped his head a little in time to silent music.

He was obviously unaware of Brian's presence until he caught a glimpse of the visitor reflected in one of the screens before him. He snatched the headset off and swiveled in his chair as Brian drew near. An embroidered nametag above his shirt pocket read, "Koslowski."

He studied the visitor's pass attached to Brian's shirt with cautious eyes. "Hello?"

"Brian McKay."

"What can I do for you?"

"You can help me by answering some questions."

"You guys already asked me a thousand questions. I mean, I don't know nuthin' else."

"Just doing my job."

"I wasn't here when it happened."

"When what happened?"

"When that kid got, uh, iced." Another television cop show fan.

"What makes you think that's what I'm here for?"

"What the hell else would it be?" The man raised upturned hands next to his shoulders. "I mean, nobody asks me questions. They just give me complaints like, 'It's a sauna on 45,' or, 'We're freezing our asses in Marketing.'"

"You're the guy found the body?"

"Yeah. It was kinda hard to miss, layin' there." He gestured to a corner.

"How about showing me?"

Brian followed Koslowski to a shadowed space next to a stack of cardboard boxes bearing the name of a heating parts manufacturer. There was a faint residue of stickum where masking tape had been affixed to the concrete floor in the rough shape of a human form and then removed. They looked at the barely visible outline in silence for a moment, like people at a graveside who'd hardly known the deceased.

"Tell me what you saw."

"This young guy's layin' facedown with blood seepin' out a hole in his head. He's got a dinky little gun in his right hand, one a them automatics. I check for a pulse, but there's nuthin' so I call the guy at the desk in the lobby. He calls the cops, who come up here and treat me like I'm a friggin' suspect. Fuckers keep me here all night, askin' the same questions over and over, 'til I'm so fuckin' sick of the shit, I 'bout blow my top. I tell 'em the same thing I just told you. That's it, everything I know. End of story."

"How much blood was there on the head?"

"Not much. About like if you cut your finger. I guess it musta been small-caliber, like the piece the kid was holdin'."

"You ever watch NCIS."

"Oh, yeah. It's like my favorite show."

"So you probably have some idea about forensics and so forth?"

Koslowski grinned sheepishly, as if he weren't sure whether he was being kidded. "Well, I don't know. Maybe a little."

"Notice anything funny about the crime scene?"

He squinted into the near distance, as if concentrating on competing theories of forensic evidence. "Okay, yeah. I couldn't smell gunpowder. Struck me as a little strange, considering this place is prob'ly the only room in the building with shitty ventilation. It's kind of, what's the word?"

"Ironic?"

"Yeah. Also, the blood was real neat. No uh, spatter."

Brian walked Koslowski through the whole scene. He'd arrived at work at seven a.m. Monday. The HVAC room was unmanned on the weekend and at night. If there were an emergency during off-hours, they could call him at home. There was a combination lock for access to the room. He'd never met Growney. The police had performed all sorts of procedures, photographing, fingerprinting, measuring, taking samples, putting plastic bags over the hands and feet, before putting the corpse into a black bag, loading it onto a gurney and wheeling it to the service lift. They hadn't told him a damn thing except *not* to wash the floor. He'd been happy as hell when they finally let him get to work.

"If you think of anything else, how about calling me. I'm on extension 4623."

"Don't tell me you work here."

"Nah, I just hold down a desk, same as you."

Koslowski smiled and gave him a thumbs-up. Just two guys making a buck without busting their asses.

When Brian returned to his office, a red light was blinking on the desk phone. He picked up and retrieved the message.

"Hey, Bri. You're set up to see Doctor Akbar at two. Good luck." Liz Wheaton's smug voice.

He consulted the office directory and got Wheaton on the line. "Who's Doctor Akbar?"

"In-house shrink."

"But I'm an independent contractor, here for a limited gig."

"Still required."

"Where's this guy hang out?"

"On 46, southwest corner."

"So what do I do, look at ink blots and tell him what they mean?"

"Actually, it's more of an interview, plus there's a written test. Anyway, we all went through it. We just need to know you're crazy enough to uh, gig here."

"What I figured."

7

While Brian was meeting with Doctor Akbar at the Belcoe headquarters in Chicago, Jerry Jensen sat at the small desk in his bedroom in Clarkville, Montana, composing a letter to Brian on his laptop. Since the murder of his mother, sheriff's deputy Laura Jensen, the year before, he'd been living with his Aunt Carol. At first, his grandparents, Herm and Melinda Jensen, had taken charge of Jerry, but they were not used to having a thirteen-year-old boy under their roof full time, and it was an uneasy alliance between the generations.

Carol, Laura's younger sister, had insisted that Jerry stay with her, and everyone involved readily agreed. Only fourteen years separated aunt and nephew, and she was pretty cool for an older woman, in Jerry's view. Her career as a small town banker afforded her a decent income and regular hours. She worked for the First Intermountain Bank, specializing in loans for growing businesses as well as home and ranch mortgages. This specialty meant she was plugged into the local business network and pending real estate activity in this ever more popular haven for big money investors and second homes in the mountains. Her three-bedroom bungalow near downtown Clarkville worked well for the two inhabitants. Carol did the cooking, Jerry took care of most maintenance chores and they each had a modicum of privacy from the other.

Carol dated but wasn't in a serious relationship. She liked it that way.

Jerry had met former FBI agent Brian McKay the previous summer when Brian came out to Montana searching for his niece, Darcy, who'd been kidnapped from the nearby dinosaur dig at Bone Mountain. Jerry's Mom, Laura Jensen had contributed in a big way to identifying the murderous thug behind the snatching of Darcy, but then Laura had been killed by the perp. Cast adrift, Jerry had endured a tough recovery over the past months. Truth was, he still had nightmares about his Mom's death. The other kids in his class treated him as though he had some kind of disease, as if they felt sorry for him and didn't want to get too close. When he walked into the cafeteria, conversations stopped. He'd learned to be alone a lot. His friendship with David Big Hair was largely conducted away from the confines of the school. They texted almost every day and met up outdoors, mainly to fish, hike or just goof around. Jerry had never known his dad, who'd deserted the family shortly after Laura became pregnant with him.

Jerry grew closer to his aunt, and they interacted almost like siblings. Jerry was OCD about the idea of Brian McKay returning to visit them. Maybe he'd even stay with them at his Aunt's house. Before he left Montana last fall, Brian had promised to visit Jerry, to go flyfishing with him. But he hadn't gotten in touch. Carol suggested Jerry write a real old-school letter to Brian, inviting him to come out and visit them. Jerry thought a text or possibly an email would suffice, but Carol was adamant. Jerry reluctantly agreed and began to compose his letter on a chilly March day after school:

Dear Brian,

I hope you remember me from last summer. You borrowed my mountain bike to go for a ride at Bone Mountain with my Mom. She said you and her were becoming good friends. I guess it wasn't meant to be, though. I stayed with my grandparents here in Clarkville for a couple of months, but now I'm living with my Aunt Carol, my Mom's younger sister. She's pretty cool. I'll be in the ninth grade this fall.

I remember you were in the FBI. My Aunt said she heard you were a detective now. Are you a private eye? There must be a lot of business for you in Chicago. There's not so much crime here in Clarkville. Mostly just guys fighting or getting drunk and doing stupid stuff. Last week, our next-door neighbors got smashed and started throwing stuff at each other. The woman fired a .22 at the man but missed him. The police took her away but she came back the next day and everything's back to normal. Maybe I'll join up with the sheriffs after high school. Mom always said it was a good kind of work, being useful to everybody, and I think she was right.

Anyway, when are you planning on coming out to see me? I can show you a kickass stream full of cutthroat. We could ride mountain bikes to it. My best friend is a Crow Indian guy in my class named David Big Hair. Kids tease him all the time about his name and just about everything else. He's what you might call an 'outsider.' I guess I'm one too. David and me go fishing a lot. He keeps his fish for his family, because his Dad can't work on account of having diabetes. I write for the school e-newspaper. Maybe you could give me some Chicago crime material to write about.

I'll have time to show you around. You could stay here with me and Aunt Carol, so it would save you the price of a hotel room. Besides, that Master's place you stayed at last year is kind of a dump. They're trying to convert some of the rooms into working space for weirdos like artists and writers.

Anyway, let me know what you think.

Jerry printed and signed the letter, popped it in an envelope and affixed a stamp.

8

Doctor Khaled Akbar formed his index fingers and thumbs into a high steeple that reminded Brian of the mudra of the Tibetan monks he'd encountered on a mountain-trekking trip in the Himalayas years earlier. A vague smile played on the middle-aged psychiatrist's lips, but his dark eyes were flat.

"Mr. McGee, are you a risk-taking man?" There was a faint trace of a foreign accent. Middle East?

"It's McKay."

Akbar consulted the sheet of paper in front of him. "Ah, yes. Well, if you would be so kind as to answer the question."

"Okay, it's yes."

"Could you expand?"

"I keep eating junk food, I probably will."

The psychiatrist removed his glasses, rubbed them unnecessarily on his red-and-black patterned silk tie. After a moment, he raised his grave eyes to Brian's. "Mr. McKay, I assure you this is a serious matter. I am a serious man, as I presume you are. I am not an opponent. Think of me as a...facilitator. So, tell me about yourself."

"That's a rather broad subject, Doctor."

"What is your fondest desire in life?"

"Avoiding corporate bureaucracy."

"All right. What do you most fear?"

"Mindless interviews."

Akbar frowned. "Let's try again. Do you fear failure in your life?"

"Nah."

Akbar made a note on the sheet of paper. "Would you say you are stronger in need to achieve or in fear of failure?"

"Yes."

"Mr. McKay, perhaps you do not realize that I have the power to judge you, to have significant input in the decision as to whether you uh, remain with us."

Akbar's face was rigid. His dark eyes had come to life. He brought to Brian's mind Charlton Heston's righteous Moses confronting his people worshiping golden idols in *The Ten Commandments*. Brian had just decided to play along enough to pass muster with the shrink, when a sudden commotion came from the outside the door.

Muffled voices became louder. A woman said, "I told you he's in conference. He can't be disturbed. Now, if you'll have a seat, I'll be sure to let him know—"

Suddenly, the door burst open. An olive-complected young man in white shirt and tan linen trousers entered, registered Brian's presence with a glance and spoke to Akbar.

"There is an emergency. He wants you in his office now."

"But, as you can see, I am consulting with an associate at the moment."

The standing man turned to give Brian a closer look. His shoulders were abnormally wide, giving the impression that his slightly-smaller-than-average head was miniscule.

"Please, come. It is an emergency," he said to Akbar, with the same faint accent as the shrink.

"Mr. McKay, I am afraid I must ask your forbearance. If you will be so good as to return to your office, I will call you the moment I am free."

"All right, Doc." Brian tossed off a two-fingered salute and got up. He lingered near the doorway as Akbar and Pinhead bustled out and over to the elevator. They said nothing while in earshot. Both men appeared agitated.

After they'd boarded the elevator and the doors had closed, Brian went to Akbar's assistant's desk. She was speaking into her phone as he approached. The nameplate on her cubicle wall read, "Mary Edwards." She was a tall brunette with a finely chiseled face.

"Yes sir, he's on his way right now. All right, Mister Spurgeon."

Brian smiled at her. "Must be something urgent to break into an interview, eh?"

"I suppose." Her eyes were neutral.

"Any idea what it's about? Spurgeon needed a quick dose of psychological counseling, maybe?"

"Mr. McKay, it's really none of my concern. Or yours."

"Who's the gentleman who just left with the Doc?"

"That's Mr. Kalif. He's in charge of some foreign locations. Egypt and like that."

"What's he got to do with Akbar?"

She bit her lower lip. "Look, I'm not really supposed to..."

"Okay. I didn't mean to press."

"I'll buzz you when he's ready to resume."

9

Akbar and Kalif were ushered into Douglas Spurgeon's immense corner office. An enormous blue, orange and cream Oriental rug covered the portion of the parquet floor nearest the desk. Floor-to-ceiling windows behind the massive mahogany desk afforded a spectacular view up the North Shore along Lake Michigan. The desktop was a rat's nest of papers. Spurgeon sat ramrod-straight in the high-backed chair, his gaze unwavering as the two men entered diffidently and approached to within a few feet.

"Sit down, gentlemen," the Chief Operating Officer commanded.

They took leather visitors' chairs and fidgeted. Akbar spoke first. "Mr. Spurgeon, we—"

"Shut up and listen," Spurgeon snapped. "We're in a SHTF situation. The goddamned FBI's investigating shipments of strategic defense products to hostile countries by American contractors authorized to ship only to friendly countries. I'm told by an informed source they believe we're involved."

"But that is impossible," Akbar began.

Spurgeon swiped a hand across the desktop, knocking his gold pen and pencil set to the floor. Akbar's mouth shut abruptly, like a puppet's. Kalif immediately sprang from his chair and retrieved the desk objects before they'd stopped moving on the rug.

"It's not only possible. It's fucking happening. I thought you guys arranged the paper trail so we're totally out of the picture. Now, I find the company's being drawn into this mess. This situation is totally unacceptable."

"Um, what evidence do they—" Akbar tried.

"Bills of lading, inventory printouts, port of entry forms. The only things missing are a treasure map and a press release. We could lose a ton of business over this."

"But sir, I specifically instructed all employees here, and those involved all the way to Damascus, as to the delicacy of these matters. I don't see how—"

"Put a sock in it, Kalif. I don't want excuses. I want results. Is that clear? Spurgeon's face flushed red and a vein throbbed in his forehead."

As the two employees left his office, Spurgeon reflected that they were as trustworthy as packrats at a yard sale. He felt his heart beating high and fast, pounding down on itself like an anvil. He took a brown plastic prescription drug container from a desk drawer, removed a couple of anti-depressant pills and swallowed them dry. Lately, everything he'd worked so hard for, everything he'd built up at Belcoe seemed to be circling the bowl. He was highly perturbed by the incompetence of the two who'd just left his office. And almost as piqued at himself for hiring them. Sometimes, it no longer seemed worth the effort. He stood and walked over to the huge windows and gazed at Lake Michigan far below. Normally, the spectacular scene soothed him. This time it did not. "Fuck!" he screamed.

In the hallway outside Spurgeon's office, Kalif spoke quietly. "What is this SHTF?"

Akbar grimaced. "It's an American expression. Shit hits the fan." He gave Kalif a meaningful look. "Not good for us. Not good at all." Akbar did not plan to call McKay back in for testing. Too many other things to worry about. He figured the disrespectful newcomer would not complain.

10

Darcy returned to her small North Side apartment, set her bulging book pack on the bedroom floor and slumped into the desk chair in the corner. Her mind was still swimming from the physics class she'd just sat through, trying to concentrate, to keep from obsessing about Matthew's death. But the lecture had been unusually dry, and her mind kept wandering back to the events of the past few days. She propped her elbows on the desk and dropped her face to her hands.

A few minutes later, she sighed as she switched on her MacBook to check her mail. She quickly deleted a spam email that offered pills guaranteed to lengthen the penis by at least three inches with no tools or gadgets. The first legitimate message was from her friend Natalie at Belcoe. It read:

Darce,

I've been so totally bummed ever since what happened to Matthew. Sorry I haven't gotten more of a chance to chat with you. Everyone's walking on pins and needles and it's hard to find the time to communicate. I know you must still feel awful. Anyway, I always thought he was one of the good ones—serious but fun. And totally incapable of BSing about anything important. One thing's for sure: no way he killed himself. I mean he had too much going on, especially you! And he would've zoomed to the top in Finance. If he could keep out of trouble, I mean. Not that he was actually IN trouble, but you know how it is. You hear things, sense things. And Matthew said something one morning when a bunch of us were having coffee in the cafeteria. Like, he knew something was bogus in Finance. Hinted the information was major. But he wouldn't say any more. The Jackster pumped him, but he like turned off. He reported to Jack, so maybe he just didn't want to say anything in front of the rest of us. Don't ask me. I'm clueless. BTW, did Matthew ever tell you what was going on? All I know was that he was working on some international stuff, and he was putting in tons of hours. But then, we all are, with the company's growth surge. You know, I've gotta think about career options. I mean, the pressure's awesome, but then, so's the payback if the stock keeps rocketing. Stock price is what drives this place. And quarterly earnings drive the stock. And, if you aren't seen by the suits as contributing to earnings growth, you're toast. Anyway, I've gotta run—just heard Massey's pet goon getting on Jack's case in the cube next door, and I don't want to be next. Rumor is, the guy threatened to throw one of the accountants out the window if he told the auditors about some adjustments we made to capital assets. I'm pretty sure that was just a figurative expression. In any case, keep in touch. Nat.

Not that he was actually in trouble? Something bogus in finance? Threatened to throw somebody out the window? What the hell was that about? She'd have to think about it a bit before responding.

Darcy forwarded the e-mail to Brian, asking for his take, then logged off. She and Natalie had once been like sisters—Nat a senior at U of I when Darcy started out as a freshman. As a volunteer in the "Freshman Mentoring" program, the older girl had drawn Darcy as her charge. They'd shared many skim lattes and talked for hours about everything from gefilte fish (Nat being Jewish and Darcy curious about kosher food) to guys. Since Nat had received her BS in Management and gone into the real world, though, they didn't see each other much. Plus, Nat was attending evening MBA classes at the Chicago Booth business school. They kept in touch by e-mail and text, mainly, and Darcy still looked to her friend for advice. What would Nat do in her situation? Darcy made a flash decision, left her apartment and headed for the Red Line elevated train station nearby.

Darcy ascended the steps to Matthew's Old Town one-bedroom, ducked under the police crime scene tape and went in. It seemed luxurious to her, with its big living room complete with wood-burning fireplace, a generous bedroom and closets galore. Matthew's job paid pretty well, and he could easily make the two thousand a month rent. She'd learned from his parents at the funeral home that the place was paid up through the end of the month. They'd left his stuff there until they could send it to their home in Evansville. She used her key, entered and closed the door behind herself.

Inside, the faint smell of Matthew's aftershave wafted in the air. She shook her head. They'd exchanged apartment keys only a few days before Matthew'd gone to the office for the last time. She dropped the key in a pocket and made her way to the living room.

Dust motes floated in the sunshine leaking in through the closed blinds of the central bay window. Darcy closed the blinds, went to the desk and pulled up the chair. A small framed photo of Matthew and her laughing in front of the polar bear viewing window at the Lincoln Park Zoo was propped up on the desk next to the computer. In the picture, Matthew's dark hair was clipped short, and his rectangular glasses lent him a studious aspect, even as Darcy leaned her head on his shoulder. They both wore self-conscious grins as they waited for the tourist who'd volunteered to take their picture to actually tap the phone. After the zoo, they'd had dinner at Mon Ami Gabi and then ended up in the bedroom in this apartment. They'd made love for the first time there, tenderly, a bit awkward in the newness of this inevitable stage of the blossoming relationship. This had been what, two weeks ago?

She heaved a sigh. Enough self-pity—a voice inside her said to stop spacing out and get to work. She needed to find a clue as to why someone would want to harm Matthew.

She clicked the computer on and entered the password Matthew had given her. She selected Excel and scanned the list of data directories. She clicked open a folder called "Belcoe." Accounting spreadsheets filled the screen, as she opened the files in order. Profit and Loss statements and related analyses scrolled by, columns of numbers with double underscores at the bottom. She mused that most people casually use the term "bottom line" with no idea it means net income on a P & L statement. Her one accounting course to date had at least taught her that much.

As she began to read the first file, she heard footfalls coming up the wooden stairs out front, echoing like gunfire in a well. She sat completely still, waiting for a knock on the door, but there was only silence.

Someone inserted a key in the lock and fiddled around trying to open the door. The doorknob rattled as it turned back and forth. Thank God she'd twisted the deadbolt home. Then came the furtive sound of metal rasping in the lock—not like a key. The noise was of something small, scraping. Could someone be trying to pick the deadbolt? Darcy's heartbeat thudded in her chest. She thought of calling 911 and immediately discarded the idea. It would be better to motor out the back door. She could call the cops from the relative safety of the street. If the intruder didn't know she'd been inside, perhaps he'd linger long enough to be nabbed.

But first, she'd try to get a glimpse of the person outside. She rose from the chair and crept to the street-facing bay window. The left pane of glass was angled toward the entryway. The narrow field of view did not quite allow her to see the person. She dug in her pack for the canister of pepper spray she always carried. There was a slight creak as someone outside shifted weight on the wooden floorboards of the porch.

Dead quiet. Then the heavy door splintered near the doorknob and cracked like an eggshell as a heavy object slammed into it. Darcy spun and propelled herself into the hallway and then the kitchen. A door in the kitchen's far wall led out back to the small yard and then the alley, she knew. As she fumbled with the slide lock, she heard a series of explosive crashes from the living room. The front door was being steadily assaulted and it sounded as if it would give at any moment. She finally managed to get the back door open and was taking a first step onto the stairs to the yard when the front door gave way in one final thunderous concussion.

Darcy glanced over her shoulder to see a large man wearing aviator shades and a black trench coat burst into the living room, pause for a moment and then come straight for her. She hit the backyard running and made for the gateway to the alley. Heavy footfalls crunched down the stairs behind her as she swung the gate open and lurched through.

11

Darcy burst into the alley and made a hard left. She remembered vaguely that the alleyway behind Matthew's apartment building was L-shaped, with one side leading to the street out front. Making a second left toward the street, she cut a look over her shoulder. Trench Coat crashed into a garbage can and fell on his butt as he clambered after her.

"Fuck!" he yelled.

Darcy sprinted the few yards of the remaining alleyway and reached the street. There was plenty of car traffic and lots of pedestrians on the sidewalk, including a half dozen men about her age, talking and laughing as they ambled along. Darcy slowed to a walk and fell in behind the young men. She sucked in air greedily as her heart hammered at her ribcage. Gradually, her breathing returned to normal.

One of the guys spotted her, turned and smiled. "Hi."

She nodded, returning the smile. "Hi." Risking a look over her shoulder, she saw her pursuer, also walking now, about twenty yards back. He took unnaturally small steps, purposely maintaining the gap. Darcy extracted her phone from her pocket and pressed the screen for Brian's cell as she moved forward.

"Hey, what's up?" Brian said.

"I got chased out of Matthew's apartment by some guy, and I'm on the run."

"Whoa. Where are you now and where's this guy?"

"I'm on Lincoln Park West, heading north, across from the South Pond."

"What about the guy?"

"He's right behind me, back maybe fifty feet. But I'm kind of with a group of guys."

"Okay, stay with them. What's this mope look like?"

"Big dude, white, shades, long black coat. He's..." She turned to check on her pursuer, but he'd vanished. "He's gone. Must've ducked into a doorway or something."

"Good. Keep moving. Grab a cab to Belcoe. I'll meet you in the lobby. We're gonna go have dinner with Uncle James. Okay?"

"Cool. But since when is he *Uncle*?"

"Well, he works for Uncle Sam, and I've got a feeling that might come in handy. By the way, how did this guy happen to chase you out of the apartment?"

"He broke into Matthew's place while I was in there looking at computer files."

"Ah, Christ. This guy say anything?"

"Yeah. The f-word, when he fell on his tush in the alley. Hey, here's a cab. Later."

12

Brian left the Belcoe offices a few minutes after five p.m. and took a seat on an uncomfortable stone bench under a garish abstract mural in the lobby. The vast space was awash in office workers scurrying for the commuter train stations, the El or the nearby city parking garages. Only the top execs were entitled to park in the Belcoe building itself. As he'd recently found out first-hand, the parking tab there was as high as the office building, but the guys with the luxury cars wouldn't care. The company sprang for the parking—an expected perk for the heavies. Even a space in one of the cheapo public parking towers in the Loop would strip 300 bucks from a patron's bank account the first of each month. He glanced at his watch. It had been forty-five minutes since he'd spoken with Darcy.

Suddenly the revolving door nearest his bench spit out a person actually entering the building rather than leaving. Amid the forest of taller individuals thronging the exit, he could make out the crown of his niece's blonde head. He stood and worked his way in her direction.

After gaining the sidewalk west of the building, Brian and Darcy headed north on State Street. They soon passed the angular tower of the American Medical Association's headquarters building with the four-story square hole near the top. North of the AMA, at street level, boutique law firms and advertising agencies jostled for position with trendy restaurants. They passed the redbrick building housing the Pellas Law Firm, whose proprietor, Christine Pellas, had been a client of Brian's the previous year. She'd been hounded by a former lover, who'd threatened to post pictures of them engaged in oral sex on the Internet. Brian had roughed the guy up and nipped off the threat.

A few blocks further the huge spire of Holy Name Cathedral loomed on the right. Leaves skittered across the plaza in front, borne by a stiff westerly breeze. Holy Name was not only headquarters for the nation's largest Catholic archdiocese, but was also the site where, in October, 1926, gangster Hymie Weiss took ten slugs from hoods firing from Dion O'Banion's flower shop across the street. Brian remembered as a boy being highly impressed by the bullet holes chipped into the stone stairs leading to the cathedral's main entrance. He noted with satisfaction that a couple of the holes were still visible as they went by. But he restrained himself from pointing them out to Darcy, who no doubt was sensitive to the topic of bullets.

They made a right at Chicago Avenue and then a left onto Rush Street, the once legendary center of the Chicago nightclub and singles bars scene, now full of luxury shops from Barney's to Bugatti.

A few minutes later, they entered the popular Brazilian steakhouse, Churrasco Brasilia. Back when the place had been called Benedetto's, reporters for Chicago's four daily newspapers and half-dozen television news operations held down stools at the bar, day and night. But the joint had gotten gentrified since those glory days of past decades. Shadowy booths had given way to white linen-covered tables with candles. The ghost of legendary newspaper columnist Mike Royko was said to inhabit the end of the curved bar nearest the east entrance, but the old-time grit and edginess was no more.

The bar was a magnet for Chicago's current media players, mostly TV.

Brian scanned the room and spotted James St. Claire, his compact offensive lineman body expertly draped in cream-colored Hugo Boss, holding down a corner table. He saw them at the same time and waved, his carved gold ring catching the light and sending a flaxen reflection across to them like a laser beam.

13

At James's insistence, Darcy took the chair facing the window and the skyline view to the west. Brian and James sat across from each other. A waiter hustled over and they ordered drinks. They chatted until the beverages were served—beer for Brian, Maker's Mark rocks for James and a margarita for Darcy. Darcy was quiet. She half-listened to the two friends trading quips while she sipped her drink and watched a spectacular sunset, heightened by a layer of swirling cumulus clouds seemingly balanced on the rooftops of the surrounding skyscrapers.

James tried to draw her out, asking questions about her classes—he seemed particularly interested in her course on ecology and evolution of vertebrates.

"Might want to take that course myself. I learned some about dinosaurs from you and your uncle here last year, when you were risking your booty on that *T. rex* thing out west," James said.

"Could you use that at work?" Darcy asked. She wasn't sure whether James was serious.

"Maybe. There're a few dinosaurs in the FBI Chicago Field Office."

"Got that right," Brian added.

Darcy rolled her eyes.

"So, how's the gig goin'?" James asked Brian.

"Charming company culture they've got. They're all driven by fear, greed and the stock price. What you'd expect from guys like this, see themselves as makers, buying out the competition, taking over foreign companies, dealing themselves options like peanuts."

"Got a rep for creative accounting," James said.

"Yes. I'm meeting the bean counters tomorrow," Brian said.

"Let me know if you come across anything ah, interesting."

"I will." Brian knew that White Collar Crime, James's department, was following Belcoe.

"Any leads on the kid?" James quickly glanced at Darcy.

"Just threads, so far."

Brian turned to Darcy. "That e-mail you got from your friend, didn't she say Matthew hinted he was onto something bogus?"

"Yeah, she did. And I've been thinking about it." She bit her lower lip. "I remember Matthew saying that Belcoe wasn't the kind of place that would tolerate whistle-blowers."

"You think he was a whistle-blower?"

"I...don't know. The subject came up when we were watching "60 Minutes," and that guy from Autonomy was spilling his guts to Scott Pelley. Told him the accountants overstated income by billions. Matthew goes, 'Not so hard to believe.'"

"But he never found anything like that at Belcoe?" Brian said.

"Not that he mentioned."

James remarked. "Used to be accountants were snooze. Now they're off the chain, usually for boosting OPM."

Darcy regarded him blankly.

"Were lame, now cool. Other people's money."

Brian said, "Reminds me, how about checking out some guys in UCR?" He knew that the FBI's online Uniform Crime Reporting program would likely reveal any criminal records of the Belcoe execs he was curious about.

"Wait a minute. We eating? And, if so, who's covering?" James looked indignant.

"Yes, and I am. The names are Khaled Akbar, Shamir Kalif, A. Hamilton Massey and Douglas Spurgeon."

James held up a hand like a traffic cop. "Whoa. Spell 'em." He pulled a business card and a gold Cross pen from his shirt pocket, and printed each name as Brian spelled it out.

"The last two, I've heard of," James said. "Massey's head of finance and Spurgeon's the prez. What're the first two?"

"Akbar's ostensibly a shrink and Kalif's some kind of business manager for their Middle East operations."

"Okay. I'll hit UCR. And, since you left the Bureau, we've added a few more tricks for mining the web. 'Course, you're gonna owe me big-time."

The waiter reappeared with menus and left again. They fell silent as they perused the bill of fare, described as world-class Brazilian-style beef dishes cooked over an 800-degree flame.

"Man, I'm ready for an RD," Darcy commented. RD was her term for a Real Dinner, an infrequent occurrence.

"Order anything you want, Darcy. The *medalhoes com bacom* looks good," James offered.

"You're a hell of a generous guy when somebody else is buying," Brian said.

"Damn right. OPM." James grinned as he flagged down the waiter. "Let's order. I'm starved," he said.

After an excellent meal accompanied by a couple of bottles of Argentinian Malbec, they went outside into the humid lakefront air. James caught a cab for the FBI headquarters building, where his prized jet-black Ford F-150 pickup waited, and Brian and Darcy walked back to Belcoe to retrieve his car. They rode in silence most of the way to her apartment.

"By the way, I called the cops and the landlord about the break-in at Matthew's on the way to the restaurant," Darcy said.

"Good. I'll run by there on my way home, see if it needs boarding up," Brian said. "I know the people to call, from personal experience." His own apartment had been broken into and tossed by a thug named Norton, a bent ex-cop, the year before.

"Thanks."

"Find anything on his computer?"

"No. I was just starting to look when that creep busted in."

"Darcy, we're gonna get the killer."

"I know."

Brian guided the Grand Cherokee into traffic. He glanced in the rearview and noticed a set of headlights a half block back. The lights were a bit higher than those of a sedan or crossover. Had to be some sort of truck.

He glanced over to make sure his doors were locked. Soon, he was in Old Town, continuing north. He found himself checking the mirrors frequently. Since Darcy's harrowing experience, his nerves had been on edge. Traffic was light. The high-set headlights stayed with him all the way.

It was possible that someone was taking precisely the same indirect route from the Belcoe building to Old Town, but unlikely. He wondered if Darcy and he were both now at risk, whether whoever had killed Matthew Growney was watching them. Suddenly, he made an abrupt U-turn and headed south on Halsted. The vehicle that had been behind him continued north, a dark-colored Suburban. He couldn't make the plate, other than that it was standard-issue Illinois. Tinted windows concealed the occupant or occupants.

He dropped Darcy off at her apartment and waited until she was safely inside. Then he found a parking space within a block of Matthew Growney's place. He grabbed the flashlight from the glove box and got out. At the gray stone building's front door, he tried the knob. Locked. The lockset was shiny and new looking, probably replaced that afternoon. He switched on the flashlight and went around back, eyeing each window along the way. All the panes appeared to be intact. The rear door was locked as well. Good-the building owner was on the ball.

On the short drive home, he periodically checked the rearview for following vehicles. Funny how proximity to violent death gets the paranoia going. *Just because you're paranoid doesn't mean there isn't someone after you.* He got home without incident, but glanced over his shoulder as he fitted his key in the front door.

14

Brian arrived at the Belcoe office building the next morning around nine. The sun was just warming the acre of concrete known as One Belcoe Plaza. Very few people were around at this hour—only a cadre of surreptitious smokers near the revolving door he'd just approached and a goggled messenger piloting his bicycle across the plaza like a kamikaze on speed. Brian walked to the waist-high iron railing on the southern edge of the plaza and looked down at the blue-green Chicago River as it flowed out of Lake Michigan. He mused about the river's peculiar history.

Back in the 1880s, the river, full of human and industrial waste from Chicago's sewers, contaminated the local water supply from Lake Michigan so badly that twelve percent of the city's population was killed by waterborne diseases. The public was up in arms, and the local politicos knew they'd damned well better find a solution. Although mankind had never before carried out such a project, the titans of Chicago decided to solve the problem by reversing the flow of the river, which they did. The twenty-eight mile-long Sanitary and Ship Canal was completed in 1900, and the Chicago River had been flushed sort of clean by the constant outflow of fresh lake water ever since. Even that solution was soon overwhelmed as Chicago's population skyrocketed, and the "make no small plans" guys constructed the world's largest sewage treatment plant. Brian smiled as he thought of the late mayor Richard J. Daley's public utterance that the Chicago River would one day be clean enough for a downtown worker to catch a fish and grill and eat it for lunch, before returning to his desk. Chances are, the guy would never make it to the end of the business day—the mercury content of his repast would turn him into a human thermometer.

Brian's phone rang. James calling.

"Hey, big guy. Got some information for you. Can you talk?"

"Sure, I'm outside the Belcoe building, loitering."

"Lemme give you the highlights. I'll fill in the rest next time we get together."

"First off, this Akbar dude's no doctor. Worked as a paramedic in Morocco, where he grew up. Flunked out of Wayne State med school in Detroit. Worked in Syria for a few years, came back to the states in 2007. Had a job in personnel for Ford Motor in Dearborn until 2015, when they canned him for reasons unknown. Caught on at Belcoe in 2016 as corporate shrink, even though he's only slightly more qualified than I am. He's fifty-seven, never been charged with anything. By the way, his Chinaman's Lou DeRosa."

"Okay. What about Kalif?"

"Dude's some kinda royalty. Came outta Saudi Arabia five years ago, went to Ohio State, got himself the job with Belcoe 'bout a year and a half back. Dad's a cousin of Crown Prince what-his-name."

"Salman?"

"Yeah, like the fish, but second vowel's an 'a'."

Brian groaned. "You know, I was just standing here, watching the river going backward, thinking of all those edible fish in it. Anyway, what else you got on Kalif?"

"Family's in shipping, ocean-going vessels."

"Big-time?"

"Like Warren Buffet's in investing."

"He got a jacket?"

"*Nada*. But we've been, uh, keeping an eye on him. The guy spreads his money around in places like Muslim temples in the Midwest, especially Dearborn, Michigan."

"Isn't that where a bunch of guys were rounded up after nine-eleven?"

"Yep, but the dudes were clean. You ask me, it wasn't the Bureau's finest hour. Meanwhile, I'm still working on this Belcoe stuff and, of course, my other job assignments."

Brian glanced up at the huge clock face on the Wrigley Building's white limestone facade a block to the north. "Okay. Hey, thanks for the info. I'd better get going. I'm supposed to sit down with the Belcoe finance staff in a couple minutes."

15

Brian entered the building, went through security and made for the elevator bank serving the top floors. He'd be a little late for the meeting with the CFO and his troops. Oh well, couldn't be helped. He got off on 47 and, following the young receptionist's directions, entered the Boardroom. The tension in the air was unmistakable. A slender man seated in a high-backed leather chair at the head of the table peered at Brian through tinted glasses. Six other people—five men and a woman—occupied chairs along one side of the long mahogany table. No one spoke. Brian approached an empty chair across from the silent six and said, "Hi, everybody, I'm—"

"Brian McKay, yes we've been waiting for you." The man in the big chair consulted a slim gold watch. "Better late than never, I suppose. Have a seat, Mr. McKay."

Brian maintained eye contact with the man as he slid into the chair. "And you are?"

"Hamilton Massey. I'm—"

"CFO. Yes, I know."

Massey's tinted glasses glinted under the fluorescent lights as he dipped his chin in acknowledgement of Brian's counterpoint. "All right. Let's get started. As you may know, Brian, I'm in charge of all financial matters for Belcoe, ranging from accounting, taxes, the treasury function, mergers and acquisitions, SEC reporting. We pride ourselves here at Belcoe as being on the cutting edge of financial innovation, endeavoring always to structure transactions in a manner accretive to shareholder equity."

The guy's voice grated on Brian. He scanned the others at the table. All kept their facial expressions as inanimate as masks. "Uh, does that mean you keep the books so the stock goes up?" Brian asked.

Massey's impassive gray eyes blinked once behind the thick lenses. "Before I answer that, may I inquire as to the scope of your background in finance?"

"MBA, a few years in the White Collar Crime unit of the FBI Chicago Field office."

"Fine. Then we'll all be able to speak the same language. As I was about to say, we do our share of innovative transactions, which is in service to maximization of shareholder value. And we are religious in adhering to GAAP."

Brian knew this meant Generally Accepted Accounting Principles, the rules of the game for financial statements of publicly held companies in the United States. "Then why did KPMG quit as your auditors? Didn't it have something to do with departures from GAAP?" Brian asked.

Massey frowned like a man who'd swallowed a mouthful of spoiled meat. "They simply couldn't keep up with us. We've been engaged in remarkably advanced financing. We are masters of creative flexibility." He shrugged. "We made a sound business decision to move away from KPMG."

"So you shopped for auditors and came up with Kimmelman?"

"We did not, as you put it, 'shop.' The Kimmelman firm are professionals, and they understand the dynamics of a best practices company such as Belcoe." He waved a hand as if shooing a fly. "Anyway, I'd like us to go round the table and identify ourselves—name and position. Tim, please lead off."

Massey nodded at the young man to his left, a towering hulk who might have sacked quarterbacks in another life. His shirtsleeves were rolled up to the elbow, revealing tanned forearms the size of baked hams.

"Yeah, okay. I'm Tim Huff. I keep the work expedited, take care of scheduling, follow-up on problems. Whatever it takes to keep things moving forward."

Brian was reminded of Darcy's friend Natalie Katz's e-mail reference to "Massey's pet goon," who'd supposedly threatened to throw one of the accountants out the window.

"What happens if someone makes a big mistake, or even worse, lets the auditors know about a big mistake?" Brian asked.

Huff brushed a golf ball-sized knuckle across his thick nose. "Somebody like that would never get hired."

"But, just for the sake of discussion, what if someone were hired and spilled his guts when he should've kept quiet?"

"Well, I'd talk to the guy and—"

"I don't see the point of exploring the theoretical. Look, we've got a lot to cover. Let's move on." Massey gestured at the man to Huff's left.

Jack Wilson, a fit-looking guy with short blonde hair and twinkling eyes, described his group management role as if he were a kindly priest discussing duty to his parishioners. "As managers, we're here to facilitate, to allow our staff to optimize their skills development. It works to everyone's advantage." Brian knew that Matthew Growney had reported to Jack. He made a mental note to speak with him separately.

Wilson was followed by Natalie Katz, a dark-haired twenty-something whose eyes were focused on the pad of yellow legal paper on the table before her as she spoke in a monotone. Her face fit the image Brian had conjured up from reading her sympathy e-mail to Darcy in the wake of Matthew Growney's death.

"I supervise the domestic and foreign manufacturing accounting groups," she said. "There are seven of us, and we handle consolidations, budgeting, trouble-shooting—"

"Speaking of trouble, you knew Matthew Growney pretty well, right?"

She met Brian's gaze for a split-second. "Well yeah, sure, we all did. If you're alluding to the uh, murder, I don't—"

Massey interrupted. "Mr. McKay, we've all been through bouts of questioning by the law enforcement professionals. So if you'll kindly limit your inquiries to fresh ground, perhaps we'll be more efficient here and we'll conclude this session on schedule. You see, this is an especially busy time for us, and—"

"My turn." Brian clenched and unclenched his hands, blew out a burst of air. "Look, Massey, in the first place, I wasn't present for the CPD's discussions with you people. Second, I've got my own concerns here, not necessarily overlapping with the police. In any case, why don't you guys finish your introductions, and I'll ask a few questions and then we can all toddle out of here. I'll follow up with you all individually."

Dead silence for a beat. Then Natalie spoke. "You're Darcy's uncle, aren't you?"

Brian nodded.

"Next." Massey's voice sounded as brittle and sharp as a sliver of broken glass.

Natalie bowed her head. Brian could see that her cheeks had reddened at Massey's rudeness. Interesting—he'd talk with her for sure.

The remaining accountants related their names and duties. Brian took notes on each. Finally, Massey said, "All right, now you know who we are and what we're about. Also, know that we wish for the same thing you apparently do, the winding up of this unfortunate, ah, incident with all due expeditiousness."

"Excellent. Tell you what: Humor me for another couple of minutes. Let's save time by everybody working on this simultaneously. I'd like each person here to jot down on a piece of paper your name and where you were between midnight and eight a.m. last Sunday morning. Give me that information before you leave the room. Also, any ideas you may have as to why Matthew was killed and by whom. Also, indicate your phone numbers, work and mobile. Finally, if any of you wish to speak with me immediately after this meeting, please let me know. I'll sit here and shut up for a few minutes, while you all scribble, and I'll stick around when you leave. And after that, I'll be at extension 4623 if you need to get in touch."

Several sets of eyes turned to Massey, who gave a short nod.

The CFO made a show of consulting his watch. "I've got to run. Meeting with the analysts." With that, he stood and marched from the room.

Brian couldn't put his finger on it, but there was something odd about the guy, and not just the sketchy accent. He looked a little like the actor Tim Robbins, only not as tall. And those glasses with the dark tint made him look somehow...secretive.

A few minutes later, each accountant had completed his or her information sheet, dropped it with Brian and left the room. All except Natalie Katz, who lingered.

When they were alone, Brian said, "Good to meet you. Darcy passed your e-mail on to me, and I've been meaning to see you."

"Yes, I...I'd like to talk with you...in private. Maybe we could go get a cup." She looked at the walls as if they might have ears.

"Sure," he said. He gathered the slips of paper he'd received from the finance staff.

They didn't speak again until they'd entered the company cafeteria five floors down. Brian pegged Natalie as a bit paranoid. Maybe she had reason—it wouldn't have surprised Brian if the Boardroom or even the elevator were bugged.

They got coffee and found seats at a table near a window, far from anyone else.

"Look, I'm probably not making much sense, but I somehow feel like, responsible for what happened." Natalie rubbed her eyes.

"In what way?"

"Matthew confided a little to some of us, I mean that something was way wrong. Like I told Darcy, I pried for details, but it was no go. If I'd pushed him, maybe he'd—."

"Hey, don't be so hard on yourself. There's nothing to be gained. Look, think back to exactly what he said when you spoke with him."

"He said that something was dubious in Finance. Not phony accounting or anything like that, he said. Jack was there, and he was like, 'What do you mean dubious?' Matthew just smiled, but not like something was funny. What was it he said then? Something like, 'Massey hears about me running my mouth, I'm toast.'"

"You think he was afraid of Massey?"

"Well, yeah. I mean, we *all* are. You've seen the guy in action. That shtick in the conference room—that was vintage A.H. The way I see it, the guy's got two goals in life: seeing the stock price zoom and making a personal fortune. The two go together. People who get in the way of either one aren't around here long."

"What happens to them?"

"You've heard about our rank and yank system?"

"Yes, and I've gotta say, I'm happy not to be part of it."

"I'd be the same way, but the money's too good to walk away. It's the same for all of us. Except maybe the marginal performers, who sweat their asses off, with good reason. But Matthew was a golden boy. You know, the consummate professional. Succeeds even though he's not into office politics. Too damned good to hold back. And everybody liked him, which is important in a place like this."

"You think whoever killed him might have been with the company?"

"I don't know." She shuddered. "Jesus, I hope not."

"You referred to 'Massey's pet goon' in that e-mail. Who's that?"

"You just met him."

"Tim Huff."

"Yep. He's the polar opposite of Matthew. Football star at Illinois, until he got tossed off the team for taking money from an alum booster. Rumor is he never graduated. Not Belcoe material, you'd think."

"So how'd he end up here?"

"Word is Massey pulled some strings. That, and he *does* have a talent—pushing people around."

"Literally?"

"Well, I've never seen it, but he gets in people's faces, especially the guys. He's an enforcer. One guy told the auditors about an embarrassing problem involving inventory valuation. Next day, the guy was gone."

"Did Huff get in Matthew's face?"

"Not that I know of."

"What about you?"

"Not exactly."

"What?"

Her face reddened. "He uh, tried to feel me up in the elevator one afternoon. I jerked away and told him if he tried it again, I'd turn him into a soprano."

"And?"

"He hasn't come near me since."

16

$\mathbf{B}$rian found Jack Wilson at 5:35 p.m. in his small private office in the accounting department. Wilson was packing some papers into a tan canvas briefcase with leather trim. He looked up when Brian stopped in the doorway.

"Hey, Brian. Some meeting, huh?"

"Yeah. Got a minute?"

"I was just leaving." Wilson looked apologetic.

"Catching a train?"

"Yep. At the Ogilvie Center."

"I'll walk you to the station. I'm going that way myself."

In the Belcoe lobby, they merged in with the hordes en route to the commuter trains. Stand still and you'd be trampled, Brian thought. Conversation was impossible in the hubbub. Brian mused about the deaths of three people in a south side club a year earlier. Pyrotechnics, part of the show of the headlining band, *Great Menace*, had set some stage draperies on fire. At the same time a scuffle broke out in the center aisle. A security guard Maced the combatants, and panic enveloped the room with the fumes and smoke. Turned out, the fire exits were all locked. People jammed into each other trying to escape. Some fell and were trampled lifeless. Others reached the exit door, only to find it literally clogged with squirming bodies. Smoke inhalation took a heavy toll. The owners of the club had somehow avoided the annual city safety inspection. Suspicion was rife that money had greased palms. And so it goes.

When they reached the street, Brian hungrily sucked in a breath of unconditioned air. "What's your take on Massey?" he asked.

"Old A.H. is one quirky mother. Y'know, he's kind of a Jekyll and Hyde guy. Smooth as silk in a road show, conning the analysts out of their Guccis. A few minutes later, he's on somebody's case like a supercilious drill sergeant. Listen to this: he's taking a cab to the office, middle of the day, couple years ago. Cab pulls up at the Wabash entrance we just came out of, cabbie flips the flag down, fare reads $4.70. A.H. hands the guy a five and waits. The cabbie figures the 30 cents is his tip, or at least part of it. Then A.H. says, 'What about my change?'"

"Don't tell me."

"Yeah. The cabbie says, 'What about my tip?' Mr. Million-a-year goes, 'If you're going to be that way about it, you don't deserve a tip.' A.H. has one leg outside the cab when the cabbie floors it, and he falls on his ass at the curb. A reporter for the Sun-Times is right there, and he asks what's the problem. Get this: A.H. tells him the whole story, not embarrassed a bit. Like the cabbie's completely at fault. Jeez. Hey, don't quote me."

Brian laughed. "Don't worry."

They reached the 42-story Citicorp Center and came to a stop outside the main entrance, as waves of commuters swarmed past on their way to the Ogilvie Transportation Center inside.

Brian raised his voice to be heard above the clamor. "One other question: what was your relationship with Matthew Growney like?"

Wilson shrugged. "I liked him a lot. Best accountant we had. Sharp guy, got along with everybody. He's gonna be hard to replace. I have absolutely no idea about the murder." He glanced at his watch. "Gotta run."

17

Eight a.m. on Thursday, Brian sat in a Yellow cab in heavy traffic en route to the Chicago Police Department's headquarters building at 3510 South Michigan Avenue to visit Dick Cissel. Seeing Cissel at Belcoe in the wake of Matthew Growney's murder three days ago had been frustrating. The tension of the situation had made the encounter almost painful. Brian and the tough cop had been close friends many years ago, in a different life for both of them.

For the past three years, Dick had been Central Area Commander within the Bureau of Detectives. He reported to the Deputy Chief of Detectives, above whom there were only two layers leading up to the top cop, the Superintendent of Police. Cissel's Central Area included the skyscraper-crammed Loop, home of Belcoe Incorporated among many other Fortune 500 companies. Even a casual consumer of local Chicago news was aware of the Central area's colorful top detective. The flashily dressed Cissel, never one to shrink from the red eye of a TV news camera, rivaled the mayor at times as the city's most visible public servant. Brian had always admired Dick's intelligence and toughness. A natural leader, he pushed his violent crimes detectives to the wall, but never asked of them anything he wasn't willing to do himself. Word was, his cops would die for him. In fact, one of his detectives had been gunned down in a crack house the week before, carrying out Cissel's highly publicized "War on Crack."

Brian was dragged back to frustrating reality by the screech of brakes and a blaring horn as his cabbie decided to pass on the right at a teeming intersection. They made it through intact, only to settle down again in the bumper-to-bumper traffic oozing south. It ended up taking nearly fifteen minutes to negotiate the two-mile route.

Brian entered the Area headquarters building just before nine, checked in with a harried cop seated at a counter behind bullet-proof glass and took a seat on a scratched orange plastic chair. After a seven-minute wait, he was buzzed in and directed to Cissel's large but Spartan office.

"You seen the paper yet?" Cissel wore a thin smile that didn't reach his eyes. As Brian approached, the cop thrust the Chicago Sun-Times across the desk. Brian dropped into a chair and began to read.

The headline shrieked, "BELCOE COO APPARENT SUICIDE." Brian quickly scanned the story. Douglas Spurgeon, 59, of Kenilworth, had been found dead behind the wheel of his Mercedes sedan in the parking garage of the Belcoe Corporation headquarters building downtown at approximately 6:30 p.m. Wednesday. A Chicago Police spokeswoman confirmed that Mr. Spurgeon had suffered a gunshot wound to the head and was pronounced dead at Cook County Hospital later that evening. The body was found by Natalie Katz, 23, an employee in the Finance department at Belcoe. The police were investigating, said it was an apparent self-inflicted wound and they did not suspect foul play, according to the spokeswoman. Company sources had not returned repeated calls.

"Christ, Belcoe's getting to be the dead zone," Brian said.

"You got it. We don't generally have two shooting deaths in a week in the same fuckin' building. How about some coffee?"

As they walked to the communal kitchen/coffee break area, Brian observed that this relatively new, state-of the-art facility somehow managed to look like all big city police stations in the most basic respects. Cops at desks cradled phones between shoulder and chin while they stared into space or tapped computer keys. A few individuals were engaged in face-to-face conversations, some hush-hush and some freight train-loud. At one desk near the front, a stocky middle-aged white officer was interviewing a young black man wearing baggy cargo pants and, despite the heat, a Tommy Hilfiger ski jacket with a black knit watch cap pulled over his ears. They were hunched over, their faces close, voices soft, like co-conspirators sharing secrets.

After they'd returned to Cissel's large private office and taken seats at the round conference table in the corner, the big cop spoke.

"You ever meet this Spurgeon?"

"No. Closest I got was two of his top lieutenants."

"DeRosa?"

"Yeah, and Massey."

"What's your impression?"

"DeRosa's kind of an enigmatic character. Massey's not very likable, but he seems intelligent and he's got a firm hold on the finance department."

"Who's in line for Spurgeon's job?" Cissel asked.

"Based on the organization chart and the little I've heard, DeRosa, for sure. Maybe Massey. Then there's a Ray Hunter, head of Sales and Marketing, whom I haven't met, Oscar Gutman, Operations chief and a few others."

"Any scuttlebutt about who's in the lead?"

"Maybe none of them. I heard they might recruit from outside the company."

"Spurgeon reported to the CEO, this guy Barry Webb. Met him?"

"Not yet."

"What're you supposed to be doing there, anyway?"

"Well, I'm a contract hired hand, not an employee. I report to DeRosa on the Growney thing."

"Look, Brian. You're in a good inside position here to get the scoop on whatever that crowd's got going. We've got a common interest. You help us, we reciprocate. With me?"

"Sure."

"Good. There's gotta be corporate feuds, rivalries, cover-ups. Maybe the company's not doing so hot. Maybe Spurgeon was about to get dumped and couldn't face up to it." He handed Brian a business card. "Look, check in with me if something shakes loose."

"You got it. What's the early word here on Spurgeon?"

Cissel's face was stony. "We're investigating hell out of it. Got two of my best guys dedicated. Belcoe's the third largest employer in the city. An employee gets whacked and one of the head honchos cashes in his chips days later, all in the company's main office building, people start talking like the city's goin' down the toilet. Hell, they might be right."

"Any chance Spurgeon wasn't a suicide?"

"The evidence points to suicide. But the guy had a lot to live for—prestige job, younger wife, big house up on the North Shore. But those kinds a jobs carry a lot of pressure, too. Maybe he couldn't handle it. We *did* find out he was taking anti-depressant meds."

"Dick, Belcoe's a strange place. Kind of like a dysfunctional town within the city. Got its own culture, hierarchy, customs, all that stuff. Competition's so fierce, I wouldn't put it past some of those people to eliminate a top guy and try to make it look self-inflicted."

Cissel pointed a finger at Brian like a gun. "Hey, I got work to do. You wanted to see the file on Growney, so far?"

"Yeah."

A few minutes later, Brian sat in a small interrogation room with vomitous green walls devoid of artwork. The table, about half the size of a desk, wobbled slightly as if one leg was a quarter-inch shorter than the others. He flipped through the slim loose-leaf homicide investigation case file on the Growney murder. The book was organized in the standard categories: chronological record, crime scene log, crime report, death report, property and evidence reports and so on. The detectives on the case, Eduardo Muñoz and Bernard Toole, had interviewed all the Belcoe employees on Growney's floor and a few others in the financial chain of command. Nobody seemed to know anything useful. They all said he was a good worker, a nice guy. Toole noted, in barely legible scrawl, "The body was moved. Someone killed him. Maybe someone in that place had it in for the kid." Muñoz noted that he "found Mr. Massey to be a difficult individual." Jack Wilson, Growney's boss, had been "cooperative but unhelpful." Neither detective seemed to have identified any suspects. There were eight-by-tens of the victim's head, fore, aft, sides and top. In the right side view, you had to look closely to spot the entry wound buried in his thick dark hair. The face looked tense and the eyes were partially open. In the write-up, Darcy was referred to as "a close friend of the deceased." She'd told them Matthew had mentioned possible financial irregularities to her. There were no usable fingerprints at the crime scene. Gunshot residue testing of Growney's hands had come up negative. The investigators concluded the body had been moved after the shooting. It was an open homicide, investigation pending.

Brian made a few notes, closed the folder and returned to Cissel's office.

"Not much there. Dick, what's your take...off the record?"

Cissel raised his eyebrows. "Between you and me, it's short odds someone works for that company punched his ticket."

"Why do you say that?"

"Everybody we talked to said the kid was good at his job, well-liked, smart, diligent, brave, trustworthy loyal, a real goddamned Eagle Scout. No enemies, no beefs. Employee of the month. Almost too good to be true. See, this outfit fires ten percent of the workers every year. Not cuz they deserve it, necessarily. It's just the way they do business. So, maybe this kid had the goods on another bean counter. Knew the guy made a mistake in the numbers, threatened to screw him in the next bump and dump, or whatever the hell they call it."

"Rank and yank, actually. But I take your point."

A quiet voice came from the doorway. "You wanted to see me, Chief?"

"Yeah, c'mon in and meet my old buddy, Brian McKay. Brian, this is my guy's headin' up the Matthew Growney investigation. He's got a special interest."

Brian turned to see a man about thirty years old entering the room. Brushy black eyebrows and a drooping gunfighter's mustache accented his pale face. Brian was reminded of a picture of Wyatt Earp he'd once seen in a museum in Tombstone, Arizona. But the guy looked familiar for some other reason that he couldn't put his finger on. The man approached, slow and cool, extended his right hand and said, "Joe G."

18

G ot time for a ride?" the pale man asked.

"Sure. Where we going?"

"Matthew Growney's apartment."

And that's when Brian realized why the man looked familiar. "You guys related?"

"Yeah. Brothers."

"I'm surprised they'd let a family member..."

"The department's what's the word...family-oriented? We take care of our own. Who's gonna work harder on a case than the victim's own blood?"

The two men walked silently out of the building to a heavily fenced parking lot full of cop cars. They boarded Joe's navy blue unmarked Ford Police Interceptor sedan with spotlights on both sides and tiny plastic hubcaps—about as inconspicuous on the street as an elephant's footprint in a wet sandbox.

"I hear your niece was already over there, got chased away," Joe said.

"Yeah. And you guys interviewed her."

"Right. Sat her down with an artist. Came up with this." He glanced down at the black vinyl portfolio jammed into the space between the vehicle's front seats, fumbled a sheet of paper out and handed it to Brian. "Here's a picture of the dude."

Brian studied the likeness: a broad face with eyes obscured behind aviator shades, possibly Ray-Bans. Neat, short haircut. Prominent chin. It reminded him of the police sketch of the man known as D. B. Cooper, who parachuted from a Seattle-bound Northwest 727 in 1971 with a bagful of extorted money, never to be seen again. Though the man in the picture looked vaguely familiar, he also looked like countless Caucasian guys.

Joe Growney looked over. "Anything?"

"Dunno. Looks like a lot of guys. Kinda like Spurgeon, from the picture of him in the paper today. Maybe even a little like you. But not particularly like either of you, know what I mean?"

"Huh."

"What did your brother tell you about Massey?"

"Said he admired the guy for his smarts, success and all. But that he'd trust him about as far as he could sling a load of truck motors."

Joe pulled the sedan to the curb a few doors from Matthew Growney's apartment. "Lucky to find a space so close in this neighborhood."

"I know, my place's near here. Used to have to circle the block for half an hour sometimes to find a spot. So, I broke down and rented a garage."

"What do they get for one?"

"Three hundred a month."

"Holy shit. No wonder I live in Skokie."

"I thought you guys were supposed to uh, reside in the city."

Joe gave him a bleak look. "I get my mail at a Chicago address."

"Works for me," Brian said as he joined Joe on the walkway leading to the entrance to Matthew Growney's apartment. The outer door was crisscrossed with yellow tape bearing the words CRIME SCENE DO NOT ENTER CHICAGO POLICE DEPARTMENT. Joe ripped the tape aside, extracted a key from a pocket and let them in. The air was stuffy. Everything was neat. The computer was on. A school of colorful fish swam around a coral reef formation displayed on the screen continuously, mindless of whether there was an audience to appreciate their efforts.

Brian sat down at the computer and tapped the ENTER key. The screen saver gave way to a login screen, password required. "Maybe I can figure out the password," he said.

"Can't let you do that. Cissel told me to pick up this machine and take it in. Our IT guys will examine everything on it."

"Maybe I could find something if I just had a few minutes."

"What, you some kinda accountant?"

"Actually, yeah. I was in White Collar Crime with the FBI."

"Well, I'm supposed to take the thing back to the station. How about giving me a hand with this stuff?"

They carted the computer and backup drive out to the city car, and secured them in the trunk.

"Let's go see Mr. Massey," Joe said.

"Okay. Tell me more about your brother. What was he like?"

"Matthew. He preferred Matthew, not Matt. All-American boy, know what I mean?"

"Good student?"

"Good? How about all-world? Perfect SAT scores. Top of his class at Illinois, captain of the debate team. MBA with top honors at the University of Chicago. Mom and Dad thought he walked on water."

"What about you? You go to college locally?"

Growney frowned. "Sorta. Got a two-year degree in criminal justice at City Colleges. Helped me get on the force, anyway."

"Were you and Matthew close?"

Joe Growney looked away. "Not really," he mumbled.

19

M r. Massey's not available at this time. Perhaps you'd like to leave word and I'll let him know you stopped by." The middle-aged administrative assistant gave him a polite smile.

"This's my card." Joe held an open leather case containing a brass Chicago Police department badge in front of the woman's eyes. "My name is Detective Joseph Growney."

Unfazed, she said, "Could you tell me what this visit is regarding?"

"Yeah, it's regarding a matter which, if Massey doesn't start talking with us in sixty seconds, is gonna make me very angry."

"Uh, one moment please." Her nasal tone reminded Brian of a long-distance operator in a 40s *film noir*.

She picked up the phone, swiveled in her chair so her back was to them, murmured inaudibly, and then hung up. She began pecking at her computer keyboard, ignoring the visitors completely.

Joe frowned and began to pace back and forth. He looked like he might erupt like some Hawaiian volcano.

"This is urgent," Brian said to the assistant.

A door in the walnut-paneled wall opened and Hamilton Massey eased his head and torso through. His face was calm, but his bloodshot eyes resembled the brake lights of an SUV at a stoplight. "Gentlemen, this way, please." He disappeared behind the door. Brian and Joe followed and caught up with him as he entered an office the size of the CPD homicide bullpen.

As the two visitors neared, Massey slid his lanky frame into a high-backed black leather desk chair that might have cost as much as the average family sedan. He gestured to a pair of chairs, but Brian and Joe remained standing.

"Please sit. I prefer eyes at a level," Massey said.

"We won't be here that long," Joe said. "How about telling us what the fuck happened to Spurgeon."

Massey's eyes narrowed. "How should I know—?"

"Stifle the bullshit," Joe said. "I want an answer."

"Detective, I've already discussed this matter in great detail with your colleagues. What could I possibly tell you that would help?"

"We'll ask the questions. And if they've been asked before, well, that's tough. When did you last see Spurgeon?"

Massey formed his tapered fingers into a classic high-steeple beneath his chin. "That's easy. I saw him in the men's room around, oh, six p.m. yesterday. He said he was leaving for the day."

A female voice came from the doorway. "You asked me to stop by, Mr. Massey."

Brian turned to see Natalie Katz in the doorway, her eyes troubled.

"Come in," Massey said. "Meet Detective Growney of the Chicago Police. You know Mr. McKay, of course." His clipped words carried just a hint of derision.

Before Natalie could respond, Massey went on, "Mr. Growney was asking about Mr. Spurgeon and his actions last night. Of course, you wouldn't have had any contact with him."

"Let her tell it!" Growney's voice was as sharp as a shard of glass from a shattered whiskey bottle. "Were you with Mr. Spurgeon between six and seven?"

"Yes. Mr. Massey, Dan Nitrick and I were with him in his office, going over the actual versus budget numbers for the Middle East Division," she said.

"This meeting was from when to when?" Growney asked.

"We started around five and went a little over an hour."

"Then what?"

"I left. I went home."

"What about Massey and Nitrick?"

"They were still around when I left."

"Okay. So what happened when you cut out?"

"I went to my office, checked my phone and e-mail, packed up and took off. That took about twenty minutes. Then I went down to the lobby, passed through the security guard area, and took the elevator down to the parking garage. I was walking to my car when I noticed the interior light was on in a big black Mercedes in the next aisle. The car looked familiar, and I thought maybe someone left the door ajar and I thought I should close it. When I got there, I saw Mr. Spurgeon." Her shoulders slumped and she looked at her feet.

"Go on. Describe what he looked like."

"He was leaning forward, with his head against the steering wheel, like he'd fallen asleep or passed out or something. I spoke to him and he didn't answer. He was like totally motionless, I mean like a statue. I tapped him on the shoulder. Nothing. I about freaked. Then I called building security and waited 'til the guard arrived. Mr. Spurgeon never moved."

"Did you see any sign of violence?" Brian asked.

"Nothing visually. But it smelled bad, like it smells after a fireworks display, and like…" her voice trailed off.

"Like excrement?" Growney's voice was soft.

"Yes." Natalie looked at the floor.

"Then what happened?" Growney said.

"The guard shook him, but he didn't react. He put his finger on his neck, looking for a pulse, I think. Then he radioed for another guy to call the police. I waited there with the guard until the police came. They pulled Mr. Spurgeon's head away from the steering wheel, and that's when the blood came into view. There was a gun somewhere in the car, I heard the guard say. I think he probably meant on the floor, but I didn't actually see it. Then two policemen arrived and they asked the guard and me a bunch of questions."

"How long did this Q and A go on?" Growney asked.

"Maybe forty-five minutes. Weird, but I remember thinking I'd be having a later dinner. Then, I realized I wasn't hungry."

"Huh. So, then what?"

"A bunch of other police department people got there. They took my contact information and they said I could go, so I did."

"Where was Massey all this time?" Growney said.

"I...don't know. The last I saw him was in here. I assume he was sitting at his desk." She nodded toward the CFO, who regarded her impassively, elbows propped on the desktop, long fingers folded beneath his chin.

"How much time was there between when the meeting ended and when you first saw Mr. Spurgeon in his car?"

"Maybe twenty-five minutes. Like I said, I had to clean off my desk and stuff."

"Okay you can go." Growney said. "Oh, and thanks."

"What do you know about Matthew Growney's murder?" Joe's voice had become almost kindly as he questioned Natalie. Now, it was back to a sharp rasp as he addressed Massey again.

Massey glanced at the thin gold watch on his left wrist. "Look, Detective, This is old news. I've discussed this with you people *ad infinitum*, and frankly, I'm quite busy.

Perhaps you could consult your department's files. I really don't—"

"Consult this," Growney said. He reached across the desk. He grabbed the executive's red Hermes tie in a sinewy hand and jerked it down so Massey's face descended slowly, almost to the desktop. Massey gurgled then said in a muffled voice, "Stop, please."

Growney released the tie, wiped his hand on the side of his trousers and remained standing, hands on hips, at the edge of the desk.

Massey raised his head slowly. His face was beet-red. His glasses had come off and lay on the blotter. "You'll be very sorry you did that, Detective."

"Don't you *dare* tell me what I'll be sorry about. This isn't some fucking accountants' meeting. It's a murder investigation. Two investigations. People around you have a nasty habit of getting killed. So don't you tell me what I'll be sorry about."

"Come on. Let's get out of here," Growney said to Brian.

At the doorway, the cop turned to Massey, who was gingerly adjusting his silk tie. "Don't you *ever* tell me what to do or not to do," Growney said.

As they retraced their steps to the reception area, Brian kept silent, but his brain was whirling. He suspected Massey deserved what he got—maybe more, depending on how the case unwound. He also knew that Joe, or any other Chicago police detective, could get away with roughing up a suspect lacking clout. But Massey wasn't one of those faceless citizens. No, he'd wield influence. Joe would be the one in a pickle now.

In the finance floor reception area, the nasal-voiced woman was nowhere to be seen.

"You really slung it into the fan up there," Brian said.

Joe shook his head. "Probably so."

Later that afternoon, after Brian had left the CPD, Joe Growney called Hamilton Massey. "I thought that went pretty well. You're okay, right?"

"Yes, I think he got the intended message. You're Mr. Intense, hot on the trail of the evil murderer. And you don't much care if a mere top executive such as myself doesn't like it. But you ruined a perfectly acceptable silk tie."

"So get a new one. What's twenty-five bucks?"

"More like one hundred twenty-five."

"Must be nice living on a one-percenter's salary."

"You'll be well taken care of…if all goes according to plan."

"Why do I worry about the parts of the 'plan' I don't have control over?"

"It's in good hands at this end. You just do your part and we'll all be fine."

20

After a night of troubled sleep, Brian stumbled from bed, showered and brewed a pot of strong coffee, which he used to wash down a bagel.

As he ate, he read through the information sheets he'd obtained from the Belcoe accounting staff the previous day. As he'd requested, all six had written their names and whereabouts from midnight to eight a.m. Sunday morning of the murder of Matthew Growney. No surprises—all of them indicated they'd been at home, except for Natalie Katz, who said she'd been out on a date and Tim Huff, who'd written, "None of your business."

By the time he'd retrieved the Grand Cherokee from the alley garage and tuned the radio to the morning news on NPR, he felt nearly awake. Although it was only a four-mile drive to the Belcoe offices, he knew he'd have a good thirty minutes in rush hour traffic, time to gather his thoughts for the day.

His personal life had taken some hits lately. Two days before, he'd had a major argument with Michelle, and they hadn't communicated since. In recent weeks, they'd gone from daily contact to seeing each other once a week, without much mutual enthusiasm. A typical Saturday night recently had been Chinese and a Netflix movie at her apartment, followed by either desultory lovemaking or their falling asleep on the couch. Brian was unsure where their relationship was going.

"Son of a bitch!"

The words were out of his mouth before he even knew he'd uttered them. A Yellow cab had cut in front of the Grand Cherokee and then nailed the brakes to avoid crunching the Jag in front of it. Brian mashed his brake pedal to the floorboard and a chain-reaction ensued, with near misses and honking horns for a quarter mile behind on Stockton.

A few days back, over beers, James had entertained him with an animated account of his most recent cab ride in from O'Hare. The young Special Agent had given the hack the address—Marina City, the 65-story twin corncob-shaped towers designed by Bertrand Goldberg, and a well-known Chicago landmark. The guy said, "No problem," and lurched into traffic. James was busy listening to messages on his phone, when he realized the cab was headed for the western suburbs instead of into the city. "Where we going?" James asked. "Cheecago downtown," came the answer. After a screaming argument as to which direction downtown lay, James badged the guy and threatened to get his medallion pulled. James was finally deposited at the curb a half hour later and sent the driver on his way, seething.

Oh well, Brian thought. You put up with a certain amount of hassle in any big city. And in Chicago, there were plenty of offsets—world-class restaurants of every imaginable ethnicity, live jazz and blues everywhere, the peerless lakeshore, the most striking urban architecture in America, two major-league baseball teams.

As Brian steered his car into a parking space at Belcoe, the radio announcer was saying, "In local business news, shares of Chicago's Belcoe Corporation are down two points to 83 in heavy trading. This amid rumors of a management shakeup at the company in the wake of the recent death of its president, Douglas Spurgeon." Hadn't the stock been in the high nineties only a couple of weeks ago? Chief

Operating Officers came and went all the time, so it seemed unlikely that Spurgeon's demise would account for a large drop in value. What else was driving the price down?

A few steps from the modest enclosed office he'd been assigned, he caught a whiff of smoke. Funny, smoking was *verboten* in the building. Inside, Mary Edwards sat in the visitor's chair near his desk, legs crossed knee over knee, her black skirt hiked up over the top thigh. He noticed that she had great legs. Slate gray smoke eddied upward to an air conditioning duct in the ceiling. A lit cigarette dangled precariously from slender purple-nailed fingers, the ash in danger of falling to the carpet. When Brian entered, she looked up, but didn't speak.

"Been waiting long?" Brian asked.

"We need to talk."

"Fire away. Hey wait. Around this place, that's a bad choice of words."

Her expression stayed flat. "Can I douse this somewhere?" She lifted the cigarette an inch.

"Here." He tapped a dark blue china mug emblazoned in gold with "FBI," a going-away present from James a year earlier. When the hot butt hit the dregs of yesterday's coffee, it hissed in defeat.

She glanced at the ceiling. "Let's go outside," she said. "Okay."

In the lobby, they pushed through a revolving door and emerged on the windswept plaza fronting the Chicago River. Mary led the way to a concrete bench overlooking the river to the south. She dug in her purse and came out with a pack of Winstons. She placed one in her lips and tried to light it with a green plastic Bic. The wind gusted and snuffed the flame before it could ignite the tobacco.

"Fuck," she mumbled.

Brian cupped his hands around hers as she flicked the silver wheel atop the lighter a second time. The cigarette caught, and Mary greedily inhaled.

"Thanks." She exhaled a cloud of smoke and smiled ruefully. "I get so needy about these things. Tried to quit, but I guess I just don't have the willpower."

"Hell, I did it a couple of times, before I finally got it right."

She nodded, her eyes solemn. "Look, there's something bugging me." She inclined her head at the pale green glass edifice towering over them. "Something up there."

"People say I'm a good listener."

"I think I might know something. I mean about Mr. Spurgeon."

"Okay."

"The evening before the one he...died, he had a visitor."

"Oh?"

"Yeah. Someone who'd been in there with him before. Several times. It might not mean anything, but..."

"Why don't you just take it from the top?"

She sighed, took a hit on the smoke and averted her gaze to the smooth dark water lapping the concrete abutment below them. "That evening, I went to his office to deliver an envelope from Doctor Akbar, and I heard something. The door was closed, and I was about to knock, when I heard noises inside."

"What kind of noises?"

Brian wasn't sure, but her face seemed to color slightly.

"Like two people involved in, you know."

"Sex?"

"Yeah, like that. Weird sex. Some kind of bondage thing, sounded like."

"All right, enough of the suspense, already. Who was in there?"

She stared ahead. "I'm not sure."

"But you've got a pretty good idea, don't you?"

"Okay. It was your friend, Liz Wheaton."

"The cold, hard *jefe* of the humans."

"Yeah."

"You're sure this was ah, sexual?"

"They were making noises like short-haired pointers in heat."

"Short-haired pointers?"

"My ex tried raising them. Thought he'd make a bundle. All he got out of it was huge vet bills, the messiest yard in the neighborhood and some pissed-off customers who tried to return the buggers after they stopped being cute little puppies."

"How long was this going on would you say? The closed door stuff, I mean."

"Maybe a couple weeks?"

"Is Wheaton married?"

"Used to be."

"What do you know about Massey?"

She smirked. "Odd duck. Never brings a woman to any company functions. But I've heard there've been 'me too' concerns. That he's made inappropriate remarks to some of the female staff, and that there was an incident with an assistant where she claims he touched her breasts. From my own experience, he never seems to even notice me."

"That's hard for me to believe."

She managed a smile. "Is that a compliment?"

"Yes." It was Brian's turn to feel a little embarrassed. "I mean, I noticed you right away."

"Nice to be noticed."

Out of the corner of his eye, Brian caught a glimpse of a large man in a long dark coat and shades standing to the west, about 30 yards from them, a phone in his left hand as he casually leaned against the metal railing. The guy looked familiar. Brian guessed the figure hadn't moved since he and Mary had arrived. He slowly angled around for a better look. The man turned away and pocketed the phone.

"What?" Mary said.

"Probably nothing. Thought I spotted someone I knew."

Mary turned to see what he'd been looking at. The man in the coat and shades was walking away. She shrugged, then glanced at her watch. "I should probably get back to my desk. They don't make allowances for us smokers, and I've been away long enough to be missed."

As they retraced their steps across the plaza, Brian asked, "Can you tell me anything else about your boss's buddy, Pinhead, I mean Kalif?"

"Sure, but not in the office."

"Well then, can I buy you a drink after work?"

"Sure."

Late that afternoon, Brian stepped into a large empty office and went to a window facing south. Outside, long deep blue shadows were infiltrating the skyscraper canyons of the Loop. Office workers streamed from the revolving doors of neighboring glass towers. A Wendella passenger boat, packed with commuters and tourists headed along the river, passing under the Michigan Avenue bridge, en route to the bustling south Loop train stations. He grinned at a boyhood memory of catching a ride on a "water taxi," as they were called, gaping up at the tall buildings. One memorable spring morning, he and his buddy, Dan, had spotted a young couple embracing *au naturel* on a balcony of a lower floor of an apartment building. They were making out, oblivious to the water-born gawkers below. As the boat motored around the bend, the couple disappeared from view, apparently moving on to more advanced intimacies.

21

After a drink at a bar near Belcoe, They'd cabbed it to Mary's apartment on the Near North Side. They sat on the couch, the outsides of their legs barely touching. They had glasses of Tia Maria in hand. Her pale gold blouse revealed the freckled top of a tanned chest, the freckles echoing the dusting on her nose and upper cheeks.

He noticed the time on the clock across the room—nearly nine. He felt a light buzz and the Tia added a touch of mellow. He guessed Mary must be feeling the same. Funny how people reacted to booze in individual ways. You wouldn't discern any change in James's demeanor, even after a long evening of tipping them back. Michelle, on the other hand, started acting silly after a couple of sips of her standby, a whiskey sour garnished with three maraschino cherries.

Mary laughed. "I couldn't believe you, yanking Akbar's chain that first day. I've never seen anybody else try it."

"I can't stand empty suits."

"And that's why you work independent."

"That's part of it." He took a short sip of the liqueur. "This human lady, Liz, she's got some clout, does she?"

Mary snorted. "That's one way to put it. Some of us, we wonder if she had something on her boss."

"Spurgeon?"

"Yeah."

"What kind of something?"

"Well, as I mentioned, she was with him the evening before he died. And he's married, so…"

"So, she could maybe have had influence over him in work matters?"

"Yes. She fawned over him, but was obnoxious to the rest of us."

He shook his head. "Reminds me of this guy, big honcho with the FBI, agent in charge and my boss. Total mediocrity in the field, but a master of office politics. Last I heard, he was in line for promotion to some assistant director position with Homeland Security. Ah, hell, this must be boring you."

"No, not at all. I like hearing your stories. Being in law enforcement, you bring a different perspective. Me, I know those guys we've been talking about are into...risky stuff, but it's not my place to get involved."

"'Akbar and his pal, the pin-headed one?"

"Probably. But it's not just those two."

"And the risky stuff being something illegal?"

"It's only a suspicion, but yeah."

"And it could involve the finance people as well, right?"

"I'd guess."

"Did they hire anyone to replace Matthew Growney?"

"Don't know. They're always adding people around there. Hard to keep track of 'em all." Mary drained her glass, glanced at his nearly empty one. "How 'bout another?"

"Thanks, but I need to be in there in the morning, just like you."

At the door, he stopped and looked into her dark eyes. Their faces drew close and their lips met in a brief kiss.

"See you tomorrow," he said.

She gave him a sad smile.

As he descended the porch stairs to the sidewalk, both doors on the curb side of a parked black Suburban opened and two heavy-set men emerged onto the parkway. Neither the men nor the vehicle looked like police. Brian headed down the walk warily. He wished he had his Sig Sauer automatic with him. When he was near the vehicle, the two men approached him, one on each side. A third man, taller and less bulky than the others came around from the far side of the truck. The shape of a fourth man loomed behind the wheel.

The spokesman, the lean specimen, stared into Brian's face. In the illumination from the nearby mercury vapor streetlight, the guy looked a little like the actor Christopher Walken. "C'mon, man, whaddaya say we go get a nightcap." It sounded more like a threat than an invitation.

The first two men had attached rough hands to Brian's biceps. He wondered if Mary were watching from her window.

"No thanks," he said. "Gotta big day tomorrow."

The man nodded. Suddenly the guys on either side started maneuvering Brian toward the open rear door of the SUV. He wrenched his left arm free and drove his elbow into the gut of the man on that side. He heard a grunt of pain. Simultaneously, he felt a sharp jabbing twinge in his arm on the other side. Had he been stabbed?

Brian felt weak, nauseous. He sank slowly to his knees. His vision blurred, and then he felt two sets of hands lifting him by the arms and legs and depositing him into the back seat of the vehicle. He was pulled into a sitting position and wedged in by bulky bodies on both sides. Car doors slammed. An engine revved. The vehicle backed once then pulled forward into the street.

The nausea slowly passed and Brian felt drowsy, like he'd wakened in the night in the middle of a nightmare. They must have jabbed him with a needle. But containing what? His head throbbed with dull pain. He slumped to the left as the truck sped up and took a corner at speed. His nose brushed the folds of a wrinkled cotton shirt, and he gagged at the pungent smell of a musk-laden aftershave apparently applied with a turkey baster. Then all went black.

99

22

Brian came to, then fell backward into a vast black dream. *He was a boy, riding in the back seat of his parents' car, Dad at the wheel, Mom in the front passenger seat. It was dark, late at night. They'd been at his Uncle Bill's house in Evanston, enjoying the annual McKay family Fourth of July celebration. A real treat for an only child: all the kids to play with, charred hot dogs and burgers, candy, Coke, ice cream, ear-splitting fireworks, including some awesome cherry bombs. The delicious sulfuric stench of burnt gunpowder. The adults drinking beer and punch, acting more and more silly as the party progressed. The best day of the year, for sure. Toward the end of the bash, as it was getting dark, he saw Uncle Bill put his hand on Mom's butt. She turned and smiled at his uncle, but then spotted little Brian staring and slapped the hand away with a laugh.*

Young Brian had eaten too much and had a monster stomachache. He'd curled up on the back seat and fallen asleep as soon as they left Uncle Bill's. He kept waking up on the way home every time the car stopped at a light, then faded back to sleep as the vehicle rolled forward again. The fuzzy cloth seat fabric tickled his nose. His parents weren't talking, not a word, which struck him as odd. Maybe they were sleepy, too.

Then, a deep voice: "He's still out."

Another male voice: "Good. He comes to, give him another jolt, just a few drops. Don't wanna kill him. Yet."

Wait a minute. There wasn't another man in the car. Just Dad. And Dad wouldn't let anyone hurt him. No, something was way wrong. Through slitted eyes, he could make out lights flashing into the car, and then dissipating. He was wedged in on both sides, head slumped forward. Brian focused for an instant, came back to the present. All grown up, a man. Definitely not his parents with him. Not going home. Going where? He'd been hurt, given a shot by bad people. Had to get out. He managed to swing an elbow weakly into the person to his right.

"Ow! Fucker's wakin' up. Better give him that jolt."

The person to Brian's left wrapped beefy arms around him, held him steady. The one on the right fiddled with something, jabbed it into Brian's arm, right through the sleeve. He immediately felt groggy, started drifting.

Brian came to in pale gray light. He lay on his side on a cold hard floor. His hands were fastened behind him with what felt like plastic handcuffs, two connected flexible zip-tie loops. He recognized them as the cheap but effective disposable handcuffs used by law enforcement and the military to quickly restrain prisoners. The loops sank into his wrists, nearly cutting off circulation to his hands. His head throbbed with the mother of all headaches. His throat and chest felt as if he'd swallowed broken glass. For a few confused seconds, he thought he had a monstrous hangover. The symptoms were all there: headache, jitters and cottonmouth with an awful taste mixed in—chemical, metallic, nauseating.

A dull pain in his right biceps reminded him he'd been stuck with a needle at least twice. It came back gradually, like awakening from the dream, finally home from the Fourth of July party. His sluggish brain tried to separate real from unreal. Three men and a large black SUV at the curb outside Mary's apartment. An altercation, words exchanged. Rough hands grabbing him, jabbing a needle into his arm. Loading him roughly into the back seat of the SUV. Everything black, then starting to awaken. The irritating realization that he'd fallen into a trap. Nobody to blame but himself for being so dumb. Wedged in by two monstrous dudes, sticking an elbow in the ribs of one, then another needle in the arm, followed by blackness again.

He realized he was naked except for his boxer briefs. His upper right arm was swollen and bloody. His fingers were numb—the damned plastic cuffs were way too tight. He wondered if they'd stanch the circulation completely, pictured his hands as puffy black gangrenous blobs incapable of function. Though aching and miserable, he could move all four limbs. Didn't seem to have incurred any permanent damage. Yet.

He struggled to his knees, nearly blacked out, paused for a few tortuous seconds and managed to stand shakily. Where the hell was he? From his FBI experience he knew he'd damn well better get out soon or he'd be toast.

It was a roughly square room about ten feet on a side, dirty white Sheetrock walls, low cobwebbed wooden ceiling with exposed joists, cement floor, no furnishings. A solid-looking wooden door, centered in a wall. Near the ceiling, a small glass block rectangular window allowed faint daylight in. No light switch on the walls.

He stumbled to the window, got up on his toes to peer through the dirty pane. Heavy wrought iron burglar bars covered the window, the fastening bolts not visible. Impossible to remove from inside. The view was of a low shrub with mostly dead brown branches. The bottom of a gray stone wall of a neighboring building meeting unkempt lawn was partially visible through the foliage. Conclusion: a partitioned-off room in the basement of a residence in a none-too-spiffy neighborhood. Probably morning, judging from the gradually expanding light.

The metal doorknob wouldn't budge when he backed up to it and grappled with a hand. In the dead quiet, his breathing sounded like the breaking of distant surf.

He leaned against a wall and considered his options. First priority would be freeing his trapped hands, then finding a way out of this subterranean jail cell. He'd have a lot better luck if he could maneuver his trussed hands in front. He knew how to achieve that, but it wouldn't be easy. He remembered the training instructor at the FBI academy in Quantico: "You guys ever jumped rope? Same concept, only the rope's a little shorter." Being double-jointed wouldn't hurt either.

He lay on his side, assumed a fetal tuck, extended his arms to the aching point, laboriously worked one foot through, then the other. Finally, his hands were in front of him, puffy and white from lack of blood. The plastic cuffs were about a third of an inch wide and an eighth of an inch thick, standard issue. Agents could undo the restraining yokes on a detainee by cutting them with a knife or needle-nosed pliers. No tool kit in sight, though.

Brian's watch was still fastened to his right wrist, the leather strap much looser than the cuffs. It registered 7:21. By extending the index and middle fingers of his left hand, he could just pinch the stout watch strap between fingertips. He managed to grasp the strap edge and nudge it a fraction of an inch sideways. He repeated this process until he'd rotated the watch around so the bulky metal case was on the inside of his wrist, close to the plastic bond encircling his left hand.

It would only take a tiny laceration and then it might be possible to gradually rip through the plastic. He tried an experimental rubbing of the protruding crown of the watchcase against the plastic cuff. The metal barely made contact. He set to work, cursing as the restraining strap remained impervious. After about fifteen minutes, he'd made a minute knick in the cuff strap. Progress.

He continued the sawing motion more violently and was rewarded a few minutes later with a slight rip in the edge of the cuff encircling his left wrist. He stopped to listen for a moment. Still dead quiet except for the belligerent chirping of an unseen robin outside the window.

He twisted his wrists back and forth, levering with all his arm strength against the cuffs. Slowly as a drunken snail, the cuff material around his left hand split. The minute tear lengthened to an eighth-inch, then a quarter, and finally the damned thing tore through and fell to the floor. His hands were free of each other, but the right one was still constricted by a blood-choking constraint. He rubbed his left wrist.

Suddenly, Brian heard a noise overhead. Footsteps. One person walking, then plodding down stairs, getting closer. The sound of a lock being opened. The doorknob rattled and turned. He swung his arms behind him, hands clasped together, and sat in a corner as the door edged open.

23

I see you are awake. Very good." The speaker's words were cloaked in a Middle East accent.

"Why am I not surprised to see you?" Brian said.

The broad-shouldered man in white shirt and dark trousers smirked. "You do not seem so cocky now." He stepped toward Brian.

Brian recognized him as the man who'd argued with Doctor Akbar outside the shrink's office at Belcoe, the guy he'd dubbed "Pinhead." Shamir Kalif.

He stopped a few feet short of Brian, sniffed the air like a nervous animal. The smirk disappeared. "You moved. What have you been doing?"

The man's eyes focused on the broken zip-tie handcuff on the floor. He stood motionless, studying the plastic strap like a medium reading a fortune in a man's palm. Brian knew this was the time to move. He extended his right leg and kicked straight out, slamming the bare sole into Pinhead's knee with all the force he could muster. A noise like the pinging last kernel of popcorn in a hot air popper came from Pinhead's left knee. He went down on his back, clutching the wounded joint to his broad chest. Brian was on his feet and astride Pinhead in a flash. He grasped the man's neck with both hands and applied clamping pressure, oblivious of the pain wracking his constrained right hand. The man squirmed like a hooked trout and grabbed with thick, hairy fingers in an attempt to pry Brian's hands loose. Snot burst from his nostrils and onto the backs of Brian's hands. Brian held on as the man arched his back and tried to buck him off. For a split-second, he thought of the bull-riding competition he'd attended with Darcy in Montana the year before, then back to business—homing in on only one vital concern, throttling the man now writhing in his grasp. Brian knew this was a potentially dangerous chokehold once used by cops but now illegal. Cutting off the man's air temporarily by compressing the trachea would cause pain and air hunger. Martial arts combatants used it to knock out an opponent. Keeping at it too long could result in death.

Pinhead's contortions slowed as his strength ebbed. Not wanting to kill his adversary, Brian let up the pressure on the man's neck, which proved to be a mistake. Reenergized, Pinhead thrashed his torso about vigorously, nearly dumping Brian on the floor. Enough of this shit. Brian raised his left hand over his head, not unlike one of those Montana bull-riders, and brought it crashing down on Pinhead's face. Blood gushed from the center of the guy's face and he brought his hands up to cover the flattened nose. Brian rose, grabbed him by the shirtfront and shoved him back so the back of his head crashed on the floor. But Pinhead wasn't done yet. He got to his feet and, bent at the waist, lunged at Brian like an enraged bull. Brian sidestepped. The top of Kalif's head smacked into the wall, the impact sounding like a ripe melon dropped from a table. He fell on his face and lay motionless. A small pool of blood oozed from beneath the man's face and spread in thin rivulets across the concrete floor.

Brian gasped for breath. His right hand had stopped hurting, a bad sign. He felt the fingers with his left hand. The right failed to register the touch—It was like grasping a Styrofoam coffee cup. He had to find something to cut through the plastic band, and fast. His eyes flashed to Pinhead. The man wore a small black leather sheath on his belt. Brian advanced on the fallen man and bent at the knees to unsnap the cover folded over the top of the sheath. As he did, he heard a sibilant snore and noticed red bubbles forming where the bloody face met the floor. The individual bubbles slowly grew in size and burst like over-inflated toy balloons.

Brian extracted from the sheath a large jackknife and thumbed open a wicked-looking, steel blade. A quick flick of the tapered blade point, and the plastic cuff was lying on the floor not far from its mate. Brian rubbed his right wrist and hand until the color metamorphosed from chalky white to rosy pink. That's when the pain came back, like an estranged relative, not unanticipated but still unwelcome. He shook the hand until some semblance of normalcy returned.

Time for turnabout. He needed something to secure Pinhead. He eased through the open door and found himself in a room about twice the size of the cell in which he'd been incarcerated. It looked like an ordinary suburban homeowner's basement workshop, with two significant differences: one, the window had been painted over with black paint and two, sitting on a wooden workbench were several handguns and some boxes of .9 mm ammunition. Next to them, a plastic bag contained some heavy plastic zip-ties. Brian selected a couple of them and quickly returned to the other room.

Pinhead lay on the floor, exactly as Brian had left him. Brian crouched with the cuffs in hand and fastened them about the man's hairy wrists. As he cinched the second strap tight, the fallen man stirred briefly, and then resumed his fitful sleep. He was still snoring as Brian exited the room, swinging the door closed behind himself. The deadbolt lock on the outside of the solid wooden door snicked home with a twist. Brian stood in place, listening intently. Dead quiet. He returned to the workshop room and picked up a Colt Defender semi-automatic pistol, checking to make sure the clip was loaded and a round was in the chamber. He headed for the nearby stairway and began to ascend.

24

The stairs were unfinished wood covered with ribbed black rubber mats. Brian placed each foot carefully as he ascended, moving fast but trying to keep the noise to a minimum. Ten steps to a small landing. A white door with a brass knob, no visible lock set. He pressed an ear to the door and listened for a moment. Nothing. He pointed the Colt at the intersection of door and jamb, grasped the knob and turned it. He sprang into the room and quickly scanned his surroundings while tracking the space with the handgun. A square room with pale yellow walls, a modest dining room table with four chairs, dregs of a Domino's pizza on the tabletop. A bunch of empty beer cans in a ragged circle around the pizza box, more on the dirty floor and in an overflowing wastebasket. Flies buzzed about the half-eaten pizza slice remaining in the grease-stained cardboard box. A shiny circular brass light fixture hung from a chain over the table. Brian's reflection in the bright metal was distorted, pulled to the sides, transforming his image into that of a fat man in a circus.

There were three doorways off the dining room. Brian checked each in turn—one led into a larger front room, another to a narrow kitchen and the third to a hallway giving onto the rear of the house. He eased into the front room, which was furnished with a maroon velour couch, two upholstered tan chairs, a 40-inch Samsung TV with satellite box on a cheap fiberboard stand and a bentwood rocker. The glass-topped blonde coffee table between the couch and TV was littered with newspapers and another discarded pizza carton. The furniture looked new but cheap, like stuff in a low rent suburban hotel suite. The curtains were drawn. The air was redolent of the ghosts of fast-food meals past. The place had an aspect of recent abandonment.

He turned and retraced his steps to the kitchen, which contained more detritus of greasy food and a sink full of dirty dishes. He made for the hallway, eased into it with the Colt out front. The door on the left gaped open. Two more doors, both closed, broke up the pale walls on the right. A quick look through the open door revealed a messy bathroom clad in green paint and gold tile. There were towels strewn about on the floor and a stinking unflushed toilet. A faint mechanical sound filtered from somewhere further inside the building.

Brian backed out of the room and swung the pistol on the first closed door across the hall. He held his breath and listened intently with an ear to the door. A low-pitched metallic hum throbbed on the other side. Otherwise, nothing. He opened the door abruptly and poked the barrel of the semi-automatic in ahead of his body. An unmade bed with rumpled sheets dominated the small room. A window air conditioner pulsated metronomically.

Head swiveling, Brian continued up the hallway to the last room, opened the door and cautiously entered with the Colt ready. Another bedroom. Empty, unmade bed. No air conditioner and no books or nightstands. Brian looked out the window. Dense shrubbery shielded the building next door, but he caught glimpses of honey-colored brick through the branches. As he moved away from the window, he heard a vehicle starting at the rear of the property, probably a pickup truck or large sport utility vehicle with a V-8, from the sound of it. The engine fired, stumbled and ran clean. Tires crunched on concrete and loose gravel. An engine revved and a tire chirped under sudden acceleration. The sound dwindled as the vehicle receded.

Brian bolted to the kitchen and out the door. He sprinted along the side of the house to a small backyard containing a postage-stamp lawn and a two-car frame garage. He approached the garage side door, which proved to be locked. He peered in through the single dirt-smudged window and confirmed the interior was empty of vehicles. A ragged oil stain marred the floor about where the engine would be in a rig parked there. Four large cardboard boxes were stacked on the floor in the right-hand space.

Brian suddenly realized he was still naked except for his boxer briefs. On impulse, he scanned the area for possible onlookers. He looked up at the brick house adjacent to the building he'd been in. He thought he detected movement in the upstairs window, but it might have been the breeze blowing a curtain to the side. For a moment, he flashed to his mother cautioning him as he dressed for grade school: "Brian, always wear clean underwear without any holes in it. If you're ever in an accident, you'll be glad you did." He'd thought, but didn't say, "If I'm in an accident, my underwear's the last thing I'm gonna worry about." He returned to the house to try to find something to cover himself with.

Further examination of the closet in the first bedroom revealed the shirt, slacks, shoes and socks he'd been wearing when the burly trio abducted him the night before, in a clump on the floor. He donned them quickly. The right shirtsleeve was crusted with blood in the biceps area. His watch registered 9:18 a.m. No sign of his phone. He began to look for a phone in the house, but decided he wouldn't use one if he found it. A phone would be a very likely repository for fingerprints of the house's former inhabitants. In any case, there didn't seem to be one anywhere.

A siren wailed nearby, getting closer by the second. The nosy next-door neighbor must have called the police. Brian quickly wiped down the Colt and replaced it in the basement. Then he went to the front door, stood just inside it and waited. The siren approached rapidly.

25

The black Ford Police Interceptor Utility bore the emblem of the Park Ridge Police. *So that's where I am,* he thought. Park Ridge was an older suburb off the northwest corner of Chicago, cheek by jowl with O'Hare International Airport. A quiet bedroom community of hardworking families and retirees. The kind of place where a nearly naked man running though a backyard would likely prompt a call to the cops from a concerned citizen.

Brian opened the door and leaned casually against the jamb, hands in pockets, as the two uniforms strutted up the sidewalk. Before they could speak, he said, "Help you, Officers?"

The older and heavier of the two, a blue-eyed, round-faced man—CASEY, per his nametag—rested his right hand on his sidearm and spoke. "Had a report of a naked guy in the backyard at this address. Know anything about it?"

"That would be me. Except I wasn't naked."

"Huh?"

"I was wearing boxer briefs."

The lead cop turned to his partner with a nasty smirk on his face. "He had his boxer briefs on. Guess everything's cool."

"You think?" the partner said. His nametag read FELTON.

A small woman with gray hair twisted into a braid like pastry dough came into view behind the two police officers. "Did you catch him?" she yelled.

Both men twitched. Casey pivoted to face the new arrival standing with arms crossed over her chest in the yard below the porch where they stood.

"And who might you be?" Casey said.

She frowned. "I'm the one who called in about the naked man. Omigod—that's him!" She pointed at Brian.

Casey nodded and turned back to Brian. "Hey, mister naked man, how 'bout some ID?"

"Can't find my wallet."

"Well, who the hell *are* you?"

Brian sighed. "Come on in and have a seat. This is gonna take a while."

Felton gestured at the woman in the yard to come on up with them and ushered her into the house behind Brian and Casey.

Brian eased into one of the upholstered tan chairs. The two policemen remained on their feet, Casey close enough to touch with an extended arm, while his partner blocked the doorway. The neighbor woman sat on the couch across from Brian and eyed him warily.

"Name?" Casey glared at Brian as he began the interview.

The younger cop pulled out a small notebook and clicked a ballpoint open with a flourish.

"Brian McKay."

"You the owner here, Brian?"

"Tell you the truth, I've got no idea who the owner is. I was snatched off the street on the north side of Chicago last night, injected with some kind of knockout drug and came to this morning tied up in the basement."

"I've never seen him before in my life," the gray-haired woman said.

"What's your name, dear?" Casey asked.

"I'm Mrs. Melissa Zemke," she replied, with an emphasis on the 'Mrs.' "And you don't know me well enough to call me 'dear.'" She crossed her arms again and slouched in the cushions like a petulant child.

"Please be quiet for now. We'll get to you later," Casey murmured. He turned back to Brian. "How 'bout taking it from the top?"

Brian knew that cops interviewing witnesses usually operated on the basis that it was better to receive than to give. He also knew that these guys were only the first in a long line of law enforcement officials who'd be interested in the case. He'd reveal only what he needed to get it over with. He sketched the events of the previous evening, starting with visiting Mary Edwards's apartment, through the abduction into the SUV, imprisonment in the basement of the house and ending with his overpowering Pinhead, and searching the house and yard. He made no mention of Belcoe or his role investigating a murder of an employee, nor did he mention that he'd previously encountered Pinhead at the company.

"You guys will want to check out the basement yourselves. This Pinhead guy's locked in the room where I was held, and there's a bunch of guns in a workroom down there that are probably hotter'n a Southside parking lot in August."

"Call for backup," Casey ordered his partner.

The younger cop got on his handheld radio to comply. Brian and Casey sat in silence.

"Car's on the way," the partner reported.

"While we're waiting, I should tell you that the Chicago Central Area Commander of the Bureau of Detectives will vouch for me," Brian said.

"Dick Cissel?" Casey said. Obviously, the suburban cop had heard of the storied Chicago commander.

"Yeah. If you'll call him, he'll verify I'm a private investigator involved in a homicide case in cooperation with the CPD."

"Fuckin' A, I'll call him." Casey extracted a phone, called the CPD and asked for Cissel. Eventually, he got him on the line and asked about Brian McKay.

Apparently, Cissel admitted to familiarity with Brian, said he was okay and demanded to know just what the fuck was going on out there in Park Ridge. As the conversation ground on, a second police squad lurched to a stop outside and another pair of patrolmen entered the room. The place was getting crowded and Brian's nerves were becoming more jangled by the minute.

As Casey hung up, Brian said, "Look, I'm kind of short on sleep. Would I be able to get out of here sometime soon?"

"Wait'll we see what's downstairs. Then, we'll need your contact information."

The four cops conferred briefly and agreed that the two latest arrivals would keep an eye on Brian while Casey and his partner headed downstairs. More awkward silence as the two new cops waited for the others to return. Suddenly, there was a burst of shouting from below, following by violent thumps. Sounded like Pinhead was not going quietly. A few minutes later the two cops staggered into the room with a bloody-faced Kalif in tow.

"This the guy played jailer?" Casey inquired.

"He's the one," Brian said.

"Fuck you," Pinhead shouted, spraying spit on Brian's face.

He extracted a handkerchief to wipe it off. "I hope you've been more polite to the officers," Brian said.

Kalif began to speak, then clamped his lips tight.

"Thinks he's a tough guy," Casey said. Then, to the two cops now clamping thick hands on Pinhead's arms, "Take him to the station and book him."

"For what?" the lanky cop on the right said.

"Kidnapping, possession of unlicensed weapons, resisting arrest and being an all-around dickhead."

"What about me?" Mrs. Zemke inquired.

Casey's stern expression softened. "Please tell us in your own words what you saw at this house this morning, Ma'am."

The back and forth about Brian running around in his undershorts took a few minutes. Then, Casey asked, "Have you seen anything weird going on here, generally speaking?"

"Well," the old woman said, "There's been that fellah with the small head. He comes and goes, sometimes carrying a duffle bag. And another foreigner has been in and out of here also. A shorter guy with a beard. They look like terrorists, ya ask me."

Eventually the interview between Casey and Mrs. Zemke wound down, he got her phone number and let her go home.

Casey told his partner to get Brian's name, address and phone number. Then, he told him to seal the house with crime scene tape and to stand by there for further orders.

After that had been accomplished, Casey said to Brian, "You're probably going to want a ride someplace, I suppose."

Brian felt embarrassed—he was penniless. "Yeah, without my wallet, I don't even have El fare."

They rolled to the Chicago city limits with Brian in the passenger seat. Casey pulled over at the Cumberland El station and handed Brian a wrinkled five-dollar bill "for public transportation." Brian felt like a panhandler. He caught the Blue Line southeast through the city and on down to Belmont. From there, it was a short bus ride east to his apartment, where he found his spare key under the lifeless potted Norfolk pine occupying a quarter of the front porch and let himself in.

After checking for phone messages, he slumped onto the couch and was asleep a few minutes later. He was awakened by the landline jangling insistently. He rubbed sleep from his eyes, managed to get to the phone on the fourth ring, and glanced at his watch as he mumbled, "Hello." It was after six p.m. He'd been sleeping for six hours.

"You owe me one." The booming baritone belonged to Dick Cissel.

"Uh, thanks, Dick." Brian's head throbbed with a merciless migraine.

"Park Ridge is transferring your guy to us tomorrow morning."

"Our guy being Pinhead?"

"Who? Oh, you mean Kalif. Shamir Kalif."

"Has he done any talking yet?"

"Only to tell us to fuck ourselves and to ask for a lawyer."

"Who's the lawyer?"

"Here's where it gets funky. Guy by the name of Menachem Sneerson. Ring any bells?"

"According to my Belcoe, Inc. staff directory, he's general counsel of the company."

"Right. He raised hell tryin' to get our friend released, but I wasn't playin'. I want you in here first thing in the morning to discuss this situation. Maybe we can work out a way to make your buddy a better communicator."

"Hey, you know me. When the big guys like you can't handle the sluggers, I come in from the bullpen."

After hanging up, Brian ordered a pizza and clicked on the TV. Unable to concentrate on the program, he looked around the living room. Had some books on the third shelf of the bookcase been moved in his absence? He wondered if someone had been inside in the apartment the night before last. Probably not. And yet, it was war now and he'd damn well be ready, not just to protect himself, but also Darcy and possibly even Mary. Either could be a target. They'd already chased Darcy and kidnapped him from in front of Mary's place. Why? Who? Kalif was a Belcoe employee. The trail led to the company.

He'd get in touch with James to find out what the FBI was doing before returning to Belcoe. He reflected that it had been a while since he'd spent a Saturday night home alone. He went to bed early.

26

The next day, Brian organized his huge collection of rock and blues vinyl and CDs while contemplating the twisted incidents he'd been exposed to at Belcoe. He chatted with Darcy on the phone. Neither of them mentioned the violent demise of her boyfriend, but Brian could tell she remained disconsolate—and angry. She again volunteered to help him with his investigation and he told her the time might come when he'd take her up on the offer. Darcy had proven herself a smart and tough investigator in her own right, both at Bone Mountain the year before and in Chicago recently with what the media had dubbed "The Cup of Chai Murder" case, where a corrupt real estate developer had tried to kill her, but she'd outwitted him. In the wake of the second case, Darcy had become a minor celebrity. She assured Brian her studies wouldn't suffer if she helped him and that she'd be available at spring break coming up soon, and then for the summer once the current semester ended in May. He realized the picture of Darcy he'd always carried was gone—he should get her to sit still for a current photo.

Brian spent most of the following morning obtaining a new phone, a temporary replacement driver's license and credit cards, along with a slim leather wallet to store them in.

The hard part was the license—he had to stand in line for forty minutes at the State of Illinois Building in the Loop, while bored-looking clerks moved with sloth-like speed in dealing with the taxpaying public. When he finally got to the service window, a pasty-faced young woman with two small chrome rings in a nostril and a purple T-shirt with the legend VAMPIRE LESBIANS ON CRACK informed him he was in the wrong line for replacement licenses and that he had to start over one floor up. He'd asked to see a supervisor, and she'd told him *she* was the supervisor. He'd reluctantly ascended a floor and received prompt, competent service, leaving the building, bemused but with license in hand fifteen minutes later.

He called James. "Kalif? Matter of fact, I got a little more intel for ya," James said. "One nasty sumbitch. Like I told ya before, raised in Saudi Arabia, part of a filthy rich family with heavy royal connections. But dig this: age of eighteen, accused of raping a twelve-year-old cousin, charges dropped. Father set up him and a brother with an Arabian horse ranch near home. Took 'em little over a year to run it into the ground. Anyway, the family encouraged him to leave town. Got a student visa to the U.S., at Ohio State he got piss-poor grades, dropped out his junior year. Started at Belcoe seventeen months back, reporting to a guy named Louis DeRosa as a quote unquote 'troubleshooter.' Doesn't have a jacket in this country. Whaddya think?"

"You're right. Sounds like a turd muffin. Right now, he's in the custody of the CPD."

"What for?"

"Let's see. There's aggravated kidnapping, possession of unregistered weapons, resisting arrest, and probably one or two more items I'm not aware of."

"Kidnapping? Sounds like the Bureau's gonna get involved."

"*I'm* involved."

"Wait, what?"

"Three hard cases grabbed me off the street the night before last, and this yahoo Kalif, strolled into the cell they put me in this morning."

"Please tell me you kicked his ass."

"Okay, I kicked his ass. Wasn't easy, though. And the other three assholes are still in the wind."

"Anybody we know?"

"Nope. But I'm checking in with Cissel later, supposed to pore over some mugs."

"What's *he* got to do with it?"

"I was snatched on the North Side."

"Let me know how that goes. I'm starting to feel a kinda proprietary interest in this, with some unknown dudes kidnapping your ass."

"I appreciate the sediment."

In the garage off the alley behind his apartment, Brian checked the undercarriage of the Grand Cherokee for tracking devices. Finding none, he hit the road for the Central Area Bureau of Detectives headquarters. Dick Cissel and Joe Growney were in Cissel's office when Brian arrived for their scheduled meeting.

"Glad you could make it," Cissel said, glancing at his watch.

Growney regarded Brian with a frown, as if resenting his presence. Brian wondered if it was the man's doubt as to the usefulness of allowing a private detective to work on a CPD homicide case. Or maybe it was animosity of a personal nature. Some people just never jelled. "Glad to see you're still on the job," he said to Growney.

"Ah, Massey never complained, if that's what you mean," Growney said.

Cissel broke in. "Not that it would've carried any weight. Anyway, your buddy Pinhead is hangin' tough."

"He say anything at all?" Brian asked.

"Said he's renting the Park Ridge house on his own. Nobody else living there. Doesn't know anything about how you ended up in the basement. Was going to let you go, seeing as how you're old buddies from Belcoe, but you jumped him and it went south from there."

"Pure bullshit. What about the weapons in the basement? He a collector?" Brian said.

Joe Growney said, "Exactly the way I put it to him. Guy says, 'Oh, yes, I collect guns for target shooting.' Can't remember where he got 'em, though, and doesn't recall where he shot at the targets. No registrations. None of 'em's been recently fired." Growney shrugged.

"Anything on ownership of the house?" Brian asked.

"We're working on it," Cissel said. "And the rent's been paid by an outfit called Midwestern Traders. Here's where it gets interesting. The owner of Midwestern Traders is a familiar name."

"Don't tell me."

"Yep. Belcoe Incorporated."

"How'd you find out?"

Cissel waved that away like a man shooing a fly. "Hell we got the goddamn lease, executed by Mr. Menachem A. Sneerson, Esquire. And a visitor to this very office earlier today." Cissel leaned back in his chair, beefy arms folded across his stomach, a look of satisfaction on his broad visage.

"This is the lawyer Kalif asked to see?"

"Yeah, and he saw him this morning."

"What'd they talk about?"

"We're not supposed to listen in on confidential attorney-client conversations."

Brian laughed. "So what'd they talk about?"

"The wanker told the lawyer he's innocent as a newborn, we're railroading him 'cause he's an Arab and blah, blah, blah. The lawyer told the wanker he shouldn't tell us dick and he'd bond him out later today. So far, he's following instructions pretty good. Bail was set at a hundred grand. Should be no problem for a guy with his connections."

"What about the other three?"

"You're gonna sit with an artist and describe 'em. Then, you're gonna go through mug shots," Cissel said.

Brian sighed. "Might as well get started."

27

Brian knew police artist Doris Niedner from way back when he'd been a rookie with the FBI. She'd been a young actress on a stint at Chicago's trend-setting comedy troupe, *Second City*, with dreams of making it big, maybe even a slot on *Saturday Night Live*. At the time, they'd both thought her aspirations at least remotely plausible—after all, look at the young comedians who came out of nowhere, learned the craft at *Second City* and ended up Hollywood mega-stars: Bill Murray, John Belushi, Dan Ackroyd, Eugene Levy, Steve Carell and Tina Fey, just to name a small sample. But the dreams died quickly when the director let her go, and Doris was forced back to waitressing at a Greek coffee shop.

One day a regular customer, a homicide detective, asked Doris out, a romance blossomed, and she ended up as a forensic sketch artist in the department. A dedicated specialist, her ability to create, revise and bring to life facial images of crime suspects was a highly valued skill. She'd had to evolve with changing technology, as computer composite imaging programs became widely available and cheap.

"Hey, you're looking very distinguished," she said as she left her workstation to greet Brian at the door of the small office. He wondered if she'd spotted gray in his hair.

"Hey, yourself. You keep getting younger. What's your secret?"

"Flattery'll get you everywhere."

She winked a pale blue eye and, for a moment, he flashed back to those days in Old Town, when they'd shared a third-floor one-bedroom on Wells Street and were like two sides of a coin. But now, Doris was married, he was on a murder investigation and this was business, nothing more.

"I understand you've got some pix for me to look at," Brian said.

"Right. The Bird himself just called. C'mon over here."

He followed her to a table in the corner sporting an iMac, its twenty-seven inch screen aglow.

"Pull up a chair," she instructed, as she sat at the keyboard and grabbed a mouse. "I've got a folder of images open which approximates the description Bird just gave me. Heavyset white male, thirties, sandy and brown, scar. With your help, we should be able to narrow it down." She clicked the mouse and a row of six blocky, clean-shaven white male faces came up, all with light brown hair and brown eyes.

"You drew these?" he asked.

"Yep, and scanned them. No facial hair, right?"

"Right."

"Any of these look familiar?"

Brian squinted at the screen, fumbling in his shirt pocket for the pair of cheap reading glasses he'd picked up at Walgreen's earlier that morning. As he donned the specs, Doris shot a quick glance at him over a shoulder and smiled. No smartass remarks. He'd always liked that about her. Tact, that's what she had.

"Hey, you with me on this?"

"Sorry. Lost my concentration for a minute there." Brian hoped his face hadn't reddened, but she was studying the screen, anyway. "Actually, that dude second from the right is close," he said. "But the jaw was a little more prominent."

Doris isolated the face as a larger single image, nearly life-size on the screen. With a few clicks, the jaw of the staring face grew, symmetrically, naturally. "That more like it?"

"Yeah, but the eyes...should be a little closer together. And the scar looked like a miniature tomato or something, just to the right of his nose."

"Not a problem" she said. After a few deft movements of the mouse, the face morphed into an image unpleasantly familiar to Brian.

"How's that?" Doris asked.

Brian was amazed. The guy who'd jabbed the needle in his arm in the SUV the night before last was replicated on the computer monitor. "Jesus, that's him. You got him. Excellent."

"Watch this." Doris clicked through several pull-down menus so quickly Brian had trouble following. But in a moment, the mug shot was replaced by a name, street address and listing of criminal charges. Doris had explained the technology to him on a previous visit—the software aligned several points on the facial image and rapidly compared them to filed images. With a 90%-plus confidence level, matches were determined and displayed on the screen with personal data. Still, there was an element of black magic, to Brian.

"Samuel Johns, LKA 4820 N. Kedzie, Chicago," he read aloud. There followed an alphabet soup of abbreviations. Brian recognized most of them right away. AB (aggravated battery), ADW (assault with a deadly weapon), BE (breaking and entering), SB (simple battery) and on and on. A habitual criminal, and one with a propensity for getting caught.

They repeated the process two more times, the result being an additional pair of repeat offenders in the violent felony business. The other two, Arthur Briley and Henry Stevko, had LKAs on the South Side, in the old Back of the Yards neighborhood, former home of the famed Chicago Stockyards.

Brian had not gotten a good look at the driver of the SUV, so they stopped at the three images.

"I'll print you some copies," Doris said.

A few minutes later, she handed him a stack of paper, three with mugs and several more listing personal data and criminal charges and convictions. Their fingers brushed as she handed him the paper and their eyes met.

"Anything else I can do for you?" she asked with a trace of a smile.

"I've got a few ideas," he replied. "But I doubt that George would approve." George, a homicide cop, was her husband.

"Well, *au revoir*," she said. She gave a little wave and disappeared into her office.

28

As Brian reached the end of the corridor, Dick Cissel emerged from his office and bellowed, "Brian!"

The chief of detectives completely filled the doorway of his office. He crooked an index finger in a come-here gesture.

Brian sighed and went to join the cop, who took the huge leather chair behind his desk. Brian remained standing.

"Well?" Cissel said.

"Doris found the three guys. You'll have it in a minute, I suppose."

A beep came from the computer on the desk. Cissel engulfed his mouse in a right hand the size of a lunch plate and clicked it once. He said, "E-mail from your girlfriend, Doris. Hmmm. Sammy Johns. Contract guy. Not connected. Does his own thing. Strong-arm stuff, mostly," he said softly, as if speaking to himself.

He clicked the mouse again and studied the screen. "Briley and Stevko are pretty much the same deal. You seen any of 'em before?"

"Nope," Brian said. "First and only time was when they jumped me and dragged me into that Suburban."

"Well, we'll pick 'em up. Joe tells me he grabbed his brother's home computer."

"You guys looked at it yet?"

"Technical wizard's going over it. Here, lemme give you his name. You two should talk." Cissel took a business card from a rectangular holder on his desk, scrawled a name and phone number on the back and handed it across to Brian. The name on the card was Jake Paulson.

Cissel was already on the phone by the time Brian hit the door, ordering some guy to get in there right away.

It was a little after noon. Brian's stomach growled as he climbed into the Grand Cherokee. He drove north up to Ontario, eased along the crowded street and nosed the car into a tight metered space on the right. He slipped his credit card into a pay station and bought a dollar's worth of time. Then, he walked a few doors east until he reached a storefront with an imposing sign, Al's #1 ITALIAN BEEF. Brian knew from experience this was no idle boast. The joint had been in business for eighty years, offering mouth-watering lean beef sandwiches. He entered the narrow space and took a place in line at the counter. When his turn came, the short, stocky register man in white apron greeted him with a voice that could have stripped paint off iron.

"Mr. FBI! How come you don't come in here no more? Whatsamatta? You go fancy-shmancy now?"

"I know, Gus. It's been too long. Changed jobs and don't get over this way like I used to."

Gus glanced at the line forming behind Brian. "Okay, what you want?" All business now.

"Give me a beef, dipped, hot peppers, provolone, fries, Coke."

Gus said, "You got it." A black youth wearing the company black tee shirt and ball cap began fixing Brian's order. As Brian moved up the counter toward the register, Gus barked at the guy assembling the sandwich, "Come on, come on. We don't got all day."

Brian paid and accepted a tray containing a white paperboard basket overflowing with lean Italian beef on a doughy bun soaked in *au jus* and slathered with melted provolone and bright, deadly-hot green peppers. A separate basket held a mound of irregularly shaped brown French fries in a shallow pool of grease. The growling in his stomach became a roar as he sat on a window stool. Not exactly health food, but hands down one of the tastiest lunches to be had in the city. Twenty minutes later, the stomach growl had been extinguished, his belt felt a notch too tight and he was ready for the afternoon's challenges.

29

Okay, Darcy, two minutes to air time."

Darcy shifted her weight in the thickly padded armchair in the WCGN television studio, trying to get comfortable. A production assistant had just touched up her makeup and clipped a lavalier microphone to the front of her shirt. She felt nervous but confident. She'd never appeared on TV before. The closest experience was playing softball as a starter on the University of Illinois women's varsity softball team for the last three seasons. That had trained her to perform before a crowd, but this was more stressful because she would be alone in front of the camera, sans teammates. She went over in her head the coaching she'd received from a friend who had interned with a network TV affiliate the summer before: know your message points, keep your answers short, make eye contact with the interviewer, slow down your speech and, above all, relax.

Suddenly, the red light and "ON AIR" sign flashed on. Catherine Keeler, the host of *Smart Talk* seated next to Darcy, went into her intro: "We're talking today with Darcy McKay, UIC-Chicago student and remarkably audacious amateur detective. You may have heard of Darcy's recent role in the Cup of Chai murder case, where she brought to justice real estate developer Arthur Stratmeyer, now awaiting trial for the killing of a North Side tea shop owner. Darcy is also known for being shot and kidnapped from the Bone Mountain dinosaur dig in Montana last summer—and then helping her uncle, Brian McKay, capture the gang involved. Meanwhile, she's majoring in Biological Sciences and plans to graduate next year."

Keeler turned to Darcy, smiling with brilliant teeth. "Darcy, welcome to *Smart Talk*. And thank you for agreeing to be our guest today."

"My pleasure," she lied.

"Darcy, tell us how you became a famous detective while maintaining an A grade point average at UIC."

Darcy released the breath she'd been holding in. "Actually, I'm just a college student who studies hard and who happened to be in a couple of situations where I was forced to react to save my own skin."

"But we know that twice you have been attacked by gun-toting criminals and managed to get the best of them. What prepared you for that level of bravery under extreme pressure?"

"I grew up with no sisters or brothers. In fact, my only living relative now is my uncle, Brian McKay. He's a former FBI agent and currently a private detective. I'd like to think that some of Brian's ability has rubbed off on me. Also, I'm pretty independent. And lucky."

"Do you plan to become a fulltime detective yourself after graduation?"

"My goal is to obtain a graduate degree in the biological sciences and to eventually work as a paleontologist in the Rocky Mountain region."

After a few more questions that Darcy fielded easily, Keeler adopted a grave expression. "Like it or not, you have become a role model for young girls. Any advice for girls who want to succeed in traditionally male-dominated pursuits?"

Darcy smiled. "Like I said, I'm just a student. But to answer your question: be yourself, do your best and don't worry about whatever you can't control."

"That's all well and good. Sounds like the Girl Scouts. How about some more hands-on advice for those mean situations where it's literally do or die?"

"Outsmart your opponent and, when in doubt, kick ass."

Catherine Keeler beamed at Darcy as though she'd just gotten the final clue correct on the *Jeopardy! Tournament of Champions*. "Inspiring words from our guest, Ms. Darcy McKay. That concludes this segment of *Smart Talk*. Stay tuned for our next feature, a visit with Mike Spector of the Lincoln Park Zoo, as he shows us 'Wild Animals You Should Never Touch.'"

The session had whizzed by in a blur. Darcy found herself wondering what the next question would be, but then realized it was all over. She wondered whether Brian had seen it. And she suspected that her friends at UIC would rib her mercilessly, especially about the "kick ass" comment. But she was pleased that she'd survived the challenge, and figured it might not hurt her chances when she applied to grad school.

30

At three-forty-nine, Brian entered his temporary 46th-floor office at Belcoe. A square yellow Post-it was attached to the computer screen: "Brian, call DeRosa immediately. Irene."

He dialed Lou DeRosa's extension.

DeRosa answered with a brusque "Yeah?"

"Returning your call."

"Brian? Hey, I gotta see ya." He sounded glum.

A few minutes later, Brian entered DeRosa's office. The executive's face, normally animated, was impassive. He gestured Brian to a chair at the round conference table near one of the tall windows overlooking Lake Michigan five hundred feet below.

"You want a drink? I think I'll have something."

"Well, it's only—"

"Yeah, it's the middle of the damned afternoon. So what? Look, I've got some Laphroaig single-malt, twenty-five years old. Goes for five hundred a bottle. Besides, when you hear what I've got to say, you'll feel like a drink."

"Okay, what the hell. I'll have one."

DeRosa made a show of extracting a tall green bottle with a white label from the sideboard in the corner. He poured a healthy dose into a chunky crystal glass and repeated the process. He took the bottle and glasses to the round table, where he joined Brian. He set a tumbler half full of amber liquid in front of Brian and held his own up in a toast. They each took a swig, DeRosa's the larger of the two by far. Brian felt the fiery whiskey warm his mouth, tickle his throat and do God-knew-what to the Italian Beef in his gut. The peaty, earthy taste was unique. This was serious sippin' whiskey, but DeRosa gulped it down like water.

"Brian, how about an update on your investigation."

"Well, I went to CPD Homicide this morning. ID'd the three guys that abducted me the other night. My friend there's got Violent Crimes looking for them. They're also looking at Matthew Growney's computer, see if anything relevant pops up."

DeRosa looked puzzled. "But we have his computer here. Information Technology's going over it."

"I mean his home computer. The one from his apartment. CPD's checking it out."

"Oh. They got anything?"

"Don't know yet. But they said they'll keep me posted."

"I see."

An uncomfortable silence ensued. DeRosa gazed out the window at the lake. Brian followed his line of view. A white sailboat tacked into the wind, headed east offshore from the James W. Jardine water purification plant, said to be the world's largest. Brian sipped his high roller Scotch. He thought he could get used to it, as long as someone else was buying.

Finally, Brian broke the silence. "What were you going to tell me that would make me want a drink?"

DeRosa turned from the window and looked at him blankly. "They uh, want me to let you go."

Brian was stunned. "I thought you guys wanted me to find out what happened to Matthew Growney."

"Hold up. I didn't say I was gonna *do* it, necessarily. Let's discuss this situation, see where our respective interests might lie." DeRosa drained his glass and set it down.

"And who's 'they?' anyway?" Brian asked.

"The Board. Had a special meeting last night. Barry had me walk 'em through what you've come up with so far. Talked about recruiting a successor for Spurgeon. Spent a lot of time on the effect of all this fucking negative PR on the stock price, which hit a new twelve month low today, by the way. Decided it's time to batten the hatches, move on."

"They don't want to know why a staff accountant was gunned down early one Sunday morning in the company's offices? Why another employee was arrested after participating in the kidnapping of an investigator contracted by the company to find out what happened? Just chalk it all up to bad luck and move on?" Brian was indignant, and he knew it showed in his voice.

"It's not like that at all. But they figure let the cops do their job and see what they come up with. Most of 'em figure you're just gonna prolong the agony. They wanted you in at the beginning when it was just the kid being killed. Thought it was a one-off. But with everything else that's happened, and the stock in the dumper, they don't want any more of Belcoe's problems aired in public."

Brian took a slow sip. By then, he'd gotten a buzz on. Not drunk, but definitely loose, a little blurred around the edges. He'd have to pace himself to stay sharp. He sensed that DeRosa might give him the heave-ho, after all. On the other hand, the older executive seemed to need someone to listen, and Brian was capable of being a wonderful listener.

"Your questions are good ones," DeRosa said. "I'm going to tell you a story. You can make of it what you like." His words were a little slurred. He tilted his head back and took a sizable swallow of his drink. His glass was nearly empty again.

Brian was silent. He knew enough to let the man talk without interruption.

"Back in the early nineties," DeRosa continued, "Bell Metals was a tired little Northwest Side steel fabricating company owned by a couple of old Swedish guys with no kids. The Swedes wanted out and sold the business to fresh young MBA Barry Webb. Within a year, the company had bought out four competitors and branched into electronics. That's when I came on board. We cultivated political connections and got cozy with the administration. Before you could say 'scratch my back,' we had a mess of defense contracts. By 2002, we'd gone public as Belcoe Inc. and had designs on the Fortune 500. Barry's one of those guys knows you've gotta spend dough to make it. Gave a million to the current president's campaign through a super PAC early on. Defense products make up more than half of company revenue. But a lot of profits come from strategic equipment exports."

"Excuse my ignorance," Brian said. "What's strategic equipment?"

"Remember 'Star Wars?' The anti-missile program, not the movies. The U.S. has never done much with it, but other countries, mainly in the Middle East, have always been interested. Belcoe missed the boat initially, but we've developed technologies designed to discover and divert conventional missiles, jam radar-dependent devices, take down military planes, even at super-high altitude and supersonic speed. Sophisticated equipment and software. Trouble is, the U.S. military plays offense more than defense. Plus, they've developed different technologies to address the national security concerns. And, as always, politics intervenes. Bottom line: the government says they can't use the stuff. So Barry's found buyers elsewhere."

"He's exporting this technology abroad?"

"Yep."

"Legally?"

DeRosa waggled his hand in the universal maybe-maybe not gesture. "It's okay to sell to approved countries, Israel topping the list. But otherwise, it gets sensitive. Especially since nine-eleven. About all I can tell ya. Hey, you're falling behind."

DeRosa picked up the Scotch bottle.

Brian held a hand over his glass. "I'm fine."

DeRosa shrugged and poured a slug into his own glass. "Anyway, with these investigations into our accounting, the market gets nervous. Rumors are flying. Say what you will about Doug Spurgeon, he complemented Barry Webb perfectly. Barry's the big-picture guy, schmoozer of politicians. Dougie built up the company infrastructure, ran the show. With him gone and the negative vibes on the street, the vultures are circling. The last thing Belcoe needs is the analysts quivering over why people've been dying like flies at the company."

"We both know there's a lot more to it," Brian said.

DeRosa lifted an eyebrow. "We've got cans of worms. Hell, we've got warehouses full of crates full of buckets of worms. The auditors are well compensated and they give us the benefit of the doubt in judgment call matters on our financial practices. But you're different. With your FBI background and don't-give-a-fuck attitude, you could be trouble to some very heavy people around here. That, my friend, is why the Board wants to fire your ass."

"And you have another idea?"

DeRosa stared at his glass, stirred the whiskey with a finger, pulled the finger out and licked it. "Maybe," he said.

Brian took a short sip of whiskey and set his glass down. He knew he needn't prompt DeRosa—the older man would tell the story at his own pace.

"Look, I think you can help with this mess. You've got the smarts and, unless I'm mistaken, some serious balls," DeRosa said. "And you've already bumped up against the tips of a few of the ice bergs floating around this joint. Speaking of ice..." He stood and carried his empty glass to the sideboard, where he extracted a plastic ice tray from a small refrigerator. He released a few cubes noisily into the glass. "Thirsty. Ice tastes good once ya get warmed up, know what I mean?" He waved the ice tray in Brian's general direction. A cube fell to the thick carpeting, but DeRosa didn't seem to notice.

"No, thanks," Brian said. He settled back in his chair.

DeRosa returned to the table with a glass full to the brim with Scotch and ice. "Look, you're probably wondering why I'm spilling my guts. After all, I'm an insider, stand to lose if this stuff gets out to the public, right?"

Brian remained silent.

"Well, I'm not gonna be inside much longer. See, they passed me over for Spurgeon's job. Say they're gonna recruit from outside the company. That's okay. I've about had enough. I'm making plans to retire in style abroad."

"Any advice for me?" Brian asked.

"Follow the fuckin' money. These guys get most of their compensation in stock. Trouble comes along, stock's gotta be propped up. Set up wholly owned offshore entities and funnel transactions through them. Disclose just enough to keep the auditors signing the reports. Follow the letter of the accounting rules, but mislead, make the financials appear a lot stronger than they are. Hell, some of this stuff's alluded to in the footnotes to the financials, but nobody pays attention. People don't read long reports, as you've probably noticed. Look at what's going on in Washington. Folks prefer their news in short simple sound bites, whether it's factual or not."

"I noticed in the last quarter financials some notes about special purpose entities. Looks like Belcoe buys assets through them but the SPEs keep the debt, so the Belcoe balance sheet looks great, regardless."

DeRosa nodded. "That's about right. Some shell game mumbo-jumbo Massey and his crew rigged up. I'm no accountant. You'll have to figure that stuff out by yourself. But I *do* know the books are sketchy. Maybe that accounting kid,

Growney, found something to prove it. 'Kill the messenger,' they say. Normally, around here, if they find out somebody's likely to cause damage, they either fire his ass or just ignore him. But now, I don't know. These are bizarre times..." DeRosa closed his eyes for a long moment, then opened them and blinked, as if trying to focus and not quite making it. He pushed his glass to the side. "Guess I've had 'nough." His words were slurred, nearly incomprehensible.

"Well, I'd better get out of your hair," Brian said. "All right if I stop by tomorrow morning, when we're both fresher?"

"Yeah, okay. Think I'll jus' put my head down." DeRosa folded his beefy arms on the tabletop and lowered his head onto them.

Brian rose quietly and headed for the door. Before he'd eased it shut, he heard ragged snores coming from DeRosa's half-open mouth.

31

Back in his apartment, Brian picked up the mail from the floor, where it had piled up next to the front door slot. Most of it was junk or bills. There was also a handwritten envelope with a return address in Clarkville, Montana. He opened the envelope and began reading a letter from Jerry Jensen, son of Laura Jensen, the Geyser County sheriff's deputy who'd been murdered last summer. Brian felt a sharp pang of remorse about Laura. They'd become friends and had worked well together investigating the dinosaur thieves up until Laura's tragic death. And there had been feelings of mutual attraction, barely expressed. But definitely there.

Jerry's written thoughts were well organized: a reminder of his and Brian's brief experience together in Clarkville, Jerry's new living arrangement with his Aunt Carol, an anecdote about a domestic disturbance next door, fishing with his friend David Big Hair. But the bottom line was: Jerry wanted to know when Brian would be making good on his promise to come out for a visit.

Brian had kept in touch with his friend Bill Thorsten, the FBI resident agent in Bozeman, a university town not far from Clarkville. The two men had become friends the previous summer. Thorsten, an avid fly fisherman, was eager to take Brian on a hike in the nearby Absaroka-Beartooth Wilderness, where a certain high country lake teemed with wild trout, so the agent said. Another intriguing recent piece of information from Thorsten: Belcoe's CEO, Barry Webb, owned a large ranch adjacent to Yellowstone National Park, about fifty miles from Clarkville. Webb's company used the ranch as an entertainment facility. The FBI's White Collar Crime unit in Chicago had expressed interest in the ranch, and indicated Thorsten should be ready to assist them with a possible related investigation. Something about electronic devices stored in warehouses at the ranch.

Brian needed a break from the corporate morass of Belcoe. He'd been feeling frazzled lately, dealing with DeRosa, Webb and the other sketchy inhabitants of the company headquarters. He'd made slow progress uncovering possible motives in the Matthew Growney murder, but not enough. He felt an obligation to Darcy to find the murderer of her boyfriend. But perhaps a break from the investigation would help. At least that was the rationale developing in his troubled mind. He'd been toying with the idea of moving to Montana someday. Making a living was important at his current stage though, and Chicago delivered. Brian's fledgling private investigations business had been successful from the start, and he knew he needed to work hard to grow it, possibly adding employees as the client load increased. And he and Michelle needed to sort out where they were headed with their sporadic romantic relationship. All that would have to wait.

He went online to see what kind of last-minute deal he could wangle on a coach seat aboard Delta to Bozeman. It was springtime, meaning the high mountain streams and lakes would still be ice-encrusted, but fly fishing would be possible at the lower elevations. Maybe he'd make a second trip in the beautiful days of September, when the aspens would be golden beacons in the deep-green conifer forests.

The next day, Brian caught an afternoon flight to Bozeman Yellowstone International Airport, still known as Gallatin Field to locals. One of the prettiest airport settings in the United States, it boasted views of several mountain ranges of the northern Rockies, including the Gallatins, Madisons and Bridgers. He exited the plane as darkness befell the surrounding peaks, claimed a rental Chevy Equinox and hit the road for the Comfort Inn in town.

32

In the morning, Brian made the thirty-mile drive to Clarkville, an old cattle and railroad town on the banks of the Yellowstone River. The weather was brisk, with occasional spits of rain—about as expected for March in that part of Montana. The beautiful valley south of town had been discovered, and was now home to many artists, writers and corporate refugees. Brian had arranged to visit Jerry and his aunt Carol. He'd corresponded with both of them by email. She'd seemed welcoming, but he'd soon find out whether he'd be staying with them as a guest or returning to the venerable Masters Hotel, where he'd lodged during his last visit to the area. He bet it would be the former; in Montana, hospitality was a given.

Carol Jensen's house occupied a small lot in downtown Clarkville, two blocks west of her deceased sister Laura's place. Brian curbed the rental and ascended the wooden porch. He was about to knock on the door, when it opened. An attractive blond-haired woman with emerald eyes opened the door and greeted him with a smile. He experienced a most pleasant *déjà vu*. With her slim figure and athletic bearing, Carol Jensen looked so much like her sister Laura that they could almost have been twins. He guessed she was the younger sister, maybe thirty. She radiated vitality, as if she spent a lot of time outdoors. Brian was intrigued.

"Jerry's told me a lot about you," she said, as they shook hands.

"I hope it's not all bad. I did return his mountain bike intact, after all." As he stepped into the living room, Brian noticed Jerry standing in the far doorway, looking a little reticent.

After introductions and small talk, Brian had a seat on the sofa next to Jerry, while Carol perched on a chair. They drank coffee while Brian and Carol slipped into easy conversation. For a moment, he forgot about Jerry. Neither of them mentioned Laura, but he figured Carol must associate him with her sister's death on some level. Carol said she had the day off. It turned out that she knew Bill Thorsten slightly through her position at the bank. She mentioned that she was on the Board of Directors of the nearby William Old Horn Dinosaur Museum, with which Brian was quite familiar from his adventure on the dinosaur dig near Clarkville the prior year. They talked museum activities and plans for a while.

The conversation flowed along seamlessly until Jerry interrupted. Addressing Brian, he said, "How about going fishing this afternoon?"

"That's a great idea," he said. "I've got my pack rod in my suitcase out there."

"Okay, boys. You can go fishing and that'll give me time to grocery shop and fix us some dinner. Speaking of luggage, bring it in and I'll show you the guest room where you'll be sleeping, Brian."

Brian and Jerry packed their fly-fishing gear in daypacks and accepted ham sandwiches and apples from Carol. "You guys be back here by six for dinner. And don't bring any trout back. We're having Montana-style steaks."

In the car on the way to the Yellowstone River, Jerry opened up. They discussed everything from fishing to detective work to girls. Brian sensed that he was providing something to Jerry that the boy had missed, a male exemplar. Not being used to kids, Brian was a little nervous. But after a while, the two-way conversation flowed. They found a deserted fishing access, donned their waders and rigged sinking nymph flies on their lines: Brian selected a size ten bead head wooly bugger at Jerry's suggestion. Within an hour, they'd each caught a cutthroat trout. The tensions of Belcoe melted away as Brian concentrated on the challenge of fooling wily native trout. Though the fish had brains the size of peas, they were capable of outwitting fishermen all too easily. And this early in the season, the fish were mostly content to hang out on the bottom of the river, rather than feed on insects above them. Brian felt privileged to catch and hold these beautiful creatures for a few seconds before releasing them back into their watery habitat.

On the way back to Carol Jensen's house, Brian stopped at a Montana state liquor store and purchased a fifth of Scotch and a bottle of good cabernet sauvignon, which he figured would go well with steaks.

Carol accepted the bottle of wine with a smile that made her eyes and teeth shine. "How thoughtful of you, Brian."

He noticed she'd changed clothes. She now wore a rose-colored blouse and tight jeans. The jeans fit her very well.

"How was the fishing?" she asked.

"Jerry's a wonderful guide. With his expertise and my tireless flailing of the water, I managed to catch almost half as many as he did."

"Well, I hope you guys worked up an appetite."

"Appetite's my middle name," Brian replied, without thinking. Where had that come from? Carol seemed to have an effect on him, amping up the ebullience factor. The wine did indeed go well with the T-bone steaks, which were garnished with locally-picked morels, fried onions and thin French fries that Carol referred to as *pommes frites*. Desert was also locally sourced, rich vanilla ice cream with huckleberries on top. If

this was small-town Montana cuisine, Brian thought he could
get used to it.

33

After supper, Brian checked in with local FBI agent Bill Thorsten on the phone. Brian gave him a quick recap of his work to date at Belcoe, including details about the murder of Matthew and the apparent suicide of Douglas Spurgeon. He asked the agent if he'd heard anything more about the FBI's interest in Belcoe's 606 Ranch down by Yellowstone National Park.

"Here's the thing," Thorsten said. "The White Collar Crime guys in Chicago tell me Belcoe is using the ranch to handle exports of sensitive electronic equipment to Canada. Just warehousing the product, no manufacturing activity. This stuff is shipped in from plants in the Midwest."

"Where's it go from Canada?"

"Israel."

"What are they warehousing?"

"Defense contract electronic devices. Related to missile tracking and interception."

"You talk with James, at all?"

"Yeah, actually. He's the lead on Belcoe in the Chicago Field Office now. He says you and he go way back. Makes you sound like some kinda hero."

"Yeah, well, he's developed into one of the best White Collar Crime agents in Chicago. Good to know he's involved with this stuff. Anyway, how far to the Canadian border from that 606 place?"

"About 360 miles to the nearest border crossing, six and a half hour drive. Probably a short flight, though. There's a little airport right at the border. It's pretty flat up there. There's a private airfield as well."

"And this 606 Ranch is in on a rough road up in the mountains? Seems like it'd be a hell of a lot easier to just warehouse the stuff near the Bozeman airport or up at the border."

"I agree. But it appears legal on the surface, proper compliance with customs and all. James asked me questions about the ranch and local scuttlebutt as to the activity there."

"Yeah, it does seem strange. Belcoe's in the arms business, and they deal heavily with some Middle East countries." Brian said. "Tricky stuff, all right. Trade with the friendly countries over there is highly regulated and trade with the hostile ones is forbidden per the sanctioned nations list of the Office of Foreign Assets Control. Makes me wonder if they're hiding something out here. Any idea what they expect you to do?"

"James said WCC wants me to make a site visit at the 606, have a look around. They've provided listings of inventory that should be on hand in a warehouse there. I'm supposed to count items in stock, look at documentation as to where they're headed and review the internal controls over storage and accounting for the stuff. Naturally, I did some research on the company and Barry Webb. Lots of coverage, good and bad: astronomical growth, SEC violations, rumors of financial fraud. James shared some information on WCC's investigation. This outfit stretches the accounting rules until they're about to snap, from what I can tell."

"My impression as well. I've got no official standing, but I'd sure like to join you when you get the call to go in."

Thorsten hesitated. "Okay, but it'll have to be off the record. Anyway, you gonna be around here tomorrow?"

"Yeah. I thought I'd explore, maybe strap on my boots and do a hike in the neighborhood of that 606 Ranch," Brian said.

"I've got some time, and I know the area. Like some company?"

"Sure."

"You know the drill, several layers of clothing, with a waterproof shell on top. We're about the same size, so if you need anything, let me know. The month of March in this part of Montana can mean any season of the year, sometimes all of 'em in one day. The forecast says chilly with possible rain and snow tomorrow, depending on the elevation."

The next morning, Brian and Bill Thorsten met for breakfast at a café in the Yellowstone River valley, a few miles north of the 606 Ranch. The temperature was in the forties in the valley, with a brisk wind and lowering clouds. The surrounding mountains looked snowy and forbidding. After bacon and eggs, Thorsten drove south to the turnoff for the ranch in his Tahoe and proceeded on a seemingly endless gravel road. After several miles, he drove past the ranch driveway, marked with a small wooden sign displaying simply, "606." As they climbed, there were puddles in the road from recently melted snow. They encountered deeply rutted spots of clay soil, known locally as gumbo, with the consistency of slippery cookie dough. The vehicle nearly bogged down, but Thorsten kept it moving ahead in four-wheel drive high range. Near the top of the road, several inches of snow slowed their progress.

"Hope I don't have to put the chains on," Thorsten muttered.

Finally, they arrived at a flat parking area with a large wooden sign indicating they were at the Valley Overlook trailhead. Thorsten parked and they got out. There were no other vehicles around. They put on their packs and rain jackets.

"What's the elevation here?" Brian asked.

"About 7,000 feet. We just climbed up about 400 on the road. We'll follow this trail on foot for about a mile, which will take us up another 500 feet. At that overlook we'll have a good birds-eye view down to the 606," Thorsten said.

Brian was out of condition for hiking at high elevations. His legs ached and he struggled to get enough air into his lungs as they switchbacked their way up the rugged path. He was thankful that his boots kept moisture from the snow and mud out. About forty minutes later, the two men crested a ridge and stopped at a wide spot in the trail atop a steep cliff. Visible to the southwest and about a thousand feet below them, a large ranch compound sprawled. A cluster of buildings was visible at the north end. Thorsten pulled a pair of olive green binoculars from his pack and focused on the place.

"Here, have a look."

Brian glassed the scene far below them. The ranch headquarters contained a huge brown building constructed of logs. Around it, there were a bunch of cabins of the same design but much smaller. A couple of imposing single-story houses that might have been at home in an upscale Chicago suburb sat side by side away from the log buildings. Further to the south were traditional farm and ranch outbuildings: a large red barn, an open-walled hay storage canopy and various other agricultural-looking structures. Brian continued scanning the property. High barbed wire fences with wooden posts enclosed the whole place. Cows grazed in three separate pastures. A couple of men were working on a corral fence enclosing a few horses.

"How big is this place?" Brian asked.

"It started out at just over 600 acres. Hence, the name. But, over the years, the owners have bought up land all around it. They've got more than ten thousand acres now."

"See that big gray building down at the south end?"

"Yeah. Looks like a warehouse. Kind of out of character with the rest of the place, eh?"

"Yeah, all metal. And I see one of those commercial vans parked at the loading dock. See that white vehicle?" He handed the binocs back to Thorsten.

"Mercedes Sprinter. Four-wheel-drive, raised suspension, knobby tires. Fit for navigating the ranch roads. And maybe some dicey roads elsewhere. These electronic products must be small, or they'd need bigger trucks."

Brian sensed movement behind them and whirled to find a lanky man wearing a ragged sleeveless tee shirt and jeans a few yards away and approaching them silently.

"Whoa!" Brian said. At the sound of his voice, Thorsten jerked around as well.

The man smiled widely. His head was bald, shiny and tanned as a cowhide glove. He was missing a few teeth. His arms were covered with prison tattoos from wrist to shoulder. Despite the cold and his skimpy attire, he seemed eminently comfortable. Brian sensed something off about the guy. His smile was mirthless and something about his eyes was troubling. He reminded Brian of a man in his army unit years ago, a southerner from a poor background who'd been dishonorably discharged under suspicion of drug dealing. That guy had also been outwardly cheerful, but with a nest of vipers inside his head.

"You guys seen another guy hikin' up here?" the man said.

"Nope," Thorsten said.

"This guy, my buddy, he's got enormous ears. Looks like a fuckin' elephant."

"We'll keep our eyes open. If we see him, we'll let him know you're looking for him," Brian added.

"My friend, he's a medical doctor. Wouldn't know it to look at him. Him and me, we hang out up here all the time."

"You know anything about that ranch down there?" Thorsten asked.

"I keep my ass away from that place. Bad dudes. They'd kill me if they could. You guys, too. Better watch your ass around that place."

"Why do you say that?" Brian said.

"Lemme put it this way. I snuck in there one time couple weeks ago. Just lookin' around, mindin' my own damn business. This security guy, looks like one a them Japanese wrestlers, sumo dudes that wear diapers? He's drivin' along in a Jeep, sees me on the road. Speeds up and aims right at me, tryin' to run me down. I dodge the Jeep, haul ass through a ditch and up away from the road. Guy sits there laughin' his ass off."

"You know anybody down there?"

"I did, but not no more. I grew up in Clarkville. Used to be a nice little town. But it's changed a lot. I hunted at that place down there for forty years, but not no more. They closed it off to us locals. Only rich guys stayin' there get to take an elk. Like I said, they run me off. Pissants."

"Well, we'll be careful," Brian said. He held out his hand to the emaciated man. "Good to meet you. I'm Brian McKay."

The guy hesitated. His smile faltered a little. "I'm uh, pleased to meet ya."

Brian: "What's your name?"

"Uh, Jimmy. Anyway, I gotta meet up with my buddy. He prob'ly went off exploring somewhere."

Brian and Thorsten left the man standing at the overlook, smiling after them as if they all shared a clever joke. The two men made their way back down the trail, slowly on the steeper parts, so as not to slide on the snowy surface. About half way down, a very tall and narrow man was making his way slowly up the trail toward them. When they were within twenty feet, Brian made eye contact with the man, who looked away shyly.

"You know a guy named Jimmy?" Brian said.

"Yes."

"He said he was looking for you. Said you were an M.D. And that you have enormous ears."

The tall guy's grin covered most of his face. "Guilty on both counts," he said. He was wearing a quilted hat with large earflaps covering his ears, so they couldn't verify Jimmy's description.

"Anyway, he was up at the overlook a little while ago," Brian said.

"Thanks, partner." He passed Brian and Thorsten and bounded up the trail on long legs.

They continued down. At one point, Brian's boots slipped in the mud and he nearly ended up on his rear end. He was happy to finally be back down at the trailhead.

On the return ride to Clarkville, Thorsten remarked, "I wonder what's up with those guys, Jimmy and the doctor. Kind of spacey, but they seemed harmless."

"Maybe."

34

After returning to Chicago via a redeye flight the next day, Brian called DeRosa's office in the afternoon.

"He's not in."

"When do you expect him?"

"If you'd like to leave word…"

"I was hoping to speak with him today."

"I really don't know when to expect him. He's been a little uh, under the weather lately." She sounded forlorn.

The next morning, Brian went to Belcoe, got on the phone and entered the code to listen in on the conference call of the latest Belcoe financial presentation to the public. He'd gotten a broadcast e-mail the day before—Hamilton Massey would be commenting on fourth quarter and annual profits for the investment community. This event was, he knew, designed to put the best possible spin on financial results concurrent with the official earnings release to the press online. The word in the Wall Street Journal was that results would be disappointing. If so, the depressed stock price was likely to go lower no matter what Massey said. Brian logged on to the company website, where the numbers would appear momentarily. He turned on the phone speaker, slumped back in his chair and took a swig of the blessedly strong coffee he'd picked up on the way in.

"Good morning, ladies and gentlemen." Massey's clipped words boomed from the speaker. Brian could hear the same words echoing from other offices down the hall. On the computer screen, a press release with tables of profit and loss numbers appeared.

"Once again, Belcoe has achieved record revenues and earnings," Massey's stern voice proclaimed. He mentioned a six percent increase in earnings per share over the comparable period of the prior year, a seven percent increase in net income, a rock-solid financing structure and expectations for a positively brilliant future. The CFO stated that Belcoe was raising expectations for the next quarter owing to "accelerated growth in electronic equipment volume, both domestic and international." Brian noticed he did not mention the results were way below expectations on the street.

After a few more platitudinous remarks, the CFO opened it up to questions from the listeners. The first few questions sounded like they'd been planted by Belcoe to put the best possible face on financial results. Hamilton glibly fielded softballs about future expansion plans and recent buyouts of competitors in the electronics arena.

Then, a discordant note: Howard Grossman, a journalist with *FORTUNE*, spoke up. "Mr. Massey, why is there no balance sheet or cash flow statement with the earnings report we see this morning? As you know, these are normally included. Is there some sort of problem?"

A long moment of dead air was finally broken when Massey, clearly irritated, said, "We'll be releasing that information soon, once the auditors have finalized their report. It'll be in the SEC filing."

Grossman responded, "You're the only major company in recent history not timely releasing balance sheet and cash flow information."

Silence again for a beat. Then Massey blurted, "Thanks very much. We appreciate your observation, asshole." A sound like shuffling papers came through the speaker. Then Massey said, "That concludes our conference call. Good day."

Brian sat up straight. Had Massey said what he thought he'd heard? The man had a temper, for sure. He made a mental note to schedule another meeting with the CFO as soon as possible—if the guy was capable of blowing up and uttering a vulgarity to a journalist while the whole world was tuned in, maybe Brian could get him to spill something useful in a more private forum. Down the hall, the sound of nervous laughter came from other offices, quiet at first, then building to a crescendo. Brian smiled.

He clicked to the Yahoo! Financial page and keyed in the symbol for Belcoe stock: BELC. The screen filled with numbers and commentary. The stock price had plummeted more than six percent already that morning. The first analyst's comment referred to "extremely disappointing results" and went on to mention "incredulous investors' reactions to the Belcoe CFO's use of a crude epithet while addressing a respected member of the equity analyst community."

"Looks like it's beginning to hit the fan."

Brian turned to see Natalie Katz in the doorway, looking tense.

"Yes, it does. Got any insights as to why your boss blew his cool?"

"As a matter of fact, I do."

35

Natalie dropped into a visitor's chair across the desk from Brian. A brown leather briefcase hung from a strap over her right shoulder. She leaned forward and jiggled her knees up and down in a nervous rhythm. "Massey's coming unglued," she said in a matter-of-fact monotone.

"Calling Grossman an asshole on the air? Yeah, that's an indication, all right," Brian said. He waited.

Natalie leaned to her left, grasped the edge of the office door and swung it shut behind her. She spoke in a low voice. "Look, I don't know if…" She trailed off, glancing over her shoulder nervously.

"What?" Brian said.

She pursed her lips in a thin line. She reminded Brian of Darcy in a serious mood. "Look. Since they killed Matthew, I haven't had a decent night's sleep," Natalie said. "You don't know what it's like to be scared to death while you sit at your desk staring at a computer screen day after day. Plus, I'm Darcy's friend, and somebody chased her down the street, like they wanted to kill her."

"I think you're smart to be worried. You need to be careful. Hell, we *all* do. You just said 'they' killed Matthew. Why 'they?'"

Natalie pulled a small packet of tissues from her skirt pocket, selected one and blew her nose. She held the tissue in her hand distractedly, all the while avoiding Brian's eyes. "'They' are people with a lot to lose…" Her voice trailed off.

Brian reached under his desk for the wastebasket and extended it to Natalie.

"Thanks." She dropped the tissue into the container and sat back. "I wonder if someone in Finance is involved, or someone higher up."

"What about Massey?"

At the mention of the finance chief's name, Natalie stiffened. In a whisper, she said, "The guy's a shiver looking for a spine to run up. How do you know he hasn't bugged this office? It would be just like him."

The possibility of surveillance bugs had occurred to Brian the first time he'd entered the office they'd assigned him two weeks earlier, and he'd taken appropriate precautions. "I've swept it a few times, most recently yesterday, so it's probably okay."

She nodded grimly. "Good. I'm too young to croak."

Brian smiled in what he hoped was an encouraging manner. "That's for sure. And you won't. But the only way we'll bring these guys down is if insiders like you step up. You're in a unique position of knowledge. You understand the intricacies of the accounting transactions. You've obviously got concerns about something that might be a strong motive to shut people up. Everything you tell me's confidential. Think of Matthew. And Darcy."

She sighed. "Okay. Here goes. There was no balance sheet or cash flow statement for the quarter analyst phone call because they were still being revised at the last minute. The boys upstairs want better numbers, to meet expectations on the street. Finance is finding ways to provide them. They don't release them until they're…ready for consumption"

"Fudged?"

"Yeah, but more than usual. And later in the game, which is embarrassing to the company and makes Massey look like a dunce."

"And he's pissed off."

She frowned. "Naturally. And I'm to blame."

"Why you?"

"Actually, it's Jack and me. We're responsible for the foreign numbers. Probably a career-ender in the next rank-and-yank."

"So what's being revised?"

"Middle East division. There's a new company added to the mix. We just got the financials. They're in Moroccan dirhams with Arabic text."

"What, Belcoe acquired an entity in Morocco?"

"Looks like it."

"What's your role in this?"

"I combine the financial statements of the ME subsidiaries, country by country. I perform currency translations, eliminate intercompany overlapping transactions, which can be quite technical, and produce financials for Belcoe's ME Division. We've got subs in Israel, Saudi Arabia, Egypt, Turkey, Kuwait, the UAE, Qatar, Bahrain and Jordan. But nothing in Iraq, Iran, Lebanon, Syria or, until now, Morocco."

"But isn't Belcoe doing business in Iraq?"

"Only as a government contractor. We provide equipment and supplies to the Army, but I don't believe we own or invest in any companies in Iraq. Not allowed to."

"How does that work?"

"Selling directly to the Iraqis or other countries on the hostile nations list would be prohibited transactions. The American Office of Foreign Assets Control, or OFAC, prohibits U.S. companies exporting goods to those governments. But there are U.S. companies doing business there under what they call exempt transactions under specific licenses. Maybe Belcoe has exemptions. I wouldn't be surprised."

"Do you have a map of the Belcoe locations in the Middle East?" Brian asked.

"Sure. Be right back."

A minute later, Natalie returned with a piece of paper, which she handed to Brian. He noticed the briefcase still hung on her shoulder, wedged to her side with a rigid upper arm. Whatever was in it, she wasn't letting it out of her sight.

Gold dots representing Belcoe locations were clustered on the right side of the map. None on the left. The company's holdings excluded the big northern African countries of Libya, Sudan and Somalia, as well as Iran, Lebanon and Syria to the east.

"Looks like you've avoided the countries the U. S. government says you can't do business with," Brian said. He placed the map on the desk between them.

Natalie glanced at the map. "Yep. "

"So, to add in this new company, you've got to translate dirhams into U.S. dollars, and you have to search for and eliminate intercompany transactions, right?"

"Yes. Took me to 'til eleven last night." She rubbed her eyes.

"But who translated the Arabic text to English?"

"We've got a translation program on the network. Specializes in business words. Not perfect, but enough to work with financials."

"Is there a name for this subsidiary?" Brian asked.

"The Excel file's called DOWNPOR."

"Mean anything to you?"

She shrugged. "Heavy rain?"

"A Hard Rain's a-Gonna Fall."

"Huh?"

"A great Bob Dylan song. Before your time. Mine too, for that matter," he said.

"Are you an expert on classic rock?"

"One of my vices, yes. Anyway, how'd you find out about this file?"

"Massey called me and said it was up on the system and I should add it into the Belcoe consolidation. This was about six-thirty last night, just as I was packing up to go home."

"He stick around?"

"Nope. Said he'd expect the final numbers this morning."

"Huh. Did you have what you needed to get it done?"

"Not really. I had a bunch of questions, so I called him at home. I knew he wouldn't like it, but he'd told me to get it done."

"And?"

"No answer on his home phone or his cell."

"What then?"

"I uh, went into his office way late. Everyone in the department was gone. The cleaning lady opened his door. Massey always keeps it locked, but they've got a key. I told her I needed to leave him a note, said I'd wait 'til they were done, would she leave the door unlocked and I'd lock it."

"And she went along?"

"Not at first. She doesn't speak much English, but I could tell she was afraid of getting in trouble. So I gave her some money, all I happened to have with me, forty-two dollars. She emptied the wastebasket, dusted off the desk and left the door open a crack. I went in and sat down at the desk. Moved the mouse and the monitor came to life. I couldn't believe it. He hadn't logged off, so I had access to his independent hard drive."

"Then what?"

"I checked for most-recently viewed files. The last Excel file he looked at yesterday was DOWNPOR2, like the Morocco one I'd worked with earlier, but with some additional notes in Arabic."

Suddenly, the office door swung open and slammed into the wall. A man in a dark suit burst into the room, bumping into the back of Natalie's chair and nearly dumping her on the floor.

"What in hell are you doing in here?" Hamilton Massey bellowed at Natalie's back.

36

No one spoke for a few seconds. Massey stayed motionless, taut as a plucked violin string. After a moment, he exhaled a huge breath and parked himself in the unoccupied visitor's chair next to Natalie and across from Brian.

Brian said, "I might ask you the same question. Why'd you barge in here? Didn't your mama teach you to knock?"

Massey worked his facial muscles as if emerging from a deep sleep. He reddened as blood flowed into his pale countenance. His eyes looked big and watery behind the lenses of his retro chic glasses. He blinked a few times and cleared his throat.

"I have every right to know the whereabouts of my staff," he said, glaring at Natalie to his left. "What exactly are you doing in here with this…contractor, when I explicitly told you I wanted you to get the financials in order ASAP?"

Natalie looked a silent plea for help Brian's way.

"Listen, Massey. I asked Natalie to answer some questions related to my ongoing investigation of the death of Matthew Growney. As you know, I am authorized to interview any Belcoe employee by the authority of the Board of Directors."

"What questions? As Ms. Katz's superior, I have a direct interest in what she says and does on company time." Massey had regained his composure and his aggressive personality was once again on display.

"That's confidential," Brian replied.

Massey stood. "All right then. Come with me, Ms. Katz." He turned on a heel and lurched out of the office.

As Brian watched the gangling executive leave, he shook his head.

Natalie rose slowly, looking like a truant kid about to answer a summons to the principal's office. She shrugged and glanced at Brian ruefully.

"Let me know what he has to say," he said.

She grimaced as she left.

Brian logged onto the Internet and checked for the latest on Belcoe. The stock price was down eight percent already that morning. There was a prominent piece dated a few minutes earlier: "Belcoe stock plunges on incomplete quarterly reporting," by Howard Grossman, *FORTUNE* magazine. Grossman, the analyst Massey had called an "asshole" during the Belcoe earnings release conference call the previous afternoon, in earshot of thousands of interested investors, employees, reporters and other sentient beings, had nothing but brickbats to lob at the company.

Grossman opened with:

"Iconoclastic Chicago-based high-tech manufacturer, Belcoe Inc., disappointed the investment community by issuing a fourth quarter P & L statement shockingly beneath street expectations during a controversial earnings release conference call yesterday. When this reporter queried company CFO A. Hamilton Massey as to the absence of the normal quarterly balance sheet and cash flow statement, that classy gent responded by calling said reporter an a__-hole. Interestingly, this vulgarism has often been used in reference to Mr. Massey himself (a play on his first and middle names, and who knows what else). In any case, Belcoe stands alone among Fortune 500 companies in failing to provide the standard balance sheet and cash flow information concurrently with its quarterly earnings numbers. A company insider revealed anonymously that foul-ups in accounting for international operations were to blame. This nameless informant, a shrewd veteran of many campaigns, suggested that a re-read of the footnotes in last year's Annual Report might be illustrative. Indeed, yours truly perused those stanzas of turgid prose and found buried in "Related party transactions" veiled references to offshore special purpose entities (SPEs) involving Belcoe's dealings abroad. I quote: 'In 2018, Belcoe entered into transactions with partnerships (Related Parties) whose General Partner is a senior officer of Belcoe. The Limited Partners of the Related Party are not related to Belcoe. Management believes the terms of the transactions with the Related Party were reasonable when compared with terms that could have been entered into with unrelated third parties.' A table of figures following that bland disclosure shows a few million here, a few million there, of funds flowing from the, ahem, Related Party, an SPE named 'SEABISCUIT,' to Belcoe in the form of loans which miraculously never showed up as debt on the Belcoe balance sheet. (This, of course, was back in the days when Belcoe actually published balance sheets). The *raison d'etre* for this cozy relationship is apparently to maximize Belcoe's cash flow while minimizing its debt. The details of these deals are between Belcoe's financial gurus and the outside auditors. Insider opinion generally concedes that God may also have an inkling as to who's involved, but I wouldn't bet the family jewels on it. Yes, what this scribe would like to imbibe is: who's the unidentified Belcoe senior officer heading up 'SEABISCUIT?' And what's the effect of these shenanigans on both Belcoe and said senior officer?"

Brian leaned back in his chair and sipped coffee. Wow. The dude was on a mission to destroy Belcoe's rep. The business press, not to mention the Belcoe stockholders, would be all over this related party stuff like a cheap suit. But why hadn't any of the big shot analysts glommed onto the issue when it first arose? He glanced at the ceiling, imagined the panic setting in on the floor above, the domain of the Chief Financial Officer and his bosses. He smiled and got to his feet.

In the hallway, a young woman carrying a stack of manila folders nearly crashed into Brian. She dodged at the last second and sighed. "Sorry...I was preoccupied."

Brian recognized her as one of the accountants he'd been introduced to on his first-day walk-around. "No problem. Have you seen Natalie Katz?" he asked.

She frowned. "I think she's with A.H.—I mean Mr. Massey."

"Thanks." Brian headed for the elevator.

On the 47th floor, he found Massey's office door closed. Massey's assistant tapped busily at her keyboard, head down.

"Is he in?" Brian asked.

"He's in a meeting." The assistant finally met his eyes, and then looked away quickly.

"Is Natalie Katz with him?"

"I uh, think so." Downcast eyes.

Brian moved to the walnut-paneled door, produced the key he'd taken from the assistant's desk drawer before he went to Montana and inserted it in the lock. He swiftly turned the key and opened the door.

Massey sat on a maroon couch across the room, near the window with his arms around Natalie Katz. Tears ran down her beet-red cheeks.

At the sound of the door opening, Massey jerked away from Natalie, his face flushed and his tie askew. Natalie, seeing Brian, covered her face with both hands. She let out a brief wail and scuttled away from Massey.

"Ah, Jesus." Brian turned and retreated through the door, leaving it open. Urgent murmuring and rustling noises came from Massey's office as Brian moved deliberately to the elevator. He felt sick to his stomach, sick of Belcoe and very tired. He returned to his own office and sat behind the desk, rubbing his eyes. He tried the coffee, but it was cold. He set the mug down on the desk. A few minutes later, the phone rang.

Natalie Katz's voice was so faint, he had to strain to hear her. "Brian, it's not what you think."

"What difference does it make what I think?"

"He was gonna fire me on the spot. I need this job. It's all I've got."

"What about the Moroccan company? What's going on?"

"Look. I've helped you as much as I can. I've got to go now." The phone clicked in his ear.

Brian wondered what to make of Natalie, Darcy's friend. Had she been under Massey's thumb right along? Leading Brian astray under the control of her boss? Or just a desperate young woman for whom the pressure had proven too much?

Brian dialed Lou DeRosa's extension. The phone rang three times and then a crisp female voice said, "Mr. DeRosa's office."

"Irene, this is Brian McKay. I need to speak to him right away."

There was a brief silence, then: "Mr. DeRosa isn't in. Would you like to leave word?"

"When's he expected back?"

"I really can't say."

"Have you spoken to him since the evening he and I met in his office?"

"Uh, actually, no."

"This is urgent." Brian put a little extra on it. "Could literally be a matter of life and death. Do you know where I can reach him?"

She lowered her voice a notch. "I'm not supposed to give out this information, but you might try him at home." She gave Brian a phone number and an address in north suburban Highland Park. He grabbed his phone and tried DeRosa's home line. He let it ring twelve times before giving up.

In the elevator ride down to the parking garage, though, he wondered if DeRosa were still in a position to help. Or if he even wanted to help. As he keyed the ignition in his Jeep, Brian glanced up at the rearview mirror. A large black sedan rolled by. It looked exactly like a Chicago police cruiser. Like the car Joe Growney drove when he and Brian visited Massey two days before.

37

By the time Brian reached the city limits at Devon, the flow of vehicles had lightened enough to allow left-lane cruising at 65, five miles an hour over the limit. He continued northbound into the prosperous North Shore enclave of Highland Park. He knew that the town's claims to fame included Ravinia, the summer home of the Chicago Symphony Orchestra as well as the homes of several well-known professional athletes and musicians.

He wheeled onto the main drag, Greenbay Road, and worked his way toward Lake Michigan and DeRosa's house. The street map showed a green oasis, Central Park, flanking the lake and bounded on three sides by winding streets. He found the park and Lake Avenue, and inched along the tree-lined road, scanning the imposing houses for address markers. Three doors in, a mammoth, vine-covered, three-story white brick colonial loomed. The number next to the dark gray door matched the one on the scrap of paper on the console next to him.

Leaving the conspicuously dirty Grand Cherokee in the semi-circular drive, Brian mounted three steps to a wide porch and rang the bell. The chimes sounded a symphonic melody—familiar but he couldn't recall the name. All remained quiet. He glanced down at the street. A vehicle bearing the Highland Park Police logo on the side cruised slowly by, made the corner and disappeared. Brian rapped his car keys on the door. Nothing.

Just as he was about to give up, he heard a faint noise from the other side of the door. Footsteps on carpet.

The door was opened a crack, its inward progress impeded by a brass chain attached to the jamb inside. A feminine face appeared in the opening. "May I help you?" The word "you" came out somewhat like "jew."

"Yes, I'm looking for Lou DeRosa."

"Mister DeRosa is not home. Who shall I say was calling?"

Her face reminded Brian of a painting of an Aztec princess he'd admired in a museum in Mexico City a few years back. Dark eyes, aquiline nose, full red lips, pitch-black hair loose around her oval face. She looked about twenty-five.

"Brian McKay. I work with him at Belcoe."

Her eyes brightened, but she did not speak.

"It's very important that I see him. Do you know when he will be back?" Brian said.

She looked uncertain. "I…cannot say. Mr. DeRosa has not come home for…a long time."

"May I come in for a moment? I just need to ask you a few questions."

Her lips twitched in what might have been the suggestion of a smile. She shrugged. "Okay. *Momento*." The door closed and he heard the chain slide off its track. The door reopened, fuller this time. The woman was wearing a white apron over a black shirt and slacks.

"Please come in," she said.

She led him through a broad tiled entryway into a large living room. "We can sit," she said. She gestured at a tan upholstered chair with small blue accents and sat on the matching couch next to it. She faced him. "What do you like to know?"

"Well, first, what's your name?"

"Paola Chavez."

"Okay, Paola, when did you last see Mr. DeRosa?"

"It has been since yesterday."

"You're here every day?"

"Yes. I live there, in the coach house." She pointed with her chin toward the rear of the building.

"So, when Mr. DeRosa left yesterday morning, did he say where he was going?"

"No. I thought he went to work."

"But he didn't return. Right?"

"Exactly."

"How long have you worked here?"

"Since just before Mr. DeRosa's divorce. That would be…four years."

"Huh. Any idea why they split up?"

"I don't really know why. It is not my place to know."

"But you must have some idea."

She hesitated. "Um, his wife and he had differences about drinking alcohol. And she did not like him flying his airplane. But I have never talked with Mr. DeRosa about these things. I am talking too much now."

"Does Mr. DeRosa have an airplane now?"

"I don't know. He has not spoken of it for a long time."

"Does he have children?"

"Yes. A son, but he died many years ago, before I came here. And a daughter in San Francisco. Jennifer. She is a college teacher."

"Have you met her?"

"No."

"Here, let me leave a card." Brian extracted one from his coat pocket, scribbled a note asking DeRosa to call him on his cell and handed it to Paola. "Well, I should get back to the city."

She glanced at a small gold watch on her left wrist. "My daughter will not be home for a while. Perhaps a drink?"

"Okay."

Paola went to the kitchen and fixed a beer for Brian and a glass of red wine for herself. When she returned, Brian steered the conversation back to DeRosa. He tried to learn more about what had happened to DeRosa after their drunken meeting in the VP's office the night before. Paola said she had no idea but that he normally came home every evening unless he was traveling somewhere.

Paola consulted her watch again. "I must go to my daughter," she said. "Her dance class is finished."

"Okay. I want to check something before I take off. Have you been in the garage since you last saw Mr. DeRosa?"

"No. I park in my space in the coach house. I come in there through the back entrance." She gestured toward the rear of the place again.

"Do me a favor and unlock the door to the garage. I'll take off after I check it out."

38

The unattached garage had three vehicle doors and a smaller personal entry door. It faced a half-acre backyard bordered by a high stone perimeter wall. The ivy-covered coach house where Paola and her daughter lived was at the rear of the property, next to the garage. Brian entered the garage and switched on the overhead light, revealing a workshop dominated by a built-in workbench covered with an array of hand tools. There was a John Deere lawn tractor parked on the concrete floor. Rakes and shovels filled a steel rack. A brick wall separated the room from the next.

He moved into the adjacent space, inhabited by an unoccupied black BMW 7-series sedan. It looked clean and polished, but a thick layer of dust covered its sleek surfaces, as if it had been abandoned.

Next to the Beamer, a silver Mercedes GLS 550 SUV was canted at a strange angle, its right front bumper grazing the wall. Brian recognized the vehicle as the top-of-the-line 7-seater with a price tag north of $100,000. He peered in through the driver's side window. The vehicle was unoccupied. He opened the driver's door and checked out the interior. Empty.

He closed the door gently and exited the garage. Sunlight leaked through the overhanging trees and collected on the ground like flecks of gold in a miner's pan. A sprawling redwood deck flanked the east side of the mansion. Nearby, in a grassy clearing ringed by maples and ashes, stood a rectangular outbuilding about twenty by fifteen feet, with cedar walls, no windows and one narrow, glass-paned door. A galvanized vent pipe protruded from the peaked roof. The rustic style struck him as incongruous there on the grounds of this posh North Shore estate.

Brian wondered if the miniature cabin was DeRosa's private retreat, perhaps a place to get away from the wife and do some serious drinking, or maybe even a home office. As he approached the building, he detected a faint wisp of burnt wood, possibly birch. Maybe this was a Finnish-style sauna.

Brian remembered vividly his first experience in a sauna. He and his girlfriend Linda had spent a glorious weekend at a rented cabin in the woods of Michigan's Upper Peninsula. The two of them sat together on a bench in the tiny log hut in their swimsuits. Sweat poured down their bodies as the glowing coals in the fire pit sizzled and popped. Brian ladled water onto the rocks suspended on a grill over the coals, and steam erupted upward like some geyser in Yellowstone National Park. Linda screamed in delight as the moist gray cloud enveloped them. Brian noticed her complexion was reddened by the heat and a rivulet of moisture trickled from her neck into the top of her two-piece.

Brian snapped out of his reverie when he noticed a jagged crack in the glass panel in the door in front of him, near the knob. The door was slightly ajar. He opened it and stepped in, his right foot coming down on something soft, which turned out to be a white terry cloth towel. Indeed, the building was a sauna. There were light-colored wooden walls, a slatted bench, a circular thermometer on the wall, a fire pit containing large round stones. DeRosa's office clothing was piled on one end of the bench. A green Scotch bottle lay on its side on the other end of the bench, flanked by an empty cut-crystal highball glass. A Samsung cell phone was next to the glass. A tri-fold glossy piece of paper lay on the floor. Brian bent and picked it up. It turned out to be a brochure advertising a vacation place in the mountains of Montana: "The 606 Guest Ranch." Interesting, the Belcoe ranch he and Bill Thorsten had observed from an overlook recently. He tucked it in his back pocket.

The thermometer inside registered only sixty-eight degrees—about the same as the outside temperature. Brian touched a finger to a fire pit stone. Cool as a mountain stream.

A flagstone pathway led from the sauna toward an arched whitewashed arbor covered with winding tendrils of ivy. It reminded Brian of the fabled vine-covered outfield walls of Wrigley Field, the Chicago Cubs' home a few miles south of where he stood. He followed the pathway through the arbor and into another secluded clearing of green space. There were more shrubs, a few honey locusts and a clump of trees he didn't recognize, with branching crooked trunks and small yellow flowers.

He was about to retrace his steps, when he noticed a pair of blue flip-flops strewn randomly on the ground. A large human foot, white as a dead man's eye, protruded from beneath a large lilac bush. Above the foot, a hairy ankle was visible. As Brian walked over, dreading what he was about to see, the view expanded to a full frontal of a motionless naked older white man. The man's body was lobsterish, like he'd been lying on a beach without sunscreen on a long, sunny afternoon.

Brian knelt beside the prostrate form of Lou DeRosa and grasped a thick wrist, placing two fingers against the radial artery, hoping for a sign of life. A faint vibration pulsed against his fingers. The skin was feverishly warm, a possible symptom of hyperthermia.

Brian secured DeRosa by the shoulders and levered him into a sitting position. It was like maneuvering a jumbo sack of potatoes. Suddenly, DeRosa's gut heaved and he emitted a raspy belch. He began to thrash about, swinging his arms erratically. Brian let go of him and stepped back. The executive drooped to the ground and lay still.

DeRosa breathed noisily through his mouth. A drop of spittle leaked onto his chin. His broad face was radish-red. Brian prodded him gently. "Lou, can you hear me? Wake up, man."

DeRosa groaned weakly. He seemed totally out of it. His breath reeked like a distillery.

Brian glanced up at the sky. Cloudy and getting cloudier. The ozone smell of impending rain pricked his nostrils. He needed to get DeRosa under cover, protected from the elements. He managed to pull him to his feet and dragged the heavier man to the rear of the house. He wrestled him inside the door and, grunting with effort, stretched him out on his back in the middle of the kitchen floor.

39

The house was dead quiet. No sign of Paola. Brian called her name as he strode through the kitchen. No response. She'd probably gone to pick up her daughter as she'd said.

Brian knew DeRosa needed medical help, and fast. He'd served in a MASH unit in the Army, so he was familiar with basic medical procedures. But he knew enough to call in the pros rather than try to revive a seriously injured man on his own. Especially a man who might have the information Brian needed to solve the murders of Matthew Growney and Douglas Spurgeon.

He dialed the local emergency number on his cell and reported an unconscious man with a possible heart attack. He gave the operator the victim's name and address along with his own name. By then, it was getting dark in the house. He flipped on the kitchen lights and eased into a chair at the large oak table.

As he waited for the ambulance to arrive, Brian scanned the brochure from the Montana guest ranch he'd found in the sauna.

Glossy photos depicted tourists on horses walking single-file up a narrow trail with snow-capped mountains as a backdrop. The breathless copy boasted of "limited space for a few of Belcoe's top performers." The brochure promised "breathtaking trail rides through sunlit sagebrush and wildflowers, casting flies to spectacular Cutthroat trout in three miles of crystalline streams, or just drinking in the purest air in the Last Best Place, the most beautiful spot in the American West—Big Sky Country." There was reference to world-class cuisine prepared by a top chef as well as a hot springs pool and spa fed by the same underwater geyser system as in nearby Yellowstone National Park. Nooks and meeting rooms were available for stretching one's brainpower or just cozying up with a favorite book. So this was a guest ranch for a limited clientele, Belcoe employees deemed worthy of the honor.

Enormous raindrops began to pelt the window near Brian's head. Lightning flashed beyond the roof of the garage in the back yard. A wall clock ticked loudly in the silent room. He glanced down at DeRosa. He was about to check the man's vital signs again, when he heard a far-off siren approaching. A few minutes later, tires crunched in the driveway and the siren dopplered down to nothing.

Brian rose and returned to the front of the house. He peeked out the window as a blocky red and white ambulance disgorged a couple of men in gray jumpsuits. Someone leaned on the doorbell as Brian reached the front entrance.

He swung the door open. The two men in jumpsuits stood impatiently on the porch, rain dripping off the bills of caps bearing the inscription HP-EMS. The older of the two, with a round pale face, looked about thirty-five. The name embroidered over his chest pocket read JON. He carried a large yellow plastic case by the handle. His partner, a dark-skinned man with the name patch LIONEL, carried an oxygen tank kit on a strap slung over his shoulder.

Jon took charge. "We got a call about a man with a medical issue. You a relative or anything?"

"A friend. He's inside. Come on." Brian stepped back to allow them ingress to the living room, closed the door and led them to the kitchen. DeRosa lay on his back, breathing raggedly through his mouth. His face remained flushed, though

Brian thought he wasn't quite as red as he'd looked when he'd found him on the ground near the sauna.

The paramedics got to work immediately, kneeling next to the patient, checking his pulse and respiration.

Jon began a mantra into his phone, as if speaking to himself. "Breaths are short and shallow, less than five a minute. Pulse is strong and bounding at 60. Blood pressure is hypertensive at 180 over 100. Skin is acyanotic, reddish color, some diaphoresis. Left pupil is blown, right is mildly reactive to light. No spontaneous movement, no vocalization or response to stimuli. No obvious sites of external bleeding. No evidence of trauma secondary to a fall." This was all spoken with a distinct Chicago South Side accent.

"He going to make it?" Brian asked.

"Don't know," the medic said. Then, to his partner: "Get the gurney. This one's a catch and carry."

Those few simple words let Brian know DeRosa's survival was iffy, that the senior executive would be under hospital care for a while. He wondered when and if he'd be able to speak with the man again. Had Louis DeRosa sipped his last whiskey? Time was short.

Lionel rolled a low gurney into the kitchen and eased it up close to DeRosa. He hit a lever, and the gurney lowered to floor level. The three of them lifted the big man onto the wheeled stretcher. Lionel tilted DeRosa's head back and levered his jaw forward to open his mouth. He quickly placed a face-sized plastic pyramid of a mask across the patient's nose and mouth. The top was attached to a tube, which led to a bag, and then onto another tube, with oxygen flowing in from a tank near the side of the gurney. He lifted a lever, and motioned for the other two to lift the bed upward.

"Let's hit it," Jon said. He and Lionel rearranged the medical supplies they'd been using, placed them, along with the oxygen tank, on the gurney between DeRosa's feet and began to roll it through the doorway.

"I'll follow you to the hospital, " Brian said.

"Okay," Jon said as he moved purposefully toward the front of the house. Brian opened the door and followed the paramedics out. He pulled the door closed, making sure it locked.

They wrestled the gurney into the back of the ambulance, its collapsing legs automatically folding underneath as they slid it into the cargo area. The two medics climbed aboard, Lionel at the wheel and Jon sitting on his heels minding DeRosa.

The ambulance lurched onto the roadway, siren blaring. Blue and red lights atop the roof flashed in a pulsing rhythm. Brian trailed behind in his Jeep.

Inside the ambulance, Jon knelt over the prostrate man, whose head rolled back and forth like that of a lifeless dummy, its motions governed by each sway and bounce of the vehicle. The medic flattened his right hand across the forehead and pressed down. The EMT pressed his left hand over the facemask covering the mouth and nose. His ring and pinkie fingers cupped the chin, pulling his jaw out, upward and open. One knee steadied his rolling head, while the other fixed the air bag against his elbow, compressing the bag as rapidly as it filled.

Finally, the ambulance slowed and jerked to a stop at a brightly lit parking area. A large hospital complex loomed before them. Lionel jumped out of the cab, leaving the door open. He and Jon raced to the rear of the ambulance as Brian pulled up behind them in his Jeep. The two medics quickly worked the gurney from the rear of the vehicle, extended the legs and pointed it toward the Emergency Room entrance a few yards away.

Brian went inside, where hospital smells of antiseptics and ammonia assaulted his nose. Then came the loud clamor of chattering voices and images of white coats, tiled floors and walls, nurses and doctors scurrying in an organized chaos, with strict economy of motion. A pair of orderlies grabbed the gurney, relieving Jon and Lionel. As Brian watched, the new runners in the relay race for a man's survival continued him on his relentless journey, likely to a trauma unit.

Jon turned to face Brian, his expression gentle now. "Guess this is where you pull out. You can hang in the waiting room, if you like. I'll tell' em you're here. They should let you know what happens."

Brian stuck out a hand and they shook. Then he went to find a place to get coffee before settling down to wait.

40

Brian took a seat in the hospital visitors' lounge. He glanced around. The other people waiting looked either worried or bored. A few slept in chairs. Some read magazines or stared at phones. A couple conversed in whispers. A young man asleep on the floor snored loudly.

Brian's phone rang.

"Yeah," he said.

"Man, you sound beat like a drum." As usual, James St. Claire's voice conveyed good-natured ribbing, with the ability to turn serious as needed.

"Well, you'd sound beat too, if you were hanging where I am."

"Which is?"

"Highland Park Hospital waiting room."

"The hell you doing up there?"

"Waiting to see whether Lou DeRosa survives."

"What happened to him?"

"I found him on the ground near his home sauna. Looks like heat stroke."

"He's your main source at that fraud factory, isn't he? Damn. Hey, reason I called, we gotta talk. It's related to Belcoe."

"Hang on. I'll go outside."

Dusk had arrived as Brian went out into the parking lot. A brisk wind whipped through, pushing Brian's hair up off his scalp. He held the phone to his ear as James said, "Was the dude drunk in that sauna?"

"Could be. Looks like he passed out and managed to get outside where he collapsed. I found him just in time."

"Assuming he makes it, I'm thinkin' he should consider AA."

"Yeah, you're probably right."

"Listen, I wanted to let you know what White Collar Crime's got, man. See, Treasury has shared some findings with us on their Middle East investigation, off the record. Plus our guys have been digging. But our investigation's been limited. Politics. Bottom line is, they've been selling stuff to some Syrians."

"Who in Syria?"

"The Prime Minister and some of the deputies. Shipping 'em electronic gear that's used with arms systems. Stuff goes from the U.S. to Canada to the Caymans to the customers."

"The way I understand it, U.S. companies are banned from selling to Iran, Syria, North Korea and some others—rogue nations, axis of evil, right?"

"Yeah, but a way around it would be for the company to set up an off-shore subsidiary, run by foreign nationals, independent of the American parent company, on paper. But their Cayman Islands outfit is a shell with only one employee. All mail there gets re-routed to Belcoe in Chicago. Belcoe does all the trading, and books the sales, clearly violating the law."

"And Treasury and WCC are both aware of this?"

"Hell, yes. Here's where it gets funkier. The CEO, Barry Webb, not only spent a fortune on the U. S. prez's campaign, but he's also been attending meetings in the Vice President's office, lately."

"Let's say the feds *did* press the issue, what happens to Belcoe?"

"They'd pay fines. Billions. Knock the hell outta their profits," James said. "Anyway, these Treasury cats tell the agency to stay out of it, while they do diddly-squat. Just wanted to let you know, man. Might affect what you've been doing with Belcoe."

"Huh. What you're telling me dovetails with what I've learned. DeRosa started to talk a little about it, said he didn't know the details, before he passed out drunk the other night. Later, I find Natalie with Massey behind closed doors in his office."

"Whoa, dude. This Natalie, is she's getting it on with Massey?"

"Looked more like coercion on his part. She says she loathes the guy."

"How reliable's her info?"

"Remains to be seen. She's under a lot of pressure. They could can her at any time."

"Maybe Darcy could help out with Natalie."

"I hate to put her at risk. She could pull it off, though. We'll see," Brian said.

As he entered the hospital waiting room, the woman at the desk looked up. "Mr. McKay?" she said.

Brian walked to the opening in the Plexiglas barrier separating reception from the public.

Before he could speak, the woman said, "You were waiting for Mr. DeRosa, I believe?"

"Yes, that's right." He didn't like the 'were.'

"Are you a family member?"

That question did not bode well. "I'm a close friend."

"I probably shouldn't even be saying this, but Mr. De Rosa has been transferred to Intensive Care. His symptoms have worsened. That's about all I know at this point."

Brian sighed. "Who's the doctor?"

"There's a team of physicians caring for Mr. DeRosa."

"Who's in charge?"

"Well, the cardiologist is Doctor Gupta."

"Here's my card. Once you know more about Mr. DeRosa, could you please call me at any time? And leave word for whoever comes on duty when you leave. I'm really concerned about him."

She took the card and placed it on the counter in front of her. "I'll see what we can do," she said. Her wan expression conveyed sympathy tempered by bureaucracy.

Outside, Brian fired up the Jeep, switched on the windshield wipers and began the long drive to his apartment.

The conversation with James had buoyed his spirits. He and James went back five years, to when he'd been the younger man's boss during the formative first years at the FBI's White Collar Crime group in Chicago. Brian had left the agency less than a year ago, after a twelve-year stint. James had stayed and done well, although the stuffy Agent in Charge, John Elgar, was not a fan of the irreverent young agent. Brian and James kept in touch, socially and professionally.

Brian looked forward to bringing down the corrupt bastards running Belcoe and, although the odds were long, he had some strong allies: besides James, both Dick Cissel and Joe Growney at the CPD could be helpful in the more street-oriented parts of the effort. Did he dare involve Darcy any further? She'd demand it.

Though traffic on the Edens was light, or perhaps because of it, Brian kept an eye on surrounding vehicles. One set of lights stayed a constant hundred yards back. He slowed from 65 to 55, and the trailing vehicle did the same, definitely not typical. Usually, on any expressway in the Chicago area, if you were in the left lane and dropped below the speed limit, you'd be passed on the right like you were standing still, often with the blast of a horn or a raised middle finger.

Brian took the Jeep up to 75. The trailing lights kept pace. He moved from the Edens onto the southbound Kennedy. Exits flashed by: Berteau, Irving Park, Byron.

Addison would be next. He decided to force the issue. He slowed abruptly and swerved right at the Addison exit, eyeing the rearview. The lights that had been in his wake since just south of Highland Park did the same. At that hour, and with slanting rain streaking across the streets, traffic was light. Brian swung left at the bottom of the off-ramp and headed east on Addison, toward Lake Michigan.

Just past Racine, he pulled into an empty space on the right and waited. The vehicle behind mimicked the move a few spaces back. Time to take it to 'em. Brian pulled back onto Addison and continued east, now with a plan in mind. He went left at Clark Street, noting the Wrigley Field sign high above the ballpark main entrance which advertised the next Cubs home game on the following Tuesday. There had been no game that day or evening, so the ballpark environs should be quiet.

Before reaching Waveland Avenue, he turned sharply right into the home players' parking lot. He doused his headlights as he pulled in behind a concrete pillar bearing a billboard advertising season tickets for next year. He pointed the Jeep toward the street, switched off the engine and lights, got out and waited. Less than a minute later, a GMC Yukon pulled off of Clark and into the lot. The driver hesitated, then proceeded slowly toward the sign concealing Brian's vehicle. He stopped short of the sign and turned off his lights. Then came the sound of a door clicking open, followed by furtive footsteps. Brian drew his Sig-Sauer, the gun he'd carried as an FBI agent, and held it close to his side.

Brian kept perfectly still, waiting now as he'd waited on stakeouts during his FBI years, quiet, focused, ready. A minute passed. The guy must be standing there in the rain, trying to figure out where Brian had gone. Might think he'd entered the ballpark. Finally, the steps came closer and stopped on the other side of the sign. A very dim light came on nearby. Brian crept silently to the end of the sign and peeked around. A tall stocky man with a crew cut was playing a flashlight beam along the ballpark wall to the north. Brian stepped from his hiding place, stepped forward and stuck the barrel of his Sig-Sauer into the back of the man's neck.

"Hands over your head. Now!" Brian yelled.

The man raised his thick arms overhead and began to slowly turn his head toward Brian. In the dim illumination from a streetlight on Waveland, Brian recognized the face of a person he'd last seen sitting at a conference room table in the Belcoe offices.

41

Turn around and face me. Keep your hands above your shoulders," Brian said.

Tim Huff, the ex-football player, the man Natalie Katz had referred to as "Massey's goon," pivoted slowly. He smirked. "What're ya gonna do, shoot me here in the parking lot? I can see the Trib headline now: LOCAL PRIVATE SNOOP SHOOTS BELCOE EXECUTIVE AT WRIGLEY FIELD."

"Don't tempt me. Who told you to follow me?"

"None of your fuckin' business." Huff's smirk was malicious.

"What were you supposed to do—convince me to stay away from Belcoe? Get me to stop looking into the murders? Or is this about the dirty stuff the company's into with Syria?"

"Fuck you."

"You're as articulate as you look. Know what? I think you're a patsy. Massey's smart enough to know a multiple-concussion case like you's not gonna keep me away. He probably hoped I'd get you tossed in jail for trying to attack me. Then, he and whoever else is in on this mess could drape the Growney killing around your fat neck. That sound about right?"

"You don't want to fuck with me, man."

"Why not?"

"Because you're getting your ass in big trouble."

"You?" Brian chuckled.

"I'm the fuckin' tip of the iceberg. There's forces involved here you can't imagine."

"Try me."

"You don't know diddly, man. Why should I talk to ya, anyway?"

"How about to save your ass? I can tell the CPD about your 'enforcer' rep. About your sexually harassing Natalie Katz. About your threatening Matthew Growney before he got killed. That what you want?"

Huff shook his head mutely.

"Where were you the night Growney was murdered?"

"I dunno. Probably at home. Hey, my arms are tired. I'm gonna let 'em down."

Brian considered. The fight seemed to have drained out of the spiteful giant. "Listen. You talk with me openly, and I believe you, I won't implicate you in any of this stuff. It's your problem that you work for an egotistical maniac who'll use you and throw you overboard as soon as the sharks start circling the leaky boat."

Huff hesitated as he rubbed circulation back into his thick wrists. "So, what if you're right? Ah, to hell with it." He turned and began to walk toward his vehicle.

Brian pocketed the automatic. "Huff," he yelled.

The big man stopped and cut a look over his shoulder. "Now, what?"

"Think about what I just said. Before this is over, heads are going to come off. Yours could be one of them unless you help me out. Here, take this. Call me at these numbers anytime." He stepped forward and proffered a business card. He flashed to handing a card to the receptionist at Highland Park Hospital earlier that day. He felt like an insurance salesman.

Huff took the card, jammed it into a pants pocket. "Don't hold your fuckin' breath," he mumbled as he turned and headed for his Yukon.

As Brian boarded the Grand Cherokee, raindrops came pelting down like needles. He drove home slowly.

The next morning, as Brian was dressing, his phone rang.

"Hello?"

"Okay, I'll talk to ya." The voice rasped like a roofing nail on corrugated metal.

"What brought that on?"

"They fired me."

"What did I tell you?"

"Don't push me, man." Tim Huff said. Then, after a long beat, "I'll talk to ya with one condition."

"What?"

"My name is never mentioned. I want to go on breathing. Know what I'm sayin'?"

"You at Belcoe now?"

"Just driving away."

"Come on over to my apartment," Brian said. "Coffee's fresh."

42

Tim Huff arrived a half hour later. Brian watched as the big Yukon backed and filled its way into a vacant parking space two doors down. A minute later, Huff trudged up the steps and rang the doorbell.

Brian swung the door open. They eyed each other silently for a moment.

"You might as well come in," Brian said.

In the living room, sitting on a large upholstered chair, Huff leaned forward, elbows braced on meaty thighs as he regarded Brian. "What do ya need to know?" he asked.

"What exactly was your role at Belcoe?" Brian said.

"It's like I said in that meeting at the office. I uh, coordinated financial projects, solved personnel problems and stuff."

"I heard you referred to as an 'enforcer' and 'Massey's pet goon.' That right?"

Huff looked offended. "Who told you that?"

"Doesn't matter."

"Anyway, I made sure the staff got the message about what the boss expected. Nuthin' physical, understand. But a big guy with an attitude gets peoples' attention."

"Did you lean on Natalie Katz? Tell her to keep her mouth shut?"

Huff hesitated. "Well, sort of. Massey said to scare her, tell her not to talk to you. If she did, she'd get fired. Or worse."

"What do you mean 'worse'?"

Huff shrugged his massive shoulders. "You know, remind her what happened to Matthew Growney."

"What *did* happen to him?"

Another shrug. "I don't have the slightest idea."

"But Massey knows?"

"You'd have to ask him. Whether he does or not, he prob'ly figured Natalie, or anyone else around there, would be scared shitless if they thought they might be next." Huff's voice was soft, barely audible.

"What's your take on Massey?"

"Well, they don't call him A.H. for nothing. He's definitely an asshole, but he's also one very smart dude. Financial genius, they say. But not a people person, 'specially with the ladies."

"What do you mean? Have there been problems?"

"The guy's a dork. A real loser. Most of the women there, if they didn't report to him, they wouldn't give him the time of day. So, he'd pressure gals at work."

"How?"

Huff sat back, distancing himself from Brian. He bent his left leg, crossing the ankle over the right knee. "See, if someone's got a performance problem, say she's afraid of the rank and yank, she could be pressured. That kinda happened with Natalie."

"What kind of performance problem and what kind of pressure?"

"No performance issues. She's good at her job. He told me to tell her to give you nothing uh, sensitive, if you asked her any questions."

"Any sexual pressuring?"

Huff looked a little embarrassed. "Well, yeah, probably. From Massey, not me."

Brian felt a little queasy. Huff had just confirmed a suspicion he'd had after walking in on Natalie in Massey's office. "What about the HR lady—Liz Wheaton? Anything going on between Massey and her?"

Huff looked puzzled. "Don't know about that."

"Tell me about Matthew Growney," Brian said. "Did you threaten him?"

"Growney was one of those uber-smart young guys, Top of his class, U of C MBA and all that. He was useful and he was going places. Not somebody Massey would give a hard time."

"So what happened to Growney, do you think?"

"Hey man, I didn't do anything to him. My guess, he found out something he wasn't supposed to and somebody in the brass or an outside professional hired by…somebody flipped his switch off."

"Who do you mean by 'brass'?"

"Nobody in particular. It's a high-pressure type of place. Lots of in-house competition. Big fish eat the little fish. Coulda been any one of the top officers. Maybe more than one. Don't know anything about Massey being involved. But then, I wouldn't put it past him."

Brian was surprised at the lengthy speech from the taciturn man facing him. "You wrote 'none of your business' on that sheet of paper I asked for. I'll ask again: where were you Sunday March 9th from midnight to eight a.m.?"

"That the night Growney got it?"

"That's right."

"At home, I guess."

"Park Ridge, right?"

"Yep."

"Did you ever visit the Belcoe rental house in Park Ridge?"

Huff looked at the floor. "Nah," he said.

Brian played a hunch. "I thought I caught a glimpse of your Yukon leaving there last Monday."

Huff cracked the knuckles of his right hand. A nervous tic, no doubt. "Huh? I didn't know you were there. Okay, DeRosa told me to drive by and check the place out, make sure it was locked up, see if it needed maintenance, like that. I parked in the alley. Went to the front door, tried the knob. No answer. The place looked like shit, so I made a note to tell DeRosa the lawn needed cutting and stuff like that. Then, I took off."

"Did you know Kalif was there?"

"Nope."

"So you worked for Lou DeRosa sometimes?"

"No, man. I reported to Massey. I've met Lou. Don't really know him. That day at the rental house was a one-off. DeRosa probably knew I live in Park Ridge and figured it would be easy for me to swing by the place on the way home."

"What's the skinny on him?"

"A very smart man, kinda operates on his own. Barry gives him lots of slack and he plays his own gigs. Rumors floating around about his extracurricular activities, though. Booze, whores, over-the top expenses, shit like that." Huff scratched the top of his head through his short hair. "But a heavy hitter. Second only to Barry in terms of clout. Definitely one of the 'brass' guys. Brass balls, ya ask me. Not somebody a guy like me ever had anything to do with." Another shrug.

"Did you go to Matthew Growney's apartment on the Tuesday before last?"

Huff hesitated. "Uh, lemme see. I might have."

"What do you mean 'might have'? Either you did or you didn't."

"Okay, yeah, I stopped by."

"Broke the door down, you mean."

"Well, I had to. See, Massey gave me a key. But there are two locks. The deadbolt was on, and the key wouldn't open it."

"The young woman in there was my niece. You chased her down the sidewalk. Scared the bejeebers out of her. Why?"

"I wanted to talk with her, ask her what she was doing there. No harm intended."

"What did Massey tell you to do there?"

"He said to pick up Growney's computer and bring it to him."

"What else?"

"That's it."

Brian had the impression Huff wasn't telling all he knew.

"How about a personal phone number, Tim."

After Huff had complied, Brian stood, signaling an end to their meeting.

As soon as Huff was out the door, Brian called Highland Park Hospital and asked for Doctor Gupta. He was put on hold. Just as he had tired of hearing the theme from the movie "La La Land" enough to slam down the phone, a quiet male voice, sounding out of breath, came on the line.

"This is Doctor Gupta."

"Thanks for taking my call, Doctor. How's Mr. DeRosa doing?"

"Ah, yes. Mr. DeRosa is improved. He is breathing on his own now. The fever has subsided. He is conscious."

"Did he have a stroke?"

"Yes. A mild one."

"I need to see him. That okay?"

"Well, yes. But please don't get him agitated."

Brian thanked the doctor again, hung up and boarded the Jeep for the long drive to Highland Park.

As he slogged north on the Edens, Brian considered his conversation with Tim Huff. He felt sorry for Natalie Katz, Darcy's friend and former mentor. A young woman who'd excelled in college, started off on the fast track at a top corporation, and found herself working for a world-class jerk in an atmosphere of daily terror, fearing for her career and suffering attacks on her dignity. And Huff's protestations that he had nothing to do with DeRosa seemed forced. Did the younger man have a working relationship of some sort with the veteran executive? Did he have something to do with DeRosa's mishap in the sauna? Did Huff know who was behind it?

Thinking of Natalie triggered the realization he'd not seen or talked with Darcy for days. He needed to get in touch with her. But first, one more thing he had to do.

43

Brian approached the reception desk at Highland Park Hospital. The woman who'd been on duty during his last visit sat at the desk behind the Plexiglas. Recognition brightened her intelligent hazel eyes.

"I hear he regained consciousness," she said.

"Great."

"And there's a gentleman with him now."

"Oh, who's that?"

"A Mr. Barry Webb. I believe he's a colleague of Mr. DeRosa's."

Brian thanked her and she gave him directions to DeRosa's room on the third level.

As he boarded the elevator, Brian mused about DeRosa's visitor. He was looking forward to meeting Barry Webb, CEO of Belcoe and former electronics whiz kid. The man calling the tune as the company he built up from nothing now faced investigations of the murder of an employee, government probes of company business and accounting practices and a plummeting stock price. He wondered if Webb's was a social visit or perhaps an effort at damage control.

He located Room 321 but stopped just short of the doorway. Inside, a man was speaking, his voice unfamiliar and barely audible. Brian cocked an ear toward the edge of the door opening. "The accounting stuff, we should be able to handle with minimal damage. The auditors are on board, most of that SPE stuff has been properly disclosed, and our staff are motivated to make it happen."

"I agree. The thing I'm still concerned about is the MTR100 sales," DeRosa said.

"I'm with you. But Doug did a good job of setting up the paper and digital documentation. They're sales to Israel only."

"Speaking of Doug, just before he bought the farm, he told me he reamed Akbar and Kalif over a fuckup in the paper flow. I hope they got it corrected."

"I checked and we should be squared away."

"Good. I'm too old for prison."

"Lou, you of all people must realize how, if we get through this, we're golden."

"Yeah, that's true. But I'm worried about this McKay guy. Why did you insist on hiring him?

"Ah, hell, Lou. The Board are adamant that this independent outside investigation is necessary. McKay provides needed cover. Anyway, he's not going to stumble on the Syria stuff. And if he does, we can take action as needed."

"Well, we'd better keep him away from the event at the ranch."

"He won't be invited. But that local FBI guy, what's his name, plans to show up and count MTR100 units in the warehouse. Shouldn't be a problem, right?" Webb said.

"Bill Thorsten is the FBI agent. I think he and McKay worked together on that dinosaur thing last summer. He should not be any trouble."

"Huh. Okay, well, get healthy, my friend. See you Monday. We'll take my limo to O'Hare. I've gotta run."

There was a rustling noise. Brian decided to enter before Webb had a chance to depart. As he cleared the doorway, he saw a man in a dark suit lean forward to shake Lou DeRosa's hand as he reclined in bed.

"Hello, Lou," Brian called. "Hope I'm not intruding."

DeRosa lay propped up at a 45-degree angle. His face was pale, but his eyes were alert. He looked a lot better, more like the two-fisted Scotch guzzler Brian remembered from their last meeting.

Webb pivoted on a shiny tasseled loafer and extended a hand with a pianist's long fingers and perfect nails.

"Barry Webb," he said. "You must be Brian." His brown eyes reflected keen intelligence.

Brian nodded. "How's the patient?"

"You can see for yourself. I was just leaving."

"May I have a word with you at your office later today?"

Webb smiled as if that were a wonderful idea. "Absolutely. Call my gal, and we'll sit down." He gave a little papal wave and was gone.

Brian stood next to the bedside, looking down at DeRosa's face. Gone from the handsome visage was the crimson hue of the man who'd been administered to by emergency technicians on the kitchen floor of his Highland Park home. Now, the patient's breathing was regular, not at all labored. His hands were folded on his chest as if he were praying.

DeRosa said, "For a while there, I didn't think we'd meet again," he said. "Not so sure it's a good idea now. But I guess I owe you."

"Hell, it'd take more than a little OT in a sauna to slow down a guy like you. But yeah, you *do* owe me."

DeRosa frowned. "Musta been in my cups the other night, eh?" He rubbed his eyes with fisted hands. "But I gave you some straight poop."

"I'd like to hear more."

"I'll bet you would," DeRosa said.

"When are you getting out of this joint?"

"Tomorrow, if I behave myself."

"I'll give you a ride home then."

"I just might take you up on that." The older man reflected for a moment. "Maybe home's not the best place for me to go, though. I should be closer to the office rather than making the long commute."

"Any chance the sauna was an accident?"

"Maybe Barry's right. Maybe I did it to myself. Dunno." He yawned expansively. "Pills make me drowsy. I've stepped on a few people in my checkered career. And I know where a lot of the bodies are buried." He laughed weakly. "Figuratively speaking, of course."

A uniformed nurse wearing purple Crocs entered the room briskly. "How are we today," she asked.

DeRosa and Brian responded simultaneously, "Fine, thanks."

The nurse regarded Brian and rolled her eyes. "The old jokes never die, do they?"

44

The crisp March weather Brian had grown up with in Chicago was only a memory now. Warm temperatures in early spring had become the norm the past few years. And last fall, the Chicago Marathon had been cut short when dozens of mid-level runners collapsed from heat exhaustion. One middle-aged male runner had died inside an aid tent in Lincoln Park.

As he looked out the window onto Aldine, a gust of wind propelled a shower of light rain against the glass. The honey locusts lining the parkway bent in the breeze, their slender branches fluttering like paper. He glanced at his watch.

At the small kitchen table he opened the Chicago Tribune to the business section on his iPad and immediately homed in on a piece entitled "Belcoe stock hits five-year low." The gist of the story: Belcoe, beset by scandal and investigations, not the least of which included police probes involving the mysterious murder of one employee and the apparent suicide of another at company headquarters, was suffering a severe image problem. The steady drop in earnings over the last three quarters hadn't helped. CEO Barry Webb was quoted: "Our fundamentals remain as strong as ever. I'm confident that near-term results will soon rebound and eclipse our historical performance. And I'm putting my money where my mouth is, accumulating Belcoe stock now that it's a bargain." Webb had purchased about a hundred thousand dollars worth of Belcoe common stock in the past week, according to the article.

Brian set the paper aside, opened his laptop and logged onto the Internet. He navigated to a favorite website specializing in reports of insider transactions among publicly-held American corporations. Here, stock purchases and sales by executives and large investors were laid out by date, share volume and dollar amount. For Belcoe, the results were anomalous. Barry Webb, Louis DeRosa, Raymond Hunter, Oscar Gutman, Nancy Northfield and Elizabeth Wheaton had each bought Belcoe shares with market values ranging from half a million to two million dollars apiece just over six months earlier, then sold off similar quantities two weeks ago, at significantly lower prices. Brian was aware that SEC rules prohibited insiders from buying and selling within a six-month period. It looked like the Belcoe quintet had engaged in unsuccessful market timing. He wondered why. Rats deserting a sinking ship? Barry Webb had made a big deal to the press of his buying a paltry hundred grand of company stock the other day, while he'd unloaded twenty times that amount just a couple of weeks prior.

He was reminded of a quote by a financial expert, "Insiders buy their shares for only one reason, because they think the price will rise. They sell them for any number of reasons."

On the way to Area 4 headquarters, Brian thought about his visit with Lou DeRosa the day before, and what he'd overheard when DeRosa had questioned Webb as to why he'd insisted on hiring Brian.

DeRosa, having survived a serious health emergency, seemed to be recovering. Brian hoped to make good on his promise to give the older man a ride home from the hospital later. Maybe he could still pump DeRosa for information. But first, he'd have to take care of business with the CPD. Jake Paulson, the computer wizard that Dick Cissel had referred him to had called first thing that morning. Paulson said he'd found some interesting stuff.

Brian entered the stark reception of Area 4 at nine a.m. A string bean of a young man with a pile of frizzy dark hair, wearing wire rim glasses and dressed in civilian clothes, leaned against the counter. He smiled and ambled forward.

"Jake Paulson," he said. "You Brian?"

Brian confirmed his identity, accepted a visitor's ID card, which he dutifully hung around his neck, and followed Paulson through a door. They walked down a long hallway into the bowels of the station. As they passed Doris Niedner's small office, she looked up, recognized Brian and offered a curled-fingers wave. They swung around the corner, and Brian noticed that Dick Cissel's large space was empty. They continued on to a glass-walled interior area with a cardboard sign taped to the door: GEEKS.

Paulson glanced over his shoulder at Brian as they entered the room. "Geeks are us," he said, waggling his bushy eyebrows.

The room contained four workstations with desktop computers, along with an assortment of other hardware and media. A fat goateed man wearing a headset glanced up from his monitor and blinked, but did not otherwise acknowledge their presence. Paulson led Brian to a computer and sat at the keyboard, motioning his visitor to pull up a chair next to him.

"First off, the interesting stuff I found was not on his computer," Paulson said.

"Where was it?"

"The officers who searched his body found a flash drive in his pants pocket. Here's the file." Paulson grabbed a mouse and clicked. The monitor came to life, displaying an Excel spreadsheet.

"See, the first pages look normal, but there're some notes tucked away six worksheets in," Paulson said. Another mouse click and a collection of text in Arabic characters appeared. Brian was familiar with the 28-character Arabic alphabet used in languages of the Islamic world. From what he could make out, the notes had something to do with sales of MTR100. He remembered that term from the overheard conversation between Barry Webb and Lou DeRosa.

"I'd need this translated to get the meaning," Brian said.

"Aha," Paulson said, a roguish glint in his eyes.

"Aha?"

"Here it is in English." He brought up another worksheet on the monitor.

Brian read the following: *22 03 19 DelivCEP4 Tangier Dmscs DOWNPOR Vetdall Dog2 CN/OOK airscn maxconf MTR100 300 x 16 25K per USD spec inv to LDR NOT BI*

"Could I have a copy of the file and the translation?" Brian asked.

"Already made you a copy." Paulson handed a flash drive to Brian. "I'm no accountant and I don't really follow politics all that much, but this stuff looks kinda…explosive."

"What do you mean?"

"Let's just say what Matthew Growney was looking into might've been illegal stuff."

"Like sales of defense stuff to the bad guys?"

Paulson shrugged. "Could be. And maybe something more, something special. You would probably know better than I. Anyway, good luck."

Brian thanked Paulson and saw himself out. Yes, Paulson was right: this information *was* explosive. Brian was now pretty sure what Matthew Growney had been looking at when he was murdered. And he had a good idea of what was going on at Belcoe. Not just illegal sales to banned countries. James said the FBI had already drawn the conclusion that Belcoe was selling to the Syrians. But Brian now understood there was a lot more to it. Something involving the titanic greed of a certain Belcoe executive.

45

As he got into the Grand Cherokee, his phone rang. "Got your wheels ready, partner?" Lou DeRosa sounded remarkably chipper for a man who'd been in the ICU two days earlier.

"I'm on my way."

Brian picked up DeRosa at Highland Park Hospital and drove him to his house nearby. As the older man fumbled in a coat pocket for his keys, the front door opened. Paola smiled at her boss. "It is so good to see you, Sir," she said.

They hugged carefully, the way old friends do. No hint of anything more intimate, to Brian's eyes. But Paola winked at Brian over DeRosa's shoulder.

"Brian, meet my extremely capable housekeeper, Paola," DeRosa said.

"We've met. Hi," Brian said.

Paola gave him a somber nod. "Hello. Would you gentlemen like coffee? Or something else?"

"No, no, we're fine," DeRosa replied. "We'll be in the study. If anyone calls, tell 'em I'm not here, you don't know when I'll be back. Okay?"

"Certainly." She gave a little bow and disappeared in the direction of the kitchen.

The study turned out to be a large corner room with a picture window facing the green sward of grass and the trees where Brian had found his host near death a few days before. A substantial oak desk dominated one side, with bookshelves behind it. DeRosa waved Brian to a leather-upholstered chair that would have looked at home in the reading room of the Chicago Athletic Club. He reached to a high shelf and retrieved a key from a space behind an unabridged American Heritage dictionary, then moved to a low cabinet behind the desk, opened it and lifted out a bottle of Laphroaig.

Without asking, DeRosa produced a couple of small glasses and poured them half full. He handed one to Brian, set the bottle on the coffee table between them and sat in a chair matching Brian's.

"Skoal," DeRosa said, raising his glass in Brian's direction. Then, "You don't know how much I've been looking forward to this." He nodded at his glass in approval.

"I can guess, though." DeRosa would perhaps be facing a delicate balance between intoxication and passing out, Brian thought.

DeRosa shrugged. "Name like McKay, I'd think you'd have an acquaintance with the stuff, yourself. What're you anyway, Scottish?"

"I grew up in an Irish-Catholic family. The Catholic part's kind of drifted away, " Brian said.

DeRosa nodded. "Well, you're not here to talk religion." He tossed back his drink and reached for the bottle. He poured himself three fingers and looked inquisitively at Brian.

"I'm fine," Brian said with a trace of impatience. He wanted to hear what DeRosa had to say before the man ended up shit-faced.

As if reading Brian's thoughts, DeRosa set his glass on the table and said, "I uh, recall that we never got to finish our conversation last time. Guess I had a bit too much to imbibe. Won't happen this time."

"Good. What were Kalif and those other guys doing in that house in Park Ridge? What's Belcoe's involvement in that whole mess?"

DeRosa scratched the side of his nose. "The company rents a few apartments and houses, various places. We use 'em for entertaining customers, prospects, visiting dignitaries and so on. As for that Park Ridge house, I don't know how it's used. I've never booked anybody there. Our places are usually more upscale."

"Who at Belcoe would know about Park Ridge?"

"Well, Barry, of course. And Nancy Northfield kind of organizes that stuff. Under Barry's close supervision, you understand." He winked.

"They have a relationship?"

"Yep."

"I haven't met her. She's Investor Relations?"

"Right. Nancy's a looker. Kind of reminds me of that gal played Jackie Kennedy in a movie…"

"Natalie Portman."

"Yeah, her."

"Tell me, why do you suppose I was grabbed off the street and taken to that house? Does Belcoe have a kidnapping division, by way of diversification from electronics?"

DeRosa frowned. "You'd be surprised, some of the tactics we've used over the years. Frankly, we're in a hardball business. I'm sure it's nothing personal, but you are no doubt seen as a threat by uh, certain parties. Hell, I may be seen that way myself." He poured himself another drink, smaller this time. He shot a glance at Brian's glass, still nearly half full.

"Why hold me in a cell? Why not just kill me."

"All I can think is they were gonna torture you to find out what you knew about some particular deal."

"Like what?"

DeRosa shrugged. "I couldn't say."

"You must be losing a lot of money as the company stock drops."

"Not really. I anticipated the drop. I've been shorting the stock for months now. I'm almost back to my peak value from a year ago in terms of unrealized capital gains. By the time it hits bottom, I'll be fine."

"SEC might construe it as insider trading, though."

"Nah. I'm careful not to trade within the exclusion dates around quarterly earnings releases. And I don't take advantage of material information not disclosed to the public. It's all out there if you know where to look. What I do is my own business. You know, you should consider shorting Belcoe, yourself, Brian."

"What about Barry? Is he taking care of himself like that?"

"You can count on it. They won't be holding any tag days for Barry Webb. But lately, he's been spending time at that ranch out in Montana. Nice place. Tax write-off. Only guests are Belcoe people."

Brian said, "I picked up a print ad for the 606 Ranch in your sauna, just before I stumbled on your carcass lying on the ground."

"Yeah, that's the place. I was looking at it as I roasted, thinking of going out there for a few days of R & R myself."

"The company has functions there?"

"Executive meetings, business and recreation, booze and music. Barry tossed a birthday bash for his wife there last year. Must've cost a million, all on the company tab. Course, some business gets done, too."

"I'm familiar with the neighborhood," Brian said. "Last summer, my niece—she's a college student—worked on a dinosaur dig a few miles from that ranch. Beautiful country."

"That it is." DeRosa Yawned. "Christ, I'm tired. Damned medication. Booze probably doesn't help, either. Tell you what. Let me catch a few zees. We'll talk in the morning. You might as well sleep in a guest room, rather than fight traffic."

"Okay."

"You got a gun?"

"Yeah."

"Keep it under your pillow, will you?"

DeRosa retired to the master bedroom upstairs. A few minutes later, Paola showed Brian to the guest room, smiled and left to join her daughter in the coach house.

Brian checked the Sig Sauer. The magazine was full and the action worked smoothly. He set the gun on the night table and clicked off the light. He dozed fitfully, occasionally rising and looking out the window at the back yard. The half moon illuminated the yard. Around three a.m. he fell into a deep sleep.

46

Brian glanced at his watch. Eight forty-five. No sign of his host yet. Obviously, the man had some sleep to catch up on after his surgery and hospital stay. He should probably let him rest for a while.

As if reading his thoughts, Paola said, "He doesn't usually sleep so long. Maybe I should—"

"That's okay. I'll check in on him in a little while." Brian sipped from his mug of Columbian.

She shrugged. "Anyway, I should be getting back to Carolina, make sure she's ready for school."

"Carolina—that's your daughter?"

"Yes."

"It's a very pretty name."

"Yes, well, it's an old name, popular in my home country."

When nine o'clock rolled around, Brian got up and went to check on DeRosa. He followed a broad hallway to the rear of the house. Along the way, he noticed framed prints of landscapes of the American west on the walls: Russell, Moran and others he didn't know. At the corner of the sprawling house, he reached a closed door and rapped his knuckles on it. Nothing.

Brian opened the door and entered a large bedroom, dimly lit by sunlight seeping in around the edges of the blinds over the two large windows. A rounded, motionless figure on the king-size bed was covered by a puffy comforter.

"Lou, you awake?" Brian said.

DeRosa groaned. "Christ, what time is it? I musta fuckin' slept a day and a half." His voice was groggy.

"We should probably hit the road pretty soon," Brian said.

DeRosa frowned. "I'm, uh, I'm not really up to it right now. You've spent enough time holding my hand. Last night, before I dropped off, I called a guy's gonna come over and keep an eye on me 'til I relocate. You know him, name's Joe Growney. In fact, he should be here any minute."

"What? Joe's with the Chicago Police."

"Was. He quit. He's my bodyguard now. Anyway, I'm thinking I'd better get my ass moved, sooner rather than later. Look, I'll let you know, once I'm settled in."

"All right, Lou. Looks like you've got things under control. Anyway, I've gotta get back to the city, catch up on some stuff, see people I've been neglecting. Whatever you do though, call me."

DeRosa nodded. "Will do. Go ahead. I'm fine. Joe's a good man. And Paola'll be around. You and she hit it off, am I right? Hey, single guy like you's gotta take his opportunities where he finds 'em." His expression sobered.

"Anyway, I'll give you a shout tomorrow."

Brian returned to the kitchen, where Paola had finished up with the dishes.

"When will you return?" she asked.

"Don't know. Take care of Lou. You'll have help. Man name of Joe Growney's coming over."

Paola's face clouded. "Oh."

"He's going to move Mr. DeRosa to an apartment in the city for a little while. Until he feels better. Let Growney in if he shows ID, but don't open the door to any strangers. Call me if anything weird happens. Okay?"

As he approached the Jeep in the driveway, a black Chevy Cruze drifted to the curb out front. The engine shut down and Joe Growney, wearing a dark blue nylon jacket and chinos emerged. They eyed each other cautiously.

"What happened?" Brian asked. "You quit the CPD in the middle of the investigation of your brother's death?"

"Let me worry about that. Lou all right?"

"He's in his bedroom. Awake, last I saw. He needs rest. And he needs a place to stay."

"Got it covered," Growney said.

"Where will you take him?"

"He'll let you know." There was a finality to his words that brooked no disagreement.

"Okay, then. Catch you later." Brian turned to the Jeep, got in and fired it up.

He worked his way over to the Edens Expressway and headed south toward the city. Traffic was light, thank God. He planned to stop at his apartment for a shower and change of clothes. Then maybe he'd check in with Darcy, see if she was free later. He yawned. Hadn't had much sleep himself, the last couple of nights.

His reverie was interrupted by the earsplitting bray of a car horn behind him. He glanced in the rearview. A maroon Cadillac sedan, lowered and tricked out with a chunky chrome grille, loomed a foot off his rear bumper. In his sleep-deprived state, Brian had committed the unforgivable sin of occupying the wide-open left lane of a major Chicago-area artery while going less than eighty miles an hour. He eased the Jeep to the right. The Cadillac shot forward like a cat with a scalded ass. Beefy arms emerged from the windows on both sides of the Caddy and shot the bird upward. Brian snapped off a military salute. The other vehicle was gone from sight in seconds.

Exits ground by: Golf, Church, Dempster, then Howard, marking the northern border of Chicago. Traffic thickened as he continued south to the junction where the Edens merged into the Kennedy, which angled eastward toward the Loop and Lake Michigan. He got off at Addison and headed east, then south on Clark. He hung a left at Aldine and negotiated the narrow street to the alley where he garaged the Jeep. A drunk stood pissing against the wall of the building across the alley as Brian remoted his garage door closed.

"Couldn't find a rest room?" Brian asked.

"Hey, when ya gotta go, ya gotta go," the drunk muttered.

Brian shook is head. He turned and walked out to the street. As he mounted the steps to his door, key in hand, he heard voices coming from inside his apartment. He stopped short and listened. Sounded like a man and a woman. Then he recognized the voices. He opened the door and went in.

47

As Brian stepped into the living room, the conversation, which had been animated and loud, suddenly stopped. Sitting on the couch with a mischievous grin, was his niece, Darcy. In the easy chair kitty-corner to the couch, James St. Clair lounged, looking equally jovial.

"C'mon in and take a load off," James said.

"Thanks. Make yourselves at home."

"We have," Darcy said. She got up and gave Brian a powerful hug. Brian was reminded that she worked out on campus several times a week—her arms were like steel bands around his back.

As they unclenched, James came over and pumped Brian's hand briskly. "We were just talking about you. Figured you were up in Highland Park. Couldn't raise you on your phone."

"Yeah, I was. Had the ringer off."

The stereo was on low, tuned to a garage rock station. Brian took a seat on the couch next to Darcy, feeling guilty he'd lost touch with her recently. "I was gonna call you," he told her.

She smiled. "I've heard that one before."

"What do I owe this dual visitation to?" Brian asked.

James spoke up. "Thought maybe you didn't love me any more, way you dropped outta sight. Plus, I got some news for ya. Darcy here kinda had the same idea, showed up same time. Let me in with her key. Great minds runnin' in the same channel, I guess."

"I'm flattered."

A song came from the speakers, a pop confection warbled by a sixties vocal duo. Brian, proud of his command of popular music history, decided to test the musical knowledge of his guests. "Know who that is?"

"What? That scratchy tune?" James said.

"Sounds familiar, but ancient," Darcy added.

"That, my friends, is the brother-sister team of Nino Tempo and April Stevens doing 'Deep Purple.'" And it was," he said, gesturing toward the sound system, "the number one song in November 1963, when JFK was assassinated. Grammy winner for best rock and roll record of 1964, too."

"Before my time," James said. "Also, kinda lily-white sounding."

"I listen to classic rock sometimes when I'm studying," Darcy said. "Good background music. Blocks out the city noise, but not too distracting."

"Anyway," Brian continued, "with 'Deep Purple,' the story goes, Nino and April had only fourteen minutes to record the song, the time left at the tail-end of a recording session at Atlantic Records. No rehearsals. Did the whole thing in two takes. Hey listen to this part."

The female vocal switched from singing to talking, reciting the words in a sort of sweet monotone, "When the deep purple falls over sleepy garden walls..." A halting male voice crooned each word, a beat behind.

"Now, you're gonna tell me this's the first ever rap cut," James said.

"April recited the words because brother Nino couldn't remember them. She was trying to give him a guide vocal to follow. But, since they had no time for editing, that's the way the track was released. And it became one of the top singles of all time."

"Brian McKay, rock and roll historian," Darcy said. "You know all about this stuff came out way before you were born."

"You *do* know a lot a trivia shit," James put in.

The song faded out. The next sound from the radio was the unmistakable seven-note guitar riff of "Smoke on the Water," the huge 1973 hit by the British metal group, Deep Purple. Nice transition, Brian thought. What a contrast in styles from 1963 to 1973. He made a mental note to check number one songs from the fall of 1983, 1993, 2003 and 2013. Maybe there was a pattern, a reflection of societal change over ten year spans. Maybe he should have been a sociologist.

He suddenly realized he hadn't had anything to eat yet that day. "I'm hungry. Anyone up for thin-crust?" he asked.

"Me," Darcy said, immediately.

James shook his head sadly. "I've gotta get to the office, man. Meeting of the WCC staff with J. Edgar. Gotta give a briefing on the METTF."

"What's that?" Brian asked.

"Middle East Terrorism Task Force. We spend over 75% of our time chasing after foreign source terrorists these days. White-collar crime's all but ignored. Insurance fraud's gone apeshit. Embezzlement's off the charts. Financial Crime's looking under rocks for sleeper cells, while the guys who swindle the crap out of everyday people get a free stay-out-of-jail card."

"So J. Edgar's surviving?" Brian wondered how the Special Agent in Charge was faring.

Another head shake from James. "Yep, but I don't see how. Bungles everything he touches, but sucks up to the honchos in D. C." James shot a glance at his watch. "But lemme give you a little update before I boogie. Like I told you at the hospital the other day, WCC's been feeding the U.S. Attorney for some indictments on this Middle East export stuff. Turns out a grand jury got impaneled, was looking to return counts. I mean big-time counts."

"Indictment of Belcoe execs?" Brian asked.

"Exactly. But now, that's in the dumper," James said.

"What happened?"

"Don't know for sure but, if I was a bettin' man, I'd say these Belcoe dudes' cozy connections in D.C. made all the difference. What I hear, the indictments've been quashed."

"Any word on what was in them?"

"Didn't see 'em, but the gist is illegal export of computer components to a Syrian national name a Mousa Abu Marzook. You might recall the name from your days with WCC. See, this Marzook dude's been classified as an SDT."

"I'm a little rusty on my acronyms," Brian said.

"Specially Designated Terrorist. Americans can't do business with 'em. Belcoe's been using their Caymans subsidiary to ship the goods to a Moroccan company fronted by Marzook that takes payment. His brother's one of the deputies reporting to the Syrian Prime Minister. So he's got plenty of clout. Interestingly, the guy was in the same fraternity at Ohio State as your pal Kalif. We've ID'd dozens of transactions. Whole thing's set up to look legit on the books. Shipping documents are phonied up, contents disguised, ultimate customer hidden."

"But the Bureau's dropping it?"

"Unfortunately, it's a combined effort: Bureau's working with Commerce on this, and it's all flowing through the U.S. Attorney for the Northern District. Politics every step of the way."

"If the details get out, the stock's gonna take another hit, regardless of whether indictments were returned. That'll hurt the Belcoe management," Brian said.

James shrugged. "Prob'ly. But it'll also kick the little guys in the ass, like the employees with company stock in their retirement plans." He turned to Darcy. "By the way, Darcy, all this stuff's totally confidential."

Darcy looked hurt. "Give me a little credit."

James held up his hands, palms out. "Sorry, I'm kinda paranoid, way things've been goin' lately."

"Any Chicago individuals named in the counts?" Brian asked.

"Two guys I know of: your buddy Kalif, who's been transferred to Cook County, by the way, and the good doctor, what's his name, Akbar. Looks like he'll slide, for now."

"But not if we can help it. Right?" Brian said.

"Yeah, right." James seemed dispirited. He looked at his watch again. "Gotta run. I'll keep you posted."

After James was out the door, Darcy said, "That crack about confidential really burned me."

"Cut him some slack," Brian said. "He's a very disappointed man right now."

"I know. I don't really blame him for being uptight. I just hate to be…patronized."

"Maybe a thin-crust at Vito's will cheer you up."

"One way to find out," she said.

A few minutes later, they sat across a table in a booth at Vito's Pizzeria, inhaling chewy slices of Neapolitan style Margherita pizza. They each paused occasionally to dab at mouths and hands with paper napkins or to take a swig of Coke. Finally, Brian wiped his mouth, burped softly and sucked some cola through a thick straw.

"Doesn't get any better than this," he said.

"Right on."

"Heard from Natalie lately?"

"We exchanged e-mails yesterday. She's thinking of ditching her job, you know. But she wants to line up something else before she leaves."

"Smart girl."

"She said her boss is making her life unbearable. I thought of that when you said that thing about James's boss. She said she'd like to kill the guy."

"But not literally, I take it."

Darcy popped a bite of pizza in her mouth and wiped her fingers with a napkin. "I'm not so sure about that," she said.

48

Monday morning, Darcy got off the El at the State and Lake station and crossed the Chicago River on the Wabash Avenue Bridge. Ahead, the 47-story glass tower housing the Belcoe headquarters loomed above a windswept plaza along the river.

While Darcy was just short of the south entrance, Natalie Katz emerged through the revolving doors, walking slowly, head down. Darcy called her name. Natalie stopped, raised her head and, spotting Darcy, waved. They converged, running the last few steps and hugged.

"Haven't been sleeping much, have you?" Darcy said.

"I won't lie. This situation here is driving me nuts. It's totally not me."

Darcy noticed a hot dog cart diagonally across the open plaza. "Let's go get a bite and you can tell me about it. How about a Chicago-style dog, my treat?"

"Okay, but let me get it. I'm the one with a paycheck…for now."

A few minutes later, they sat next to each other on a stone bench formed by one side of a massive planter shaded by a diaphanous honey locust. Like many of downtown Chicago's skyscrapers, the Belcoe Building was surrounded by a sizable plaza broken at intervals with square cutouts containing well-tended trees. Raised concrete planters were scattered around the plaza. In each planter was a thriving bed of colorful perennials. Say what you would about the city, it promoted trees, flowers and parks like nowhere else. The city regularly repurposed huge swaths of former industrial land into new parks. City Hall sported a "green roof" covered with thriving gardens. Chicago's official motto, *Urbs in horto*, (city in a garden) never seemed more apropos. Lunchtime office workers took full advantage of the *horto* near their buildings.

Darcy looked around with a faint smile on her lips. Dozens of men and women dined al fresco from paper bags. Some played chess. A few bopped to tunes through ear buds. Others studied phones. While Darcy had consumed her hot dog and was working through a sack of rough-cut fries, Natalie had hardly touched her food. Her eyes remained focused on the ground near her feet.

"C'mon eat something. You'll feel better," Darcy said.

"I'm not hungry." Natalie carefully folded the top of the food bag closed and set it on the bench next to her. "Look. I'm getting paranoid as hell. Every time I hear footsteps in the hallway, I look up, expecting to see some huge security guy coming over to escort me out of the building. Or worse."

"Is it really that bad?" Darcy asked.

"Oh yeah. At night, I keep waking up, thinking I hear a weird noise. Like someone breaking in. Sometimes my phone rings and there's nobody there. Blocked number, anonymous. I don't know. In the morning, I'm a complete basket case. I chug about four cups of coffee just to stay conscious. But I keep on going into the office every day, pretending to myself and the whole world that everything's okay."

"Can't you take some vacation time?"

"It'd be a waste, 'cause I'd still be miserable, only at home."

"You really think you're like in physical danger?"

Natalie scuffed a shoe on the concrete plaza surface. "After what happened to Matthew? With Massey suspicious that I spilled my guts to your uncle? Yes."

"Look, it's already after one. Why don't you take the rest of the day off? You can stay at my place tonight. A change will do you good."

Natalie considered for a moment. "I can't..." She raised her eyes to Darcy's. "Maybe you're right. I don't have any meetings this afternoon or tomorrow. And I really don't want to go back in there."

"Let's do it. You got your car?" Darcy said.

"It's in the parking garage."

They tossed their lunch detritus in a mesh trash container and picked up Natalie's Subaru in the Belcoe building.

"I'm glad you suggested this," Natalie said. "We can catch up and maybe, just maybe, I can get my mind wrapped around something other than my problems at this place." She keyed the ignition and backed out.

Natalie worked her way through typically heavy River North traffic, a mixture of harried locals and dawdling tourists. At Grand, she made a right and headed toward Lakeshore Drive. Midday, traffic on the drive wasn't bad. Natalie eased the car up to fifty and stayed in the right lane. She seemed to relax a bit as a fresh breeze filtered through the tipped-open sunroof. A moment later, the vehicle began to vibrate.

"Feels like you need an alignment," Darcy said.

"With all the potholes around here, I wouldn't be surprised if I need a whole new car."

The vibration got steadily worse. The Subaru shuddered and swayed. Natalie took her foot off the gas. Darcy reached for a grab handle on the door. Suddenly, the right front of the car dipped toward the pavement, and there was a loud series of thumps along the side of the vehicle. It fishtailed wildly as Natalie pumped the brakes.

"Hang on," Natalie yelled.

The car rocked back and forth as it gradually slowed, shimmying and bucking and threatening to roll. At twenty miles an hour, Natalie eased the wheel to the right and they moved toward the shoulder. A horrendous scraping noise came from under the front-end as the car continued to oscillate like a rodeo bucking horse. Horns blared behind them. Finally, they came to rest on the shoulder, out of the flow of traffic.

The two women sat motionless for a moment, breath short, expressions dazed. Natalie began to cry softly.

The honking of horns continued. Darcy turned around and glanced behind them. Cars were weaving around some low, roundish object in the right lane, coming perilously close to the Subaru's left rear fender. After a moment, it registered to Darcy what the object was: a tire.

They got out and stood on the shoulder together, the lopsided car between them and the steady stream of traffic. Cars whizzed by, buffeting them in the slipstream. The Subaru's problem was obvious: the right front wheel had come off. Natalie called 911.

"Did you have the tire repaired recently?" Darcy asked.

"No. I've never even had a flat on this car. I know what you're getting at. But no, there's no reason for the wheel to come off. None that I know of, anyway."

"Unless someone went into the parking garage and loosened it up this morning while you were at your desk."

Natalie wiped a tear from the corner of an eye. "Those sons of bitches. Didn't even have the nerve to kill me face to face." She shook silently as the tears continued to come.

A siren howled in the distance and drew near. A few seconds later a Chicago police car eased to a halt behind their disabled vehicle with its rear-end sticking out into traffic, causing motorists to veer around both the errant tire and the squad car. A pair of young uniforms with matching bulky builds, shades and dark mustaches emerged from the sedan with its flashing blue rooftop lights and approached them slowly.

The taller one with the name badge reading "McFetridge" tilted his cap back with a knuckle and said, "Looks like you ladies could use some help."

Natalie said something then that Darcy would remember with affection for years: "The bastard that did this to us is the one's gonna need help."

The other cop, whose badge identified him as "Grabowski," risked his life as he retrieved the tire from the surface of Lake Shore Drive. He rolled it over to the gaping wheel well and said, "Now all we need is a jack and some lug nuts."

His partner grinned. "Only lug nut around here is you."

"Ya gotta allow for him. Cracks himself up at the weirdest times," Grabowski explained to Darcy and Natalie with a wink.

Turning to his cohort, McFetridge said, "You want to call a wrecker for these good-lookin' gals, so they don't hafta hang around here all day?"

Darcy was grateful for the indefatigable good cheer of the two flippant officers as the four of them waited for a tow truck to arrive. McFetridge was particularly attentive. He even managed to make Natalie smile as he related a long, complicated joke about a twelve-inch pianist. As the rescue truck pulled in, he asked for and received Natalie's phone number.

A little while later, the women were underway, Darcy driving, four wheels underfoot, one of which sported a new set of shiny lug nuts. The car seemed fine. The officers, though sympathetic to Natalie's suspicions, had advised against a police report, as nobody was hurt, nothing was damaged, and, as Grabowski had put it, "Ya couldn't prove diddly-squat."

"I wonder if they should have taken finger prints off the wheel," Darcy said.

"I don't know about that, but I think I have Dave's fingerprints on my shoulders," Natalie replied.

"Dave?"

"McFetridge. He asked me out."

"You going to go?"

"I might. He's pretty decent-looking. Plus, I could use a body guard."

Twenty minutes later, they were entering Natalie's North Side apartment. She looked up and down the street carefully before shutting the door.

49

Brian went into his home office, where he read an e-mail from Darcy. There'd been an accident, possibly an attempt on Natalie's life, and Darcy had almost gotten caught up in it. A wheel came off Natalie's car on Lake Shore Drive and they'd nearly crashed in heavy traffic. Rescued by a pair of cute cops. Brian frowned. Seemed like Darcy lived a more dangerous life than he did himself as a PI. He picked up his phone, got her recording and left a message to call.

His phone rang. Lou DeRosa. "Where are you?" Brian asked.

"Lincoln Park. Nice quiet place."

"You sure you're all right?"

"Yeah, yeah, I'm fine. Feelin' stronger every day."

Brian thought of the hit song of that title from 1973. "I tried to reach you earlier. I was worried about you, man," Brian said. "Is Joe with you?"

"No, he had to go take care of something."

"I'm mystified by his leaving the CPD. I thought he was busting his ass to find the guy that killed his kid brother. And now he's working for you instead."

"Well…Joe's a good man. He's entitled to choose his employment. I'm paying him a hell of a lot more than a cop makes."

"Was he close to his brother?"

DeRosa hesitated. "Don't know. He said the kid was a star at everything he did. Jibes with what I heard about him at the company. Very smart kid. Joe seems more…down to earth. Anyway did you hear about the latest at Belcoe?"

"What do you mean?"

"I checked in with my assistant a few minutes ago. She says somebody took a shot at Barry. Fired a round through his office window."

"Was he hit?"

"Nah. His typical luck he backed away from his desk just as the shot came in."

"Isn't his office on the 47th floor?"

"Exactly."

"Give me your address and I'll be by in a few minutes."

DeRosa gave him directions to an upscale condo building on Lincoln Park West called *The Pierre*, where units started around a million dollars. Brian wondered how the hell a shooter got a crack at Barry Webb inside an office with opaque green-tinted windows more than forty floors above street level. Could it have been an attempt to scare the executive, send him into hiding? He grabbed his car keys and went out the door.

On the way, Brian mused about the plethora of violence plaguing Belcoe and its employees over the past month. It had started with young Matthew Growney, shot in the head point-blank in the office early on a Sunday morning. Then the Chief Operating Officer, Douglas Spurgeon, dead in his car in the company parking garage, apparently a suicide, but the police investigation was ongoing. Next, Darcy was chased from Matthew's apartment by a guy in shades and trench coat. Then Brian himself had a taste of the craziness when he'd been abducted off the street at Mary's place and taken to a basement prison in a Park Ridge house overseen by Pinhead. A few days ago, DeRosa had been unconscious outside his sauna and nearly broiled alive. Just yesterday,

Natalie's vehicle, with Darcy aboard, lost a wheel and nearly crashed on Lake Shore Drive. And today, someone had tried to pop Webb in his office. What did it add up to?

He left the Grand Cherokee in an illegal space near *The Pierre* and approached the ivory-colored stone building. Twelve stories of apartments rose above Lincoln Park West. Each had a wall of windows facing east toward Lincoln Park and beyond to the blue expanse of Lake Michigan. Inside, the ornate lobby contained Corinthian columns, a ceiling painted to evoke an azure sky with cottony white clouds, crystal chandeliers and a fireplace capacious enough for roasting oxen. The lobby gave onto an alcove housing an elevator. Brian thumbed number three and waited as the door took its sweet time closing. The small car ascended silently. At the third floor, he exited into a short hallway sporting cream-colored walls and a pair of framed charcoal drawings of nude women in the style of Picasso. He proceeded to a door bearing a brass number 3-A and knocked.

Lou DeRosa let him in and went to a large easy chair in the corner of a sparsely furnished living room. A chunky glass of amber liquid and a whiskey bottle stood sentry atop a low rectangular table in front of him. Astonished at DeRosa's pounding down hard liquor while convalescing from heat exhaustion, Brian stayed on his feet. "Lou, are you always this self-destructive?"

DeRosa frowned. "Don't be so fucking judgmental, me boy. This is mother's milk." He looked a little sheepish for an instant. "At least it works for me."

Brian took a chair across the table from DeRosa. He turned his attention to his host. "What's all this stuff about a shooter going after Webb?"

DeRosa grimaced. "I only got the bare bones from Barry. He just called. Said he's finished up with the cops. Wants me to stop by his office, have a little powwow." DeRosa got to his feet. At the door, he reached down and grabbed a leather suitcase, which he carried out to Brian's vehicle and tossed in the back seat. Brian did not comment.

Brian welcomed the opportunity to visit Webb on his home turf. He was curious about the enigmatic Belcoe CEO's personality and even more curious as to why someone had attempted to punch the man's ticket.

50

They rode in silence. Approaching the Belcoe building, DeRosa finally spoke. "Y'know, Barry and I go back to the days of the giants. I owe my career to the man. He's no saint, but Christ, think of the good he's done. Employs twelve thousand people. Creates jobs all over the world. Pays enough taxes to finance the average Central American economy. I wouldn't be too quick to point the finger at Barry Webb."

"So you're nominating him for sainthood? The man hasn't had much to brag about lately. He's accused of bribing government officials over the years and disregarding inconvenient laws so he could make his dirty money. His people have been killed on the job. The stockholders and employees who bet on his company and his ability to lead it have lost their ass."

In the parking garage, DeRosa grabbed his suitcase and Brian locked up the Jeep. After security, an elevator whisked them up to the 47th floor. Neither man commented on the fact that the Belcoe video screen was blank. Brian figured the in-house propaganda budget might have been slashed as a cost-cutting move.

Brian noticed that most of the individual office doors were closed, including DeRosa's. At the corner, DeRosa stepped to Webb's office door and rapped his knuckles on it.

"Lou, that you?" A tenor called.

Brian grasped the doorknob and eased the door open. He went inside with DeRosa behind him. Webb sat in a high-backed black leather swivel chair behind a desk large enough for badminton. There was nothing on the desk except one of his Italian loafer-shod feet. If he was surprised by Brian's presence, he didn't show it.

"Gentlemen. Come in. Sit." He waved at the array of visitors' chairs.

Brian sank down into the soft cushion and found himself looking up at Webb's tanned, impassive face across the desk. He noticed that the CEO's dark hair had receded up his forehead, which had the effect of making him seem cerebral like a university professor. Brian glanced to his right and noticed the ceiling-high windows affording a view northward along the shore of Lake Michigan's blue waters. Except that one windowpane was boarded up with plywood.

Without preamble, Webb spoke. "At first, I wasn't sure where the shooter was. But now I think I know. To the north, the closer-in buildings are lower than this one. And the taller ones are quite distant. But one dominates and there's a clean line of sight. Have a look."

Brian stood and went to the boarded-up window, then to the one next to it. Looking north, there was, as Webb had said, a series of buildings shorter than their current perch. About a half-mile to the northeast, right on the lake, came Lake Point Tower, 70 stories of residential units. The John Hancock Center's 100-story facade loomed over Michigan Avenue due north.

"Somebody with the right weapon could send a round here from the Hancock," Brian said. "It's about 800 yards."

"Let's be analytical here," Webb said. "Say we're talking about a sniper rifle. They vary all over the map, from semi-auto rifles, to bolt actions, to long-range 50-calibers. There's even an assault rifle with a low-power scope. I guess if I were looking at a kill from 800 yards, I'd go with a bolt-action, a damn good one. Remember, as distance increases, the bullet drop increases greatly. The difference between a 400 and 450-yard shot's minimal; the difference between an 800 and 825-yard shot is enough to cause a miss. I'd want a superb scope and I'd be sure to adjust for 10-yard increments past 700 yards or so."

"So what would the ideal weapon be in these circumstances?" Brian asked.

"The best sniper rifle for the job would be a Remington M24," Webb said. "It's bolt-action, heavy, .308 caliber, has a 5-round magazine. With a good tripod or similar setup, you could easily get 800 yards out of it."

"But the windows in the Hancock don't open," Brian said.

"Remember that suicide there a few years back? A woman weighing 130 pounds knocked a window out and jumped," Webb replied. "The windows are double panes a quarter inch thick. Wouldn't be too hard to cut out a sniper's port from a condo window facing this way."

"Say an expert had an M24 and used it on you from the Hancock. How could he see you through the green glass building skin here?"

"The lights in my office are bright halogens. I happened to be in the Hancock observatory one night a while back and looked over this way. You can see the office occupants well enough."

"How did he miss?" Brian said.

Webb managed a small grin. "Maybe because I just happened to back away from my desk as he fired. I swear I could hear the bullet whiz by in front of me. The police pried it out of an engineering manual in that bookcase." He nodded to his right at a tall walnut bookcase full of business and engineering books.

"Of course, the round was nearly spent. But if it had struck a soft target like my chest instead of wood, I don't think we'd be chatting," Webb said.

"Rifle like that's got a 1.25 moa, right?" DeRosa interjected.

"That's right, Webb said."

"Whoa. What's moa?" Brian asked.

Webb said, "I guess you could say it indicates a tool of surgical precision. Supposed to be capable of quarter-inch groupings at 100 yards, an inch at 400 and 4 inches at 800."

"I wonder why he only fired once," Brian said.

"He knew he only had the one chance. Either he hit me or not. "

"So who's got a weapon like that?" Brian said.

"The hell of it is, Belcoe's got secure warehouses full of 'em. See, we sell them to law enforcement nationwide."

"Any exports?" Brian asked.

Webb and DeRosa exchanged a look. Then DeRosa turned to Brian sitting at his side and said, "Yeah. To friendly nations only."

Brian started to speak, but Barry Webb held up a hand like a crossing guard signaling a motorist to stop.

"Look," Webb began. "I know you've got more questions, but I'm about fizzled out. Had a hard time sleeping the last couple of weeks, with the company's problems, the stock plummeting, and now this." He stood abruptly. "I've gotta get going."

"Can we talk some more tomorrow?" Brian asked.

Webb reached for the suit jacket hanging on a wooden coatrack near the desk. "Afraid not. I'm going to be on the road for a few days and quite busy. Maybe when I get back."

As Webb shrugged into his coat, he said, "Lou, are you ready to go?"

"I'm gonna hit the restroom first. Meet you downstairs in a few minutes."

"Okay," Webb said as he breezed out of the room.

"Where are you guys going?" Brian asked.

"Barry's invited a few top management people to his place in Montana for a kind of retreat. Future of the company's on the line. We need to discuss possible solutions."

"What about me? What if I show up?"

"You'd never get past the gate. When Barry invites you, you're in. If not, you're not."

51

The two men exited the Belcoe Building, the revolving door shunting them out into a maelstrom of pedestrians moving purposely toward Friday evening destinations. Though slanting rays of late-afternoon sun reflected off the upper stories of the surrounding steel-and-glass skyscrapers, it was nearly dark at street-level. As Brian watched, an entire block of streetlights lit up with the orange blush of mercury vapor illumination. A block east along the river, the glazed white *terra cotta* façade of the Wrigley Building glowed as if lit from within. Brian knew that the building, erected to house the Wrigley chewing gum headquarters, was hand-washed occasionally to maintain its gleaming aspect. As night fell, massive floodlights would bathe the façade, making it stand out as the southern anchor of the fabled Michigan Avenue shopping district known as the Magnificent Mile.

Pedestrian traffic was heavy. A solid wall of office workers surged across windswept Belcoe Plaza, some headed to train stations, others to bus or El stops. More than a few would linger in nearby watering holes, waiting for rush hour to be over, or simply celebrating another week of survival in the corporate trenches. An unbroken line of yellow cabs flanked the curb on Wabash. A black Lincoln stretch limo was double-parked parallel to the cabs.

As Brian and DeRosa neared the street, the rear door of the limo opened and Barry Webb's head emerged. "Hey Lou, let's go."

"Brian, I'll catch up with you later," DeRosa said.

A uniformed driver with *café-au-lait* skin and built like an NBA power forward, got out of the car and opened the limo's trunk. After he'd stowed DeRosa's suitcase, he stared at Brian blankly for a moment. The guy looked familiar, something to do with professional sports, but Brian couldn't place him. DeRosa made his way into the vehicle, moving quickly and smoothly, almost like an athlete himself. Brian wondered whether the older man had been sandbagging him for some reason.

Once DeRosa was in the passenger compartment, the driver got back behind the wheel and turned to listen to something Webb was apparently telling him through the car's interior Plexiglas divider. Suddenly, the motor revved and the limo accelerated into traffic, acing out a cab just pulling out behind it. The limo quickly disappeared in the surge of traffic.

Back in his apartment, Brian wondered which other company execs would be with them in Montana. And he questioned whether he himself would have a role in Belcoe's future, whether he would remain in touch with the man whose life he'd saved, his last link to the company's inner circle.

He thought about the FBI's interest in Belcoe's 606 ranch near Yellowstone National Park. What the hell. He opened his laptop, went online to United Airlines and booked a nonstop flight to Bozeman the next morning. At such late notice, he felt lucky to get a seat. And the airfare was astronomical. Chances are, he'd have to eat the expense. He reflected that he hadn't seen a check from Belcoe since the advance Lou DeRosa had handed him two weeks ago. He knew it wasn't entirely rational to set off on an unpaid, uninvited visit to Webb's hideaway. But, whatever happened, he knew he'd regret it if he backed away now.

Before packing his rolling carryon case, he sent emails to Darcy, James and Bill Thorsten, letting them know about his travel plans.

At O'Hare in the morning, Brian found a coffee stand and picked up an Americano along with a cranberry scone, then walked to the gate and settled in to wait. He'd packed light, but made sure he wore his hiking boots and had his mini-Maglite, night vision goggles and his laptop. As for armament, he knew a guy in Clarkville, the little town between Bozeman and Webb's ranch, who could probably fix him up with a weapon.

As he popped the last of the scone in his mouth, two men sat down in chairs behind him. He'd seen their photos on the Belcoe website, though he couldn't place their names. He pretended to read his iPad and listened.

The short, dark-haired fellow directly behind Brian spoke quietly to his companion. "He wants numbers. It is always numbers with the guy." The man's English was accented, reminding Brian of a trip he'd taken to Saudi Arabia back in his days with the Bureau.

"That shouldn't be a problem," the short man's companion said, speaking with the inflection of a native Chicagoan. "Numbers we've got. Question is, will Barry buy them?"

"If he doesn't, you can, what's the phrase, kiss your ass farewell," Saudi Arabia said.

"It's goodbye. Kiss your ass goodbye. Anyway, I'm thinking it might be time to move on," the Chicago guy replied.

"How long do you think we'll need to stay at this farm?"

"It's ranch, not farm, and we stay two days."

"A long time in isolation."

"It's not so bad. A few meetings, musical entertainment, best liquor and wines. Outdoor stuff, too, if you're into it—horseback riding, fishing, sporting clays course."

"What is this sporting clays?" Saudi Arabia asked.

"Shotguns, clay pigeons."

"Hmmm. I know shotguns. But what is—"

"Clay pigeon's a target. You shoot right, you blow it to smithereens. And don't ask what's a smithereen." A pause, then, "Mo, you do okay. Don't know that I'd do any better in Arabic."

Brian glanced over his shoulder, to see the man who'd just spoken raising his coffee cup to his companion in toast. The man's eyes met Brian's. There was a split-second of awkwardness. The man looked away hurriedly. Was he the Marketing VP, Hunter? He glanced down at his watch and began to assemble his belongings in preparation for the trek onto the plane and three hours ensconced in a seat designed to comfortably hold the average ten-year-old.

52

The plane was full. Most of the passengers appeared to be either vacationing skiers or Montanans heading home. There were people talking about Big Sky, others fiddling with electronic devices, a generally relaxed vibe. Brian's seat was at a window near the back. A large woman wearing a flowered sack dress anchored the aisle seat in his row. He prayed the center seat at his right elbow would remain empty, and it did, as the plane was pushed away from the gate.

The aircraft taxied for fifteen minutes and was aloft. Brian watched the cityscape below as the MD-90 twin-engine jet banked over Lake Michigan, made a long turn to the west and climbed. The tallest skyscrapers poked through light cloud cover. As an architecturally aware Chicagoan, Brian knew that his hometown was the birthplace of the skyscraper. The 110-story Willis Tower, rising above the south Loop, had been the tallest building in the United States until being overtaken by One World Trade Center in New York City in 2013. 875 North Michigan Avenue had condominiums as high as 92 floors above the city. Construction was in progress on the Vista Tower, the tallest building in the world designed by a woman architect, Jeanne Gang.

He caught a glimpse of his own Lakeview neighborhood, and seconds later, they were inland, crossing over a vast interlaced web of expressways, main thoroughfares and side-streets, the commercial and residential buildings stolid and lacking the glamour of their sky-seeking brethren to the east. The low-rise structures sprawled on for miles, into a dense jigsaw puzzle of city neighborhoods and suburbs old and new. There were railroad tracks, factories, warehouses, office campuses, apartment complexes, enclaves of single-family homes, golf courses, Forest Preserves and endless lines of traffic everywhere. This, he knew, was the beating heart of economic activity in the Midwest.

The flight was a little choppy as they headed west. Brian occasionally broke away from his novel to eye the scenery below. After a little under three hours of cruising over flat prairie topography, the corrugated folds of the Rockies appeared. Snow mantled most of the peaks. They passed over Yellowstone National Park, dominated from above by forested ridges and multi-fingered Yellowstone Lake. Then it was a gradual descent into the Bozeman airport.

Brian grabbed his bag and headed to the Hertz counter, where he rented a silver Toyota 4Runner, a truck-based SUV with four-wheel-drive. It looked thirsty but capable.

An hour later, in downtown Clarkville, Brian eased to the curb on Main Street, outside the venerable Masters Hotel. He'd stayed there the previous year, when he'd been to Bone Mountain. The hotel building evoked a bygone time of cattle drives and cowboys. He knew that celebrated film director and hell-raiser Sam Fletcher had lived the last few years of his life in a suite in the Masters. Fletch had reportedly shot holes in the ceiling and arm-wrestled buddies like Steve McQueen at the bar in his apartment. The hotel's website advertised that the two-bedroom "Fletcher Suite" was available by the night.

Brian used his Visa card to rent a room. It turned out to be a high-ceilinged space furnished with western art, a queen bed and a minibar. He got out his phone, called old Army buddy Mark Briggs and arranged to meet him in the Masters bar in an hour.

At 3:50 p.m., Brian took a stool at the end of the Masters' horseshoe-shaped bar and ordered a locally brewed Scottish Ale. The place was nearly empty. A half hour and a pint of beer later, a large hand rested on his shoulder. A familiar voice boomed from behind, "Jesus fucking Christ. They'll let anyone in this place."

Mark Briggs had put on a good twenty pounds since they'd served together in the Army. Mark's hairline had receded conspicuously and his long beard was mostly gray, but he still had a contagious smile and alert eyes.

"What's keeping you off the street?" Brian asked.

"Even a half-assed carpenter has work around here. Me, I'm swamped as much as I want to be. Ain't complaining, though."

"Looks like you're uh, prosperous." Brian poked a finger gently in Briggs' belly, which looked like a bowling ball under his loose tee shirt.

"Life around here agrees with me. None of the big-city bullshit you have to put up with. You should try it."

"I'm hoping to come back out in the fall. But first, I've got to get this damned case cleared up."

"You say you're investigating some company out of Chicago?"

Brian hit a few highlights of his work at Belcoe and the reason for his visit to Montana, concluding with, "So, I couldn't bring my piece on the plane, and I knew you'd come through."

Briggs drank the last of his beer, set the mug on the bar and wiped his mustache with the back of a beefy hand. "Got it covered, compadre. We'll stop by my rig later. You gonna need any help on this deal?"

Brian hesitated. "I hate to drag you into this mess. These guys are desperate sons of bitches, and they haven't a clue I'm coming. But at least they know me and probably figure they can't disappear me. Not right away, anyhow. With a stranger, there'd be no guarantees."

"You said something about the old 606—right?"

"That's the place."

"Just so happens, I've done some work out there. Big remodel job up at the main lodge last year. 'Course I was dealin' with the ranch manager. Never met the owner. But I know the setup there like my left armpit."

"Good. You can fill me in. I saw the place from a trail overlooking it, but don't really know what's where."

"Look, I can draw ya a map." Briggs found a pen and piece of paper in a shirt pocket and began sketching. Brian watched as he drew a cluster of boxes representing buildings, with double lines representing roads leading in and out. As Briggs worked, Brian glanced around the bar. No one seemed to be paying attention to them.

"They've got a ton of acreage. Main lodge, guest cabins, two big houses, all here." He tapped a spot on the paper. "Barns and equipment sheds along here. Hay barn there. And way over in the southwest corner, this metal warehouse."

"What's that lodge building like?" Brian asked.

"Well, they put up guests there, and there's a so-called great room with a rock fireplace, huge windows facing the mountains, leather couches, shelves full of books, bar, open floor space for a band, dancing or whatever." Briggs labeled each building and added some notations on the entry and exit roads, of which there were two.

Brian swiveled on his stool and scanned the room. The bar had filled as people got off work in the late afternoon. There was a mix of office workers, blue-collar guys, ranch hands and tourists. Judging from snippets of conversation in the air, there were a few lawyers and real estate brokers. Every barstool was occupied, and Brian felt a little uncomfortable talking about anything related to Belcoe or the 606. He knew that, in a small town, the walls had ears, and a sprawling ranch owned by a rich Chicago businessman would likely be an object of interest for others in the bar.

"Thanks." Brian folded the sheet and tucked it in a pocket. He caught the bartender's eye and signaled for two more beers. He punched Briggs lightly on his arm and said, "How's the love life?"

They chatted until about 5:30, when the restaurant in the building opened, then headed there for dinner. The homemade meatloaf with mashed potatoes was delicious, as was the cherry wine from Montana's Flathead valley.

After they'd finished dessert, and Brian had snagged the bill, Briggs said, "Tell you what: we get done here, let's take a walk, and I'll get the uh, item we discussed earlier."

Outside, Briggs led the way half a block down the street and unlocked a late-model Ram three-quarter ton pickup with a large diamond-plate steel toolbox in the bed. "Hop in," he said.

Seated behind the wheel, Briggs said, "Don't normally bother locking up in town, but..." He bent forward and removed a brown paper bag from under the driver's seat. He handed it to Brian, who opened it and extracted a new-looking Smith and Wesson .38 revolver with a two-and-a-half-inch barrel. He could tell by the weight—a little over a pound and a half—it was loaded. A box of cartridges occupied the bottom of the bag.

"This looks okay. What do I owe you?" Brian said.

Briggs made a face. "Nada, man. Give it back before you go. And here, take this for backup." He handed Brian a wicked looking Spyderco locking folding knife with a four-inch blade.

"Okay, I probably won't need to use either of these things, but if I do, they could end up anywhere. In which case, I'll pay you market value."

"All right. But if you need to use 'em, you'll probably need some backup. Call me anytime."

53

Brian walked back to the Masters Hotel and took the stairs to his room on the second floor. He was drowsy from the flight, the beers and the big dinner. He glanced at the Clarkville newspaper he'd picked up in the lobby. The headline read, "LOCAL MOUNTAIN MAN SURVIVES GRIZZLY ATTACK." He began reading the piece, by a writer named Sam Logan, who he knew had authored a book on grizzly bear attacks. "Self-styled mountain man Rob Kenton remembers grabbing the bear by the nose with both hands as it tried to bite his face and throat. Doctors needed more than a hundred stiches and staples to secure Mr. Kenton's scalp to his skull. As he wrapped a hooded sweatshirt around his head to stanch the bleeding, another problem occurred: 'My pants fell down around my ankles,' he related. He had to lie down on the ground to pull the drawers back on before hiking to a nearby ranch to seek help." But the best part was the final sentence: "The undeterred former logger said from his hospital bed Monday that he's already planning another trip into the woods alone with his horse, Numbnuts."

Brian dressed in a black long-sleeve fleece pullover, dark jeans and hiking boots. In his nylon daypack, he inserted the Smith and Wesson, a ball cap, bottle of water, energy bar, small Maglite, night vision goggles and Gore-Tex rain jacket.

He stuffed in a Google map of the 606 Ranch area and the map Briggs had drawn as well. He was on the road a few minutes later.

Clarkville was quiet at that hour. Most retail establishments were closed. Only a couple of bars showed activity, with vehicles out front and music leaking from inside. As Brian drove by the false-front Whiskey Barrel Saloon, a thin bearded man in a Carhartt cap lurched out the door and sat down on the sidewalk, a perplexed frown on his face, as if he were trying to figure out how in hell he had gotten there.

Brian headed west on Main Street and then south on Highway 89, where the two-lane road was narrow, traffic light and the likelihood of a deer crossing high. He set the cruise control at seventy. As the moonlit countryside flashed by, he mused about the situation he was about to confront. A little research on Natalie's part in the Belcoe accounting records had revealed that Webb's Montana retreat had been paid for with Belcoe funds to the tune of 12 million dollars. Furnishings had run another couple of mil, also on the company. A staff of a dozen or so worked at the place. Brian imagined Webb ran the payroll and other operating expenses through Belcoe. Even DeRosa, jaded as he was, seemed to tread lightly around the man. With the company stock spiraling downward daily, the SEC and FBI closing in, and an attempt on Webb's life in his office, the CEO must be distraught. Whatever this powwow at the ranch was about, it had to include a high-stakes attempt to salvage the company and Webb.

He thought of James's recent comments on the FBI's White Collar Crimes unit's progress investigating Belcoe. Despite pressure from unnamed political powers, WCC had uncovered enough admissible evidence to threaten Webb and several other execs, including DeRosa.

Brian's reverie was interrupted by a pair of fluorescent shining eyes off the right side of the road about a hundred yards ahead. A whitetail doe stepped slowly into the roadway, followed by a pair of last year's fawns. The trio gazed blankly at his vehicle as it hurtled toward them at a hundred feet per second. Instinctively, Brian braked and cranked the wheel to the left. The 4Runner cleared the standing animals by only feet. As he corrected and veered back into the right lane, he was happy he'd taken a three-day Bondurant Racing School high-performance driving course in Arizona a few years earlier. He remembered a line from a young racecar driver/instructor at the school: "When you get out of control, remember CPR: correct, pause, recover. Or, as some would say: choke, puke, retch."

Forty miles later, he turned right on a gravel road and crossed the Yellowstone River on a single-lane bridge that rattled noisily under the weight of the vehicle. A climb came next as the road switchbacked up an-ever-steeper grade through a forest of pines and firs. Brian remembered his ride on that road with Bill Thorsten at the wheel a few days earlier. Light rain began to fall. The road narrowed in spots, so the vehicle barely fit through a tunnel of trees. There were a few muddy stretches where the rear wheels spun, but he didn't need four-wheel drive. All in all, it was a road for driving a rental.

Occasionally, the entrance of a ranch appeared alongside, with a winding drive leading to a house accompanied by a few outbuildings, all faintly illuminated by yard lights on poles. Horses and cows regarded him idly from behind barbed wire fences. He encountered no other traffic, which was a good thing, since there was barely room for one vehicle at a time. He turned in at the side road marked by the "606" sign.

Brian glanced at the odometer. A couple of miles to go. After driving just short of that distance, he saw a flat clearing with a clump of Douglas firs on the right. He eased the SUV off the road and around the far side of the trees, which left him about twenty-five yards from the road. He switched off the engine and lights and got out of the vehicle. He listened intently. The only sounds were the ticking of the cooling engine and the wind rustling the trees and grass around him. He placed the bulky 4Runner key on top of the rear tire on the driver's side, put on the rain jacket and ball cap. He shouldered his pack and began to walk.

At the road, he looked back toward the vehicle. Satisfied that it was pretty well-hidden, he began hiking the rest of the way, all senses alert. The wind had picked up and was coming straight toward him, pushing raindrops in his face. Good—the sounds of weather should mask the noise of his approach. In a few minutes, he saw a faint glow of light ahead. Shortly after that, the sound of guitars and drums drifted down to him. It was a Buddy Guy blues tune, "Damn Right I've got the Blues," played expertly by a live band. In fact, the singer sounded a lot like Buddy. Could it be him? Nah. Soon, a massive steel gate barred the road. There was a keypad on the left, convenient to a driver's window. It occurred to him there might be surveillance. Sure enough, a video camera topped the gatepost, aimed toward the road. He moved swiftly around the far side of the gate, hopefully out of camera range, ducked through a new-looking buck and rail fence made of peeled logs and headed toward the cover of trees between the gate and the place where the music emanated. At the small grove of aspens, he stopped and listened as the song, "Feels Like Rain," wound down. There was a burst of applause and some hooting and whistling. Sounded like a pretty good-sized audience. The rain had stopped, but the wind continued to blow moisture around in swirls.

Brian's position afforded him an excellent view of a cluster of low buildings, most of which were dark. The entrance of a massive log structure blazed with lights. He was about to pull Briggs' map from his pack for a review by flashlight, when a couple emerged from the doorway of the building and strolled outside. The light atop the entrance revealed a thirty-something woman sporting a low-cut white blouse tied at the midriff, skin-tight blue jeans and high-heeled boots. Brian made an immediate identification: Liz Wheaton, the hard-edged Human Resources executive who'd interviewed him at Belcoe. Her slightly younger companion, a guy with a buzz cut, wore western apparel and a smug smile. The man looked familiar—was it someone he'd seen at Belcoe? As Brian watched, the couple drifted toward him. He held his breath as they entered the trees. They stopped a few yards short of his hiding place and locked together in a clinch, punctuated by the sound of sloppy kissing. While the man was clumsily unbuttoning Liz Wheaton's shirt, the sound of an engine approaching from below was barely audible. As it grew louder, a pair of high beams split the darkness and swung toward the aspen grove. Suddenly it was awash in illumination. Wheaton let out a shriek, and the couple stood frozen, much like the trio of deer Brian had narrowly avoided on the main highway below. As Brian watched, the vehicle rolled into view. A dark Suburban rumbled up the drive and rolled to a stop at the front entrance of the log building.

"Shit. We'd better get in there. Don't want to miss the man," Wheaton's companion said.

She sighed theatrically. "And just when I was going to fuck your boots off."

Brian suddenly recognized the guy with her, Jack Wilson, who'd been Mathew Growney's boss.

54

As Brian watched, the couple in front of him stood up, buttoning and straightening their clothes. They cut nervous glances toward the Suburban, which had eased to a stop at the main entrance of the massive log building. Its headlights illuminated a cluster of sizable cabins with stone chimneys scattered among evergreen trees in the distance. To Brian, they looked like very luxurious accommodations, considering the remoteness of this high mountain aerie. A slender man of medium height, dressed in a dark suit without a tie, emerged from the vehicle's rear seat and stretched backwards, hands on hips. Barry Webb, his dark hair backlit by the coach lamps flanking the lodge entryway. He straightened and reached to open the rear door of the SUV. A second man, taller, of substantial girth, emerged from the passenger side and stepped to the ground.

"C'mon, Lou. You're gonna enjoy this," Webb said. His voice carried clearly through the thin mountain air.

As Brian watched, Webb held the building's entry door open and waved Lou DeRosa inside.

After the door closed, the blues band started playing again, this time "Sweet Home Chicago." A round of cheers and applause came through the walls. Brian wondered if it was for the entrance of the two Belcoe execs or the familiar tune.

Liz Wheaton and Jack Wilson followed the men a minute later as the music continued. Brian removed his small backpack, extracted the holstered gun and put it on, with the butt of the weapon handy at the small of his back. He put his pack on the ground next to a lone towering tree, where it would be easy to locate later. He inched forward in the darkness, leaving the cover of the trees, and approached the building. Instead of going to the main entrance, he crept into the shadows at the near side of the structure. A window glowed with light about twenty feet down along the rough log wall. He glanced at the illuminated hands of his watch. Eleven twenty-five. The band finished the song and launched into another. Men and women, their voices obviously lubricated by plenty of alcohol, shouted to be heard above the music. The din was easily audible through the double-glazed window near Brian's head. Suddenly, the music stopped.

"Folks, Mr. Webb would like to talk to you for a moment." The speaker, a man with a clipped baritone, sounded familiar: Hamilton Massey, the Chief Financial Officer who, among other obnoxious acts, had abused Darcy's friend, Natalie Katz.

"Quiet, please. That's better. Thanks. And now, Mr. Webb will address us."

A round of applause and cheers swelled, rose and ebbed. "Thanks, Hamilton," Webb began. "And thanks to all of you for humoring me by schlepping here to the middle of nowhere for this little gathering."

He paused for a round of applause. A beery male voice proclaimed, "Yowzah!"

Webb resumed, "As you all know, Belcoe stock has declined precipitously the past several months. The naysayers in the media have written us off. Another Enron in the making, they say. Financials don't look healthy. Allegations of fraud. Feds closing in. Employees dropping like flies. Barry Webb has lost the golden touch. They're bailing the boat with a food strainer lined with Swiss cheese. Am I right? Isn't that what the *Wall Street Journal* says? *CNBC*? *New York Times*?"

There were murmurs of agreement. A man spoke up. "Yeah, that's what they're saying. But they're wrong. Belcoe's strategic plan is world-class. We'll have the last laugh." Brian recognized the voice, the guy in the departure area at O'Hare who'd explained idioms like 'kiss your ass goodbye' to his pal. Brian guessed he'd been speaking from a pre-arranged script.

Webb spoke again, softer. Brian edged to the window and listened, straining to catch the words. "Thanks, Ray. Folks, I can tell you that the media hypesters selling Belcoe short are totally and absolutely full of crap."

Ray? Must be Ray Hunter, VP of Sales and Marketing. The mention of selling Belcoe short reminded Brian of Lou DeRosa, whom he had not heard speaking since the man entered the party room.

A cheer went up. A harsh female voice cut through the noise. "Right on, Barry. We've been down before and we'll be back!"

"That's right, Nancy. In fact, we *are* back. I am pleased to announce that the SEC has dropped their investigation of the company. We've been given a clean bill of health. I've also been told they've concluded no material violations have occurred. Of course, there may be fines for minor infringements, but nothing material." More cheers and applause. Nancy would be Nancy Northfield, the Investor Relations honcho, Brian guessed.

"But the main announcement I have for you this evening is that we have just signed a deal which will ensure Belcoe's return to its rightful place of leadership. As of yesterday, Belcoe has become principal supplier of defensive weaponry to several allies of the United States in the war on terror: Saudi Arabia, Kuwait and Pakistan. At the same time, we retain our strategic supply contracts with other Middle East nations. Estimated sales volume from the new contracts will exceed four billion U.S. dollars annually."

More cheers. A crackle of sound from a microphone, as though someone had inadvertently brushed against it.

"These innovative partners will aid us in leveraging applied technology on the leading edge. We will continue our retention and evaluation programs for all strategic product lines." Webb went on in the same vein for a while and concluded the speech. More applause and cheers, and the band started to play again.

55

Brian decided it was time to go public. No need to stand outside in the rain. He entered the lodge and scanned the crowd. Finally, he spotted Webb in conversation with an overweight middle-aged man with a shaved head. Brian raised his hand and caught Webb's eye as he made his way over to the Belcoe CEO. "Barry, could I have a word?"

Webb's eyes widened and then he reverted to his customary in-control self. "Brian, meet our VP of Operations, Oscar Gutman."

Brian shook hands with Gutman, and then turned to Webb. "I need to talk with you right away," he said.

Webb shrugged, impatient. "All right." As he spoke, he scanned the room, apparently a habit, ascertaining where the other players were on the court.

As they moved away from the Operations chief, Brian said, "Aren't you afraid a trespasser like me might try to choke the truth out of you?"

Webb shook his head ruefully as if disappointed by an unruly child. "How about listening to me for a minute? You came here to find out what's going on, right?"

"Yes."

"You know, you could have just joined the party anytime." He eyed Brian's rain-dampened clothes. "We would've accommodated you as a guest."

"I heard you tell your people the SEC gave the company a clean bill of health. Was that bullshit?"

"I'm going to be frank with you. I realize the company's still in trouble, despite what I just told my management people. The FBI can still cause us significant problems. Stock's at its nadir, in my opinion. My personal finances are nearly beyond redemption. Look Brian, I hired you because I thought you were a pretty sharp guy and I thought you could do Belcoe and me some good. Let the public know we're a decent company capable of making a comeback. You want information. So do I. I'm a reasonable guy. Maybe we can work together, after all. I'm enough of a businessman to know you don't get something for nothing. You with me?"

"I'm listening," Brian said.

"I want a chance to save Belcoe. It's that simple. No one else can do it. But I need a clear shot. I can't turn the company around if I spend all my time dealing with investigations, requests for documents, subpoenas, you name it." He waved a hand dismissively.

"What makes you the savior?" Brian said. "You're the guy who's been at the controls while the company's in free fall."

"Fair question. The answer is that nobody else has the knowledge, the drive, the smarts to pull this recovery off. I admit my mistakes. Won't make them again. I just need a little breathing room."

"Where do I come in?"

"You could speak with your friends at the FBI. You could also come to work for me full-time. Act as a liaison with the investigators. All above board. No games. You get all the resources you need. You can feed your friend James St. Claire, make him a hero. I don't care, as long as Belcoe survives with the prospect of returning to industry dominance."

"But what if the investigations result in you taking a fall? What if the company's uh, questionable export sales are proven? Who's a hero then? And why me? Don't you have people who are intimately familiar with the Company's operations? Insiders who could handle these matters much more efficiently than me? What about Lou DeRosa? He's been with you from the beginning."

Webb shook his head. "Lou's got issues, including one obvious one."

"He drinks like a fire engine."

"Yes, and he's past his prime. And frankly, I wonder if he's gone rogue. I understand he's been shorting company stock. Which shows a complete lack of confidence."

"So, why's he here?"

"He needs to help us in the short term. And he's still a formidable resource."

"Luckily, I happened to be around and found him before he died there on the ground by his sauna. Helped conserve a Belcoe resource, you might say."

"Lou probably just got drunk and fell asleep in the sauna, then came to and managed to get himself outside. Or, maybe he gave up and decided to end it. Perhaps he'll tell us some day."

"Lou told me you guys wanted to fire me. Is that true?"

"Wait, what? No, absolutely not. It was my idea to hire you in the first place. Lou resisted, for some reason. I wonder why in hell he would tell you such a thing. Does he want you out of here? I understand you've spent a lot of time with him. Makes me wonder if he was using you, somehow. Lou is many things, but selfless is not one of them. Though he did say you were an accomplished listener and a pretty fair whiskey drinker."

"You mentioned my possibly working with you. What would the terms be?"

"You've been looking at the murder of the Growney kid, which is very important to me and the company. It's a cloud I want lifted. And you could also investigate that gunshot through my office window. I'll pay you to resolve both issues. We'll enter into a brand new agreement. How about a retainer, say a hundred thousand to start?"

"I'll think about it. Meanwhile, I need to talk to a couple of people back home. Looks like there's no cell coverage here."

"No, but you can use a landline. Or a satellite phone."

Brian glanced at his watch, noticed it was now after midnight. "You'll be here tomorrow?"

"Yes. I'm in meetings with key people early, free in the afternoon. Most of the guests are leaving tomorrow, so it'll be quiet."

"Let's talk tomorrow afternoon. And I'll take you up on that sat phone."

"Of course. I'll get you set up with everything you need in the morning. Meanwhile, let's sleep on it."

Webb guided Brian to a nearby cabin, let him in and bid him good night. No mention of how Brian got there or his vehicle. Inside the cabin, there was a rustic living room, a bedroom with king-sized bed, a small kitchen with fridge and a bar with a selection of liquor. Brian wanted to also see Lou DeRosa tomorrow for sure. Suddenly, he felt exhausted. He lay on the bed fully clothed, resting his head on a soft pillow. He began thinking about the conversation with Webb. He didn't know who to believe regarding his status with Belcoe—Webb or DeRosa. Within minutes, he was asleep.

56

Brian awoke to brilliant sun beaming through a gap in the curtains. He glanced at the digital clock on the radio atop the nightstand. Nine-oh-eight. Sleeping in felt good. His black Mountainsmith duffle lay on the floor just inside the door. Someone must have found his vehicle concealed in the trees outside the ranch gate during the night. He knew he'd hidden it pretty well. Which meant somebody competent had gone looking for it. Probably searched the vehicle and looked through his duffle as well. Fortunately his phone was protected with a strong password. A white envelope lay on top of the duffle. He removed a handwritten note.

> Brian, here's your stuff. Your vehicle's outside the cabin—we took the liberty of moving it. Breakfast anytime you're ready in the lodge dining room. Then have a look around. No secrets here. Mackie can fix you up with a computer, sat phone, whatever you need. There's Wi-Fi. Catch you this afternoon.
>
> Barry

He tossed the note in the wastebasket, stood with arms over his head and arched his back in a catlike stretch. The big muscles of his lower back were sore, and he reflected that he was approaching his middle years now, past the age when most professional athletes retired. Perhaps his physicality was diminished from too much time sitting at a computer. Maybe he should join a health club, get a trainer when he got home. He got some ibuprofen from the duffle and washed a couple down with tap water.

The dropping off of his luggage in his cabin while he slept seemed to constitute delivery of a message: *You're not as slick as you think, pal.* He had a hunch he couldn't afford any more carelessness. Something was about to be resolved soon, and he'd need to be at full alertness. His stomach growled, and he realized he hadn't eaten anything since the energy bar on the drive to Webb's ranch the night before. He dressed in jeans, tee shirt and hiking boots and left the cabin.

Brian entered the main lodge building, where a deserted great room greeted him. A leather couch and cluster of chairs near the fireplace were all empty. Framed prints of western landscapes hung on the log walls. The air was still and silent. He decided to delay breakfast. There had to be offices somewhere in this place. Maybe he could prowl around and learn something useful. He walked into a hallway and began to explore. Voices came from the far end of the building. He moved cautiously in that direction. Light seeped from under the door of a room in the corner. As he approached, he heard Lou DeRosa speaking.

"Barry means well, but he's deluded. What he just told us is a fantasy. If you want to get out with more than the shirts on your backs, you'd better move now. Cut your losses. Sell your shares while there's still some market value. Then take the company into Chapter 11 and hope to reorganize."

"Barry will never go for Chapter 11." Hamilton Massey's voice was tense.

"I'll handle him." DeRosa.

"What about that McKay ferret? What's he doing out here anyway?"

"He's an uninvited visitor. Same answer: I'll handle him."

Liz Wheaton: "There's an FBI agent in Bozeman, a friend of McKay."

"Yes, Bill Thorsten. And he'll be here soon to look at some inventory in the warehouse. I'll show him around and get him on his way expeditiously," DeRosa said.

"We're already highly exposed with law enforcement in Chicago," Massey said. "The company's ah, financial difficulties, the Growney kid, the attempt on Barry and that Katz girl's car accident. Not to mention the company's existential problems. We can't afford any more negative PR."

"Agreed. The kid in accounting was Barry's doing, as far as the outside world is concerned—I've got some related evidence that'll come to light," DeRosa said. "Doug Spurgeon was a suicide, which was actually the case, as far as I know. Poor bastard was taking medication for depression, he told me. The shot at Barry, no evidence exists, so it's another mystery. Maybe a disgruntled shareholder. That Katz gal's accident, who knows?

"All right, folks. If there are no other questions, we'll wrap up this little confab," DeRosa said. "Joe, please stick around." There came the sound of people getting up and moving chairs.

The last thing Brian wanted was to be discovered eavesdropping outside the meeting room. He spotted another door nearby and went to it. Turned out to be a utility closet with cleaning supplies. As he eased the door closed, he could hear several people emerge into the hallway and walk down the hall in the direction of the great room. As soon as it quieted down, he eased out of the closet and went back to the door of the meeting room.

Lou DeRosa's voice came through the door. Brian strained to catch the words. "Here's the deal, Joe: you will address Barry today in a very professional manner. No blowback to us. He should be at his house in an hour or so.

You can catch him then. I'll take McKay and Thorsten to the warehouse in a little while. I will do as I told you earlier and you will do your part and will use those two fellows, the big one and the acne-faced one, as you see fit. Just make sure there is no fucking up."

"I'm on it, Lou." Sounded like Joe Growney's voice. Was the former Chicago cop and older brother of Matthew Growney moonlighting as a hired killer? Brian wondered if Joe was the sniper who'd taken a shot at Barry Webb in his office. And, as unthinkable as it should have been, could the ex-cop have murdered his own brother? If so, at whose direction? DeRosa? DeRosa's statement about Webb and Brian being addressed with no blowback sounded like, what— a contract for murder? And this warehouse business—what was that all about? He'd have to warn Webb as well as Thorsten when he arrived. He checked the Smith and Wesson in his waistband.

DeRosa continued, "And, of course, as time permits, you'll need to load the van and get the materials to the plane ASAP. Can you handle all that?"

"Not a problem." Once again, Joe Growney speaking.

"Okay, then. Let's get to it," DeRosa said.

Brian moved away quickly and smoothly. He remembered reading a tip from a well-known racecar driver: to move fast, the most important thing is to be smooth, not abrupt. He seemed to avoid detection as he walked steadily out of the hallway and into the lodge building's massive lobby. He crossed through and continued into a large dining room with a ceiling supported by logs with the girth of 55-gallon drums. At the far end, a wiry man in western clothes stood, looking out a window and chewing on a toothpick. He regarded Brian impassively from under the brim of a tan cowboy hat. His faded jeans looked like they'd been spray-painted on. The guy reminded Brian of the country singer Dwight Yoakam.

He approached Brian, slipping the toothpick into a shirt pocket. His pale gray eyes were dull like dusty stones. He stopped a few feet short and said, "Name's Mackie. Ranch manager. Mr. Webb said you might need a few things."

"Breakfast would be good."

"Have a seat. I'll get 'em to rustle up some food."

Brian eased into a chair at a table set for one near a window, while Mackie disappeared into the next room. He contemplated the view, a lush lawn separated from a rolling pasture of tall grass by a three-rail jack fence. Horses with multi-colored coats grazed in the pasture. He guessed they were Paso Finos.

"Will this be okay?"

Brian looked up at a slim woman holding a plate of eggs and pancakes. Dark hair in a pageboy framed a toothy smile. She wore a black shirt and jeans under a white apron.

"The food be just fine," Brian said. "Would you like to join me?"

Lou DeRosa's housekeeper, Paola, grinned like a co-conspirator. "Thank you, sir, but I have work to do. Perhaps we will see each other later." Her accent sounded musical to Brian.

As she returned to the kitchen, she gave her hips just the slightest bit of extra motion. At the door, she glanced over her shoulder to see if Brian was watching. When she saw that he was, she raised an eyebrow and disappeared through the doorway.

She must have come out at DeRosa's request, Brian thought.

Mackie returned with a coffee pot and a couple of heavy mugs. He filled them and took the chair across from Brian. He carefully set his Stetson crown-downward on a nearby table.

"You two acquainted?" He asked.

"We've met," Brian said. He had the feeling that Mackie had been watching him, and he wondered if the surveillance went back to the night before. Perhaps he was the one who'd looked for and found Brian's rental vehicle camouflaged outside the ranch entrance. Maybe Webb had assigned him to keep an eye on Brian. In any event, he'd need to ditch him soon. He had a few things to find out, and the taciturn man at the table needn't be part of it.

"Good. Well, go ahead and eat," Mackie said, raising his mug in toast.

"Seems quiet. Did the party people leave?"

"Pretty much. A few stragglers will be taking off later today."

"When did they get here? And what's the schedule?"

"Most of 'em were here for the weekend, riding and fishing and such on the ranch, then there were meetings yesterday and the party. There's an executive get-together today and that's about it."

Brian decided to use the satellite phone to call Thorsten rather than a landline—less likelihood of someone listening in. He needed to speak with Barry Webb ASAP. Assuming DeRosa's comment to Growney was correct, Webb should be at his house soon. He ate his meal in silence, while Mackie drank coffee and gazed out the window.

Finished eating, Brian said, "Barry mentioned I could use a sat phone. I'd appreciate it if you could point me to it."

"Let's get 'er done." Mackie rose, donned his hat in a deft motion and headed toward the door. Brian followed him out of the lodge to a small frame building about a hundred yards away, near a large house with floor-to ceiling windows aimed at the Absaroka mountains in the distance.

"Phone's in here," Mackie commented, as he unlocked the door to the small structure.

Inside, a desk held a laptop computer and a large mobile phone with a thick antenna.

"This here's a LEO phone. You familiar with it?"

"Low Earth Orbit," Brian said. "Yes, I've used them before. Looks like it'll work best outside."

"That's right. Well, I'll leave ya to it, then. If you need me, I'll be in my office in the admin wing. Anyone can tell you where it's at." Mackie touched his hat brim and left. Brian could hear the ranch manager's boots as he clomped away.

He waited a moment, then took the satellite phone outside the building and switched it on. He knew that the phone required line of sight to an orbiting system satellite to be effective. Each satellite had a usable pass of four to fifteen minutes, with the adjacent satellite taking over at the end of the pass. But occasionally, there'd be a slight blip in service as the signal transitioned between satellites. In theory, one could have gapless coverage anywhere on Earth. He also knew that a sat phone could be insecure, so he'd have to tailor his conversation accordingly. As the phone sought a satellite to hook up with, he looked around at the firs and pines, the huge house nearby, the jagged mountain peaks rimming the horizon, the blue sky, the clouds gathered above like great boneless birds of prey.

Brian punched in the appropriate country code, area code and Bill Thorsten's cell phone number. After three rings, the agent answered.

"Bill, I'm at the 606."

"Doin' all right?"

"Yes. Anything new at your end?"

"I'll be there around four p.m. to attend to that matter we discussed on our hike. And I spoke with your friend, James. He's on his way out to work with me. Your niece is joining him. Spring break, James said. They arrive BZN this afternoon. I expect they'll be at the ranch around the same time as I am."

Brian winced. Fine for James to be coming. But Darcy? He hated to think of her in harm's way in Montana for the second time in less than a year. "Roger that," is all he said. He decided to wait until the afternoon to discuss with Thorsten face to face DeRosa's orders to Joe Growney. He considered why he hadn't received a text or email from Darcy and decided she didn't want an argument. Rather, she'd just show up. Probably thinking she could help close out the investigation of

Matthew Growney's death. Not the first time she'd acted impulsively.

Brian switched off the sat phone and returned it to the desk in the little building. Outside, as he pulled the self-locking door closed, he caught a glimpse of a lean man disappearing around the edge of a distant structure. Had Mackie been listening in on his conversation?

57

Without hesitating, Brian marched over to the rambling single-story home a few yards away. Based on the map he'd gotten from Mark Briggs, he knew it was Barry Webb's *pied-a-terre*. At the front door, he looked over his shoulder. Seeing no one, he tried the knob, opened the door and went in.

Inside the door, he listened intently and then called out, "Hello. Anybody home?" Silence. The windows afforded expansive views of the Absarokas across the valley. The furnishings were modern, impersonal, expensive but unused-looking. He glanced at his watch, decided to use the professional burglar's *modus operandi*—get out in five minutes. He quickly walked through a formal dining room and into a kitchen that would have done a Chicago North Side posh eatery justice. Down the hall, he found a guest room, bed made, no personal effects in sight. Then he entered a sparely furnished office room with a desk, an iMac and a phone. Next, on to the master bedroom, also empty. Finally, to the last room. At the door, he stopped to listen. He heard a faint buzzing coming from within. Brian grasped the doorknob, turned it as slowly as the second hand on a clock and eased the door open a crack. Sunlight filtered in through a window next to the king-sized bed. A lone figure lay on her back on the bed, atop the covers, snoring softly. She wore a filmy pale blue nightgown that revealed tanned thighs. Brian recognized her immediately. He eased the door closed, hoping that the slitted eyes hadn't been cognizant or even subconsciously aware of his presence. He headed back to the study. The gentle snoring continued, barely audible now.

Brian checked his watch. The five minutes were nearly up. He entered the office, sat at the desk. The computer was in sleep mode. He moved the mouse, bringing the screen to life. The usual array of icons appeared in the dock. He clicked on the mail symbol. A list of e-mails in Webb's inbox revealed six unread messages. One was from Lou DeRosa.

He was about to click on the message to read it, when he heard footsteps approaching the front of the house. He froze as someone opened the door and stepped in. A familiar voice called, "Mr. Webb? You there?" Then the sound of heavy thudding feet. Mackie had apparently walked into the kitchen, some fifty feet from where Brian sat. He heard running water in a sink, perhaps Mackie getting a drink. Brian had a choice: go out and greet the ranch manager as if he owned the place and wondered why the other man were there, or hang loose and then get the hell out, preserving a slight edge of secret knowledge. Before he could make a move, Nancy Northfield's groggy voice called from the bedroom. The Belcoe Vice-President of Investor Relations. Probably not there for a business meeting.

"That you, Barry?" She said.

The heavy feet quickly retraced their steps to the front of the house and exited. Brian moved silently into the recently vacated kitchen and reached the back door. As he let himself out, he heard lighter footsteps, Nancy on her way out of the bedroom. He checked his surroundings. He was on a flagstone patio with a few Rocky Mountain junipers on the perimeter, then open grass for many yards, bordered by a shelterbelt line of Colorado blue spruce. He knew a person who happened to look out a south-facing window could easily see him moving away from the house. He maneuvered between a pair of junipers just off the edge of the patio and crouched down. A nervous rattling "cack-cack" noise sounded near his left ear. He slowly turned toward the racket. He found himself looking into the glassy black eyes of an adult magpie, sitting astride a ragged globular nest of straw and sticks. Brian blinked; the bird did not.

58

James and Darcy were on their way to O'Hare airport in a taxi. James on the job as a White Collar Crime agent with the FBI Chicago Field Office, and Darcy on spring break from the University of Illinois. She had five days without classes, and she wanted to see Brian, who was at the huge 606 Ranch, not far from the dinosaur dig she'd been on last summer. She hoped her uncle was making progress on solving the murder of her boyfriend, Matthew Growney, but Brian hadn't been very communicative lately. She certainly wasn't going to ask his permission to come out to Montana. As always, she decided to move ahead rather than wait for circumstances to dictate her actions.

James had been ordered to fly out and meet Bozeman Special Agent Bill Thorsten at the 606 Ranch. They were to conduct an audit count of electronics inventory stored in a warehouse there. The electronic devices were to be used in missile defense systems by select U. S. allies overseas. Brian had told James on the phone a few days back that he and Thorsten had hiked in and viewed the ranch, including the warehouse, from an overlook. The FBI had learned that Belcoe shipped the devices to Canada and then on to the Middle East. The question was: to which countries? Ones on the no-trade list? If that was true, government contracts could be yanked from the company, effectively eliminating a significant chunk of their revenue. Long-term, such an action could put Belcoe out of business. So, there was a lot at stake, especially for major stockholders like Barry Webb and Lou DeRosa.

James and Darcy had each packed hurriedly and booked tickets on Delta Airlines. After meeting at a coffee shop on the North Side, they'd caught a cab on Halsted and hit the road to catch a flight to Bozeman, Montana. The plan was to rent a car there and drive to the 606 Ranch. They'd meet up with Brian there late that afternoon. They'd dressed in jeans and trail runners.

"Traffic on the Kennedy sucks, as usual," James muttered.

Before Darcy could reply, the cab driver, a middle-aged man wearing a wool cap and full beard said, "Ah, but it is by far the best way to go at this hour. If we go surface streets, you never make your flight."

"Fine," James said.

"Don't worry. We've got plenty of time," Darcy said.

James glanced at his watch. "Maybe, but I wonder about Brian. How much time has *he* got?" Noticing that Darcy's expression had turned pensive, he added, "But that uncle of yours, he can take care of himself."

"I hope so. He takes chances." She sighed. "I can relate to that, though."

"You know, the man taught me a big chunk of what I know, professionally speaking. I owe him big-time," James said.

"He owes you, too. He told me about a couple of cases you guys were on with the Bureau. You were the key on that Central Soybean fraud deal, according to Brian."

"Yeah, well…" His dark features reddened a little.

She knew that, despite having a healthy ego, James, a deacon at his church, was basically a modest man.

They made their flight just in time. Both had roll aboard carry-ons, barely stowable in the scant overhead bins.

But the flights were on time, the two-across seats reasonably comfortable. In Bozeman, they picked up a rental Ford Escape. Knowing there was no cell signal at the ranch, James called the main number and asked for Brian. The person who answered said she had no idea where Brian was and couldn't promise anything, but that she would try to get a message to him, when she had time. Not exactly a candidate for hospitality host of the year.

James phoned Bill Thorsten next. Thorsten confirmed he would be at the 606 that afternoon as well. He said he had a detailed inventory listing for the electronic components they needed to see. He sounded happy at the prospect of seeing Brian and Darcy again and to finally meet James. James thought the guy sounded a little lonely. He figured Thorsten worked alone most of the time on small town stuff and that the influx of Chicagoans and the nature of the job, involving a shady but ginormous defense contractor would likely be the biggest case of his career. Brian had found the man to be capable when they'd worked together on the Bone Mountain case the summer before.

They were away from the airport and on the road to the 606 Ranch by late afternoon. Darcy navigated, while James piloted the car along the Interstate to Clarkville, then south on Highway 89 toward Yellowstone National Park.

"How're your classes going?" James asked.

"Okay, I guess. I'm glad to be away from organic chem."

"What's your favorite course so far?"

"It's called 'Ecology and Evolution.'"

James smiled. "Very scientific sounding. What's that degree you're workin' on?"

"Bachelor of Science with a major in Biological Sciences. The idea is it brings several scientific disciplines together within biology. I'm working on how biomechanics and morphology shape the way an animal's skeleton develops and how that may have driven the species' evolution. I'm especially interested in the Saurischian dinosaurs."

"What's Saurischian?"

"Uh, lizard-butt. They had tail bones similar to those of modern lizards."

"Reminds me of the Chicago Agent in Charge. What you gonna do after U of I?"

"I'm thinking about a doctorate in Vertebrate Paleontology at the University of Chicago. There's a professor there you might have heard about, Paul Smith, specializes in dinosaurs and drifting continents, goes on expeditions to Inner Mongolia, places like that. The kind of work I'm interested in. But there's also a good program at Montana State University, and I could see living and studying close to the source of *T. rex* skeletons in Montana. Anyway, I've got to make a decision soon."

"Your senior year starts this fall, right?"

"Yes, and that means I've got to apply for grad school ASAP. But it can wait until I get back to Chicago."

"Jesus. I can see the novel now: *The Girl With the Dinosaur Tattoo*."

They turned off Highway 89, immediately crossed the Yellowstone River on a narrow bridge and proceeded up a gravel road into the Gallatin Mountains. They rode in silence as the road became a rough two-track winding ever higher. The sharp-edged peaks of the Gallatins looked almost close enough to reach out and touch. They came to a wooden sign on a post displaying the numbers "606."

"According to Google Maps, we're a couple of miles from the ranch," Darcy said.

"Might as well head up there," James said.

"We're expected?"

"I am. Don't think you are. Anyway, let's just march right in like white folks."

Darcy frowned in mock disapproval. "C'mon, James."

At the main entrance to the 606 Ranch, a heavy steel gate barred the way. James noticed a security camera and a keypad to the left. He braked at the barrier.

As he buzzed his window down, a metallic voice came from a speaker below the camera: "Welcome to the 606 Ranch. Please state your business."

"James St. Clair, here to see Mr. Webb," James said.

"Just a moment, please."

They waited for several minutes. Then the voice, with a hint of wariness: "Please show your ID at the camera next to the keypad."

James did as directed. Another two minutes passed.

The metallic voice: "You're going to drive in and park where directed."

The gate rolled open, and James drove in for a few minutes on a gravel driveway, arriving at a parking area designed for several dozen vehicles and about one-third full. A lean man in western clothes ambled up to the driver's side. James eyed the man, who looked back at him blankly.

"You can park right here." He pointed at a space bordered on one side by a new white three-quarter-ton Chevy crew-cab pickup with a long bed and dually tires and on the other side by a dusty Tahoe. James thought the pickup looked about as maneuverable as a lake freighter. Once the Escape was parked and James and Darcy had emerged, the man said, "If you folks would follow me please, we'll get ya checked in."

They entered a lodge building that reminded Darcy of a slightly smaller-scale version of Yellowstone National Park's Old Faithful Inn. Following the greeter, they crossed a cavernous high-ceilinged room to a small office occupied by a stern-looking woman of about forty with a sallow complexion.

"Have a seat," she said, beckoning them into a pair of chairs across the desk. "I'll issue you visitor ID tags, which you'll need to wear while you're here. Names, please."

After answering a few more questions, they put the proffered ID cards on cords around their necks. There was no mention of accommodations. James guessed the cheerless woman was the one he'd talked with earlier on the phone.

"I'm afraid Mr. Webb is engaged for the next hour or so. Would you like to wait in the lodge dining room? You can order refreshments, if you like and I'll let him know you're here when he's available."

"What about Brian McKay? He available?" James asked.

The woman pursed her lips. "Hmmm…I'll have to check." She entered a two-digit number in her phone, listened for a few seconds and hung up.

"He's not answering at his cabin. Shall I leave a message?"

"Where's his cabin?" Darcy said.

She gave them directions and they walked to a nearby wooded area where several deluxe-looking one-story log cabins were grouped. They found number 12 easily, ascended the two steps and knocked on the door. No answer.

"Let's wait inside," James said.

They opened the door and began to enter. The interior was neat as a pin, the bed made, Brian's duffle and toiletries all lined up with military precision.

"Must have maid service," Darcy said.

Suddenly Brian appeared from behind the door with a gun in his hand.

"Don't shoot," James said, smiling as he raised his hands above his head.

Brian returned the smile. "Sorry, I heard voices and wasn't expecting you so soon. I just got back here myself."

Darcy hugged her uncle. James reflected that these two were like peas in a pod, but that made sense, as each was the other's only living relative. Brian looked troubled. James knew that he was protective of his niece and that he no doubt did not want her here where she might well be in danger. But

Brian wouldn't try to send her away, either. He valued his niece's intelligence and fortitude; he was not about to insult her by telling her to vamoose while the adults—all men—handled the current challenges.

A man sitting quietly in a chair in the living room rose and said, "Darcy, good to see you again."

Darcy jerked around to see who was speaking. Bill Thorsten stood and greeted her with an affectionate hug. The two had forged a bond the previous year when they'd teamed up with Brian when the dinosaur dig turned into a treacherous experience for the McKays. Brian introduced James and Thorsten, and then they all got down to business.

Brian filled the others in on what he'd seen and heard since arriving. Thorsten was astonished at the report of Brian's eavesdropping on the meeting in the lodge. Thanks to DeRosa, Barry Webb, Brian and perhaps even Thorsten had apparently been set up for hits at the hands of Joe Growney. Brian said he'd been at Webb's house earlier in the afternoon, that a woman was sleeping there, but that he'd seen no sign of Webb.

"Let's go find him," Brian said. "We could take him into protective custody, get him out of harm's way where Growney couldn't easily find him. There's no cell coverage up here, so it'll be hard to communicate if we separate."

"Let's stick together for now," James said. "Where to first?"

"Let's try the meeting room in the lodge," Brian said. "I have a revolver. Bill, I assume you're armed."

"Of course. James, you set?"

"Yep. I checked my weapon on the plane."

"What about me?" Darcy said.

"I know it won't do any good to tell you to wait here," Brian said. "Here, take this." He handed her the mean-looking folding knife Briggs had given him after their dinner in Clarkville.

Brian led the others to the main lodge building and the room where DeRosa's meeting had taken place earlier that day. They saw no one else—the building seemed as deserted as a cemetery.

"Maybe Webb went back to his house," Brian said.

They followed a wooded path to the large home Brian had searched earlier. He rapped loudly on the front door. No answer. He grasped the doorknob. Locked. He wondered if Nancy Northfield had left and locked up.

"Might as well try his next-door neighbor, Mr. DeRosa," Brian said.

As they approached the nearby home, the front door slowly swung open.

Paola, DeRosa's housekeeper stood in the doorway frowning. She looked at Brian and said, "Mr. DeRosa is not here."

On a dirt track in the trees behind the two large houses, Mackie coasted to a stop in a John Deere Gator. He raised a radio to his mouth and murmured, "They're outside your house talking with the Spanish gal. Okay, will do."

59

As Brian and his companions stood just outside the front entry discussing their next move, Lou DeRosa rolled up in a dark red Jeep Rubicon four-door. The older man stepped out of the raised vehicle and smiled at Brian. Paola looked on from the doorway of the house, and then disappeared inside.

Brian made the introductions, after which DeRosa surprised him.

"Okay, I know why you FBI guys are here. Darcy, you are a charming surprise." DeRosa bowed toward her as a Japanese businessman might to an American visitor.

"I think we can all fit into my Jeep. Anyway, It's not a very long drive to the warehouse. I know you gentlemen need to see the export electronics inventory. I'm only too happy to cooperate."

James spoke up. "I'm going to stay here. I'd like to find Mr. Webb and have a word." He glanced at Brian, who nodded agreement.

Brian got in the Jeep at shotgun, with Darcy and Thorsten in the back seat. Having heard DeRosa's conversation with Joe Growney earlier, Brian was glad he had the Smith and Wesson and that Thorsten was along and armed. As to Darcy, he knew that, if anything happened to her on this excursion, he'd regret it for the rest of his life.

DeRosa looked healthier than when he'd last seen the man—clear eyes, rosy cheeks and upright posture. Maybe the mountain air was therapeutic. His safari-style khaki shirt complete with shoulder epaulets was wrinkle-free and spotless. Interesting, too, that the man seemed unperturbed by the presence of Darcy.

As they bumped along a rough two-track heading north, Brian said. "Can we see Barry later then?"

"Sure. We'll catch up with him after the tour. Your friend James will probably be with him."

DeRosa continued at a leisurely pace as the track looped around the developed part of the ranch and headed north. Brian noticed there was a staff housing area composed of the ubiquitous log cabins, though these were smaller than the high-end guest ones like the one where he was staying. As they gained elevation, Brian could see the main lodge building, surrounded by those guest cabins in a clearing among the pines below. Further out, there were new-looking barns, a corral, equipment sheds, tractors, haying equipment, a couple of men at work repairing a corral fence, Paso Fino horses in one pasture and black cows in another. There were miles of seven-strand high-tensile smooth-wire fence indicating the western boundary of the 606 Ranch in the distance. Everything was neat, orderly. Brian was reminded of the Arthur Sands bison ranch near Bone Mountain.

"Is this a dude ranch?" Darcy asked.

"This place is used for company events, but it's also an honest-to-God working cattle ranch."

"About all I know about cattle is they eat grass," Darcy said.

"After your visit here, you'll know enough to pass for a cowgirl," DeRosa said over his shoulder.

Brian had never experienced DeRosa so upbeat, as if he were more proud of the ranch than the company for which he'd toiled his entire adult life. On a hunch, he said, "Lou, you sound like you own the place. Do you have a financial interest?"

DeRosa gazed ahead as he piloted the Jeep. "No, I'm a city boy. What would I do with a place like this?"

After a mile or so, the road became rougher, with rocks embedded in the surface. In a few spots, mud wallows and puddles covered the roadway. DeRosa demonstrated remarkable aplomb as he shifted into four-wheel-drive low while navigating through the muck, never losing traction, even as they sluiced through water deep enough to hold fish. All the while, he kept up a running commentary on their surroundings. Finally, he wheeled the vehicle to a stop at a gray steel-walled building several miles from their starting point. No sign of human existence other than the building, the track leading to it and the nearby perimeter fence. Beyond them, grass and sagebrush gave way to foothills with the Gallatins framing the horizon.

The warehouse was constructed of metal corrugated walls and roof, one large vehicle door, a smaller door for people. There did not appear to be any windows. Before they had a chance to exit the Jeep, the large white warehouse door rolled up, rattling in its tracks. DeRosa jerked in apparent surprise and muttered, "What the—"

A white commercial van, like the one Brian and Thorsten had spotted several days prior from their lookout perch above the ranch, roared out of the warehouse and headed over to the nearby fence. A man got out of the truck and opened a gate. Brian squinted through the Jeep's dusty windshield glass. The guy looked familiar. He drove through the gap, got back out and closed the gate behind him. He shot a glance toward DeRosa and the four visitors before jumping into the truck. He blasted down the road outside the fence, throwing up a rooster tail of dust. Heading south, in the direction of the ranch headquarters. Brian now knew who the driver was: Joe Growney. Brother to Darcy's murdered boyfriend Matthew Growney and the guy DeRosa had apparently charged with eliminating both Barry Webb and Brian himself.

DeRosa shifted the vehicle into park and opened his door. "Hop out, folks. You all can look at the inventory and then we'll go have a drink."

They got out of the Jeep. DeRosa unlocked the smaller warehouse door and shepherded his charges into a large open space. Beefy crosshatched trusses supported a metal roof high above. Fluorescent fixtures hung from the ceiling came on as they entered, the work of a motion sensor. Tall steel racks on both sides of a central aisle held wooden pallets, most empty, a few stacked up with small white cardboard boxes. Thorsten had a computer listing of inventory items attached to a clipboard.

Brian was curious as to whether a load of boxes had just left in the van with Joe Growney. He thought of the notes translated from Arabic that Jake Paulson had shown him at the CPD three days ago.

DeRosa turned to Bill Thorsten. "The export electronics inventory you'll want to observe is stored in that secure cage over there. As you would expect, those MTR100s are small precision parts designed for maximum efficiency and accuracy. Nothing but the finest technology for our Israeli allies. They're packed sixteen to a box." He gestured toward an enclosure constructed of heavy diamond-pattern steel mesh in a corner. The cage contained racks of white cardboard boxes similar to the ones stacked on the nearby pallet outside the cage. "Your printout will tie in with the product descriptions, all of which are on the boxes in inventory item number order. You'll find our perpetual inventory system is bang-on correct. Come on in, everyone."

They trooped into the cage, a cube measuring fifteen feet on each side. Brian noticed the top was covered with the same heavy mesh material as the walls. DeRosa brought up the rear. When they were all in, DeRosa suddenly backed out of the enclosure, grabbed the open door and swung it shut. A metallic noise came as the bolt of an automatic lock snicked home.

Brian grabbed the doorknob and twisted. No dice. They were trapped inside with no way out. He yelled, "Hey, Lou, this's not funny at all."

"Not meant to be. Now, if you folks will excuse me, I have more important matters." He strode toward the exterior doorway, waving a hand above his shoulder. A moment later the door to the outside opened and slammed shut again. The overhead light went off, leaving the vast interior as dark as an undertaker's suit. They heard the Jeep start up and idle outside, as if DeRosa were waiting.

Thorsten pulled his service gun from a holster in the small of his back. Before he could attempt to shoot the door open, they heard a hissing noise coming from the ceiling. Then some sort of gas began to descend on them, barely tangible as an odorless, fog-like emanation from above, slowly drifting over their heads, enveloping them down to the floor.

"What is this stuff?" Darcy said. She began to cough.

Brian answered, "My guess is it's what they call BZ in the military. It's a psychedelic gas. Very powerful. It'll slow us down, maybe knock us out. Fortunately, it will eventually disperse through the mesh of this damned cage."

Thorsten said, "I learned about this stuff at the Academy. It's illegal, but not that hard to get ahold of. Screws up your system pretty bad." He coughed. "Stuff's making me jumpy."

Darcy: "I feel awful. I'm gonna lie down."

Before he could react further, Brian's legs became rubbery and weak. He sank to the concrete floor. Remorse overtook him, even as he struggled to keep calm. His arms and legs began to twitch involuntarily. Why in hell had he dragged Darcy into this mess? Darcy had a whole beautiful life ahead of her—he hoped. He knew she would be a star in the field of paleontology. If they somehow survived this treacherous work of the madman whose life Brian had inadvisably saved, he'd make it up to his niece and his agent friend. *If.*

As his body spasmed, Brian heard Darcy groaning as if in acute pain. He closed his eyes tight. Yellow lights seemed to appear. Reopening his eyes, a blurry, barely focused scene formed on the floor in front of him. A baseball game played by Lilliputians was in progress under miniature ballpark lights. He watched, fascinated, as the tiny pitcher delivered an off-speed pitch to the plate. The batter, clad in a gray road uniform with a script "C" on the chest swung mightily and missed. An appreciative round of cheers emanated from an invisible crowd of miniscule fans. A diminutive runner took a modest lead off second base, as the batter rearranged the crotch of his uniform pants.

Brian heard Thorsten yell out, "Stand back. I'll take care of it." He turned his head in the direction of the voice. In the inky dark, it was impossible to see his friend. When Brian swung his head back in front of him, the ball game had vanished. He knew that one of the effects of exposure to BZ was hallucinations dominating one's field of awareness. Darcy whimpered—God knew what weird scenes were playing out for her.

A few minutes later, after the three visitors had settled into a fitful sleep, DeRosa re-entered the warehouse, unlocked the cage and gathered up the pistols from Brian and Thorsten. He regarded the trio breathing unevenly as they lay on the hard concrete floor, oblivious to his presence. He re-locked the cage and made his way back to the exit door. As he reached it, the motion sensor automatically switched the overhead lights off. A man unable to control a slight tendency for drama, he yelled over his shoulder as he eased the door closed, "*Hasta la vista,* kiddos."

60

Brian dropped into an unsettled sleep finally, but not before undergoing a traumatic series of involuntary body-wrenching impulses, while horror movie scenes played out in his head. He later awoke with a splitting headache, fell asleep again and finally regained consciousness. It was dark as a moonless midnight inside the steel cage. The air was stale, with a faint trace of the debilitating gas. No sound except the uneven breathing of his two companions. His face and head were maddeningly itchy. As he lay on his side on the cold concrete floor, he reached for the revolver he'd had when the gas hit them. Not there. He felt around on the floor. The weapon was gone.

His voice thick and scratchy, he called out, "Anybody awake?"

No reply. Brian knew they needed to get up and out of the steel cage. Their lives might depend on it. No telling what DeRosa planned on doing with them.

Sounding half-asleep, Thorsten spoke. "Why in hell'd you go and save that evil snake's life?"

Brian shrugged, though he knew Thorsten couldn't see him. "Didn't know he was evil at the time. But I had my suspicions. They say, 'keep your friends close, and your enemies closer.'"

"I know that line from somewhere," Thorsten said.

"Yeah, Michael Corleone in *The Godfather*," Brian said. "Though, some attribute it to Sun-tzu, a Chinese general back in 400 B.C."

The sound of epigeal rustling came from nearby as Darcy came to. "Are you guys all right?"

"Yeah, but my damn gun is gone," Thorsten said. "You okay, Darcy?"

"What I am is pissed off," Darcy said.

They sat on the floor and conversed in muted voices for a few minutes. The effects of the gas seemed to be dissipating, but they all felt nervous, jumpy, with itchy skin and an occasional involuntary movement of limbs.

"What time is it?" Thorsten asked, rising to his feet.

Brian checked the luminous hands of his watch. "Around seven p.m."

"No food since the so-called snack on the plane this morning, but I'm not hungry," Darcy said. "Very strange."

Thorsten rummaged around among the cardboard boxes on the shelf near him. "Empty. DeRosa never planned on letting us see anything. Just lured us in here to get us out of the way and gassed us to what—disarm us?"

"Could be," Brian said. "Joe Growney probably took that missing inventory in the van. DeRosa seemed surprised though when he took off as we arrived here. Maybe Joe's gone rogue and DeRosa's chasing after him. In any case, we'd better find a way out of here."

61

After the others left for the warehouse, James made the short walk back to the lodge building. He strolled around on his own, but encountered no one. The reception area was deserted. He made a circuit of the guest cabins, all of them except Brian's locked and apparently empty. He headed to Barry Webb's house to see if the executive had returned.

Just before he arrived, two men, one huge and the other slight, exited the house and, seeing the approaching agent, hustled away, pretty sure they had not been seen.

James rapped on the front door in the way of officers of the law everywhere, long and loud. Silence. He tried once more, longer and louder. Finally, he twisted the doorknob. Unlocked. He entered and stepped onto a vestibule, then ahead into a living room full of high-end furniture, carpeting and artwork. The place had the sterile feel of a rental apartment awaiting the next tenant.

Something else was off, not obvious. Then he realized that his olfactory sense was giving him unsettling news, an intimation of an ominous disturbance. He flashed back to a day early in his career as an FBI agent. A man had died violently on the North Side, and James had been with Brian when they'd come upon the body in the storage area of a closed barroom.

Like then, the air now held the aromatic perfume of rotting fruit.

James drew his gun from his compact belt holster and made sure the safety was clicked off. On the far side of the living room, an arched opening gave onto a formal dining room with plenty of space for ten. There was a framed Mondrian abstract piece on the wall. He gave it a look as he slowly eased by—the damned thing looked like it might be real. With people as rich as Barry Webb, you never knew. He passed into a sizeable kitchen that might have been taken from a posh Brazilian steak house like the one where he'd recently had dinner with Brian and Darcy in Chicago. On he went to the hallway leading to the rear of the building, where he cleared each room without incident. One of the rooms had a rumpled bed, as if someone had slept in it the night before. On to the last closed door. He took a deep breath and pushed the door open, but its inward progress stopped abruptly as it encountered resistance. James put his shoulder to the door and his let his 190 pounds work at moving it in the rest of the way. The disturbing olfactory news was now overwhelming. The unmistakable odor of recent death.

Barry Webb lay on his back, unseeing brown eyes staring up at the ceiling. He might have fallen asleep from sudden fatigue, except that his neck was bent sideways at an impossible angle. An agent with less experience might have thought a freakish accident had occurred, Webb tripping and falling to the carpeted floor. But James knew the more likely scenario: someone very strong had grabbed the man from behind, put him into a lateral vascular neck restraint and then went a step further. The assailant had squeezed his arms tight around Webb's neck and wrenched it sideways with force and speed, snapping the executive's cervical vertebrae like breaking a dry twig. Webb would have died in seconds. The unpleasant odor came from the man's pants—he'd voided his bowels as he died.

James stood still and listened. Silence stretched out like a membrane ready to tear. He went back to the office room and found a phone. He needed to report the crime to the locals at the Geyser County sheriff's office and to his boss at the FBI Chicago Field Office. But the phone line was dead. There was a computer, but it was off. He left the house.

62

The Jeep carried two men as it bounced and juddered along on the rough track toward the warehouse in the far corner of the 606 Ranch. At the wheel, the larger man spoke in a deep voice: "That wasn't so hard. Thought the little fucker would put up more of a fight. Y'know, that guy was the head honcho of the whole damn company." His un-tucked black tee shirt couldn't disguise a belly of hard fat the size of a watermelon. His features were Asian, and he did in fact resemble a clothed sumo wrestler, as Jimmy had described to Brian and Thorsten six days ago on the trail above the ranch.

The smaller man, with a pockmarked face and thinning blond hair, said in a high-pitched whiny voice, "Man, that was cold, the way you grabbed him and wrenched his neck over like snapping a piece of kindling."

"Next stop should be pretty easy, too. Mr. DeRosa said these people'd be out cold and unarmed. Should be nothing to it."

"Yeah, but, if it's such a fuckin' piece a cake, why not do it himself?"

"Dunno. But he's a rich executive kinda guy who don't get his hands dirty, contracts out the wet work to peons like us. We're being paid pretty damned good to do what he says. So let's get 'er done."

"What if they already came to? Could be kinda risky. I heard those guys are FBI agents."

"Look, dude, we can't have the man know we fucked up and let those people get away. We'd lose our jobs. Or hell, he might even kill our ass. Anyway, don't be a pussy. Let's rock and roll."

They approached the entry door cautiously. Sumo drew his pistol and reached for the door handle as Pockmark hung back a couple of steps.

Brian, Darcy and Thorsten listened as they lay on the floor in the dark confines of the metal cage. They'd heard a vehicle pull up and two male voices outside, but couldn't make out the words. They heard jangling keys at the door, and then footsteps as two men entered the dark room. The overhead lights blinked on, bathing the entire space in harsh fluorescent light.

Sumo and Pockmark approached the cage and looked through the diamond-shaped holes in the black steel mesh walling in the three captives. Two men and a younger woman lay sprawled out on the floor, apparently unconscious. Sumo considered firing at them through the holes in the mesh wall, but decided it wouldn't work—the barrel of his gun wouldn't fit through. As he unlocked the cage door, he barked a laugh. "You guys don't look so damned tough. What you look like is fuckin' fish in a barrel."

As Sumo stepped closer, Brian suddenly reached out an arm and grabbed the big man's jeans cuff, yanking as hard as he could.

Sumo yelled, "What the fuck—" He went down in a heap, his Glock clattering to the floor outside the cage as Brian, Thorsten and Darcy sprang to their feet.

Pockmark stood rooted in place, uncertain for a moment. Then he seemed to awaken and began to fumble for the gun still tucked in his waistband.

Back on his feet, Sumo directed a kick at Brian, who rolled away. The massive man's momentum caused him to slip. He fell heavily onto his broad back, cursing like an enraged sailor. Meanwhile, Pockmark regained his wits and grabbed for his own gun. Without hesitating, Brian dove for Sumo's pistol, grabbed it and snapped off a shot at Pockmark from one knee. The bullet missed the smaller attacker, but he froze in place like a deer lit up in a vehicle's headlights.

Sumo scrambled to his feet once again, looming over the others like a huge dark colossus. He ignored his sidekick, who had finally gotten hold of his gun and was edging toward the open cage with it aimed ahead. Sumo seemed to be considering another attack.

Brian aimed the Glock at the muscle-bound man's face. "Don't even start to think about it," he said.

"Fuck you!" Sumo yelled. He came straight at Brian, giving him little choice. Brian pulled the trigger just before the man buried his block of a head in his stomach. Sumo slowed, and then it became a rugby scrum. Sumo pounded a meaty fist against the side of Brian's head while Thorsten fell on the attacker and methodically banged his right fist against the big man's neck. Sumo ignored Thorsten and continued to smash into Brian, alternating hands. Gradually, the big man's movements slowed, like an old clock winding down. He slumped forward onto Brian and lay motionless.

Pockmark had hung back, afraid of accidentally shooting his monstrous partner. Regaining his nerve, he aimed his gun at Brian's head. Before he could fire, Darcy screamed, "No!" and lunged at him with the open Spyderco knife clutched in her right hand. Darcy had always been a little squeamish when it came to knives. She remembered vividly the time her mother nearly cut her own little finger clean off in a bloody misstep with a chef's knife while slicing a flank steak for dinner. Her dad had driven his panicking wife to the emergency room, where they'd used ten stitches to close the wound. Nevertheless, Darcy screwed up her courage and plunged the serrated stainless steel blade deep into the man's stomach and held on as he screamed and jerked his body away from her. He dropped his gun and fell onto his back howling, "I'm fucked! I'm fucked!"

Brian struggled to his feet, his breath coming in ragged gasps. Sumo lay inert, a large red stain emanating from his chest, turning his shirt crimson and quickly creating a pool on the floor next to him. Brian grasped the man's thick wrist, felt for a pulse. It flickered for a few seconds and then there was nothing.

Pockmark lay groaning on the floor, twisting his bent legs back and forth. His eyes looked as messed up as broken marbles. Blood seeped from the wound in his gut. Brian guessed the knife had not severed an artery, but the guy would need medical help, and soon. Darcy looked as shaken as Brian had ever seen her. He tried to imagine what she was feeling, but gave up. He was just grateful to her.

Brian, Darcy and Thorsten made a ragged group, gasping for breath, looking at each other and gradually understanding that they all seemed uninjured.

Darcy suddenly jogged outside to the idling vehicle and located a first-aid kit in the cargo area. She hurried back inside the warehouse and over to the man she'd knifed. With assistance from Thorsten, she taped all the gauze bandages in the first aid kit to Pockmark's gut, where blood oozed steadily through his shirt. The man kept moaning and whining while they worked on him. Brian noticed Darcy's face was red and tears had run down her cheeks. She'd saved her uncle's life. But she'd feel guilt, Brian knew, and there'd be nightmares.

Brian's head still throbbed with dull pain where Sumo had repeatedly hammered him. He slowly eased it back and forth, testing the connection with his neck—it didn't seem likely to fall off anytime soon. "Let's get this guy outside so we can find some help," Brian said. They carefully carried Pockmark out and folded him into the back seat of the Jeep.

Brian and Thorsten now had the two .9 mm Glocks from Sumo and Pockmark, along with full magazines, except for the two rounds that Brian had fired.

"Let's go see Mr. DeRosa and find out what he has to say for himself," Brian said.

"Good plan," Thorsten said.

The threesome climbed aboard the Jeep, Thorsten at the wheel, Brian riding shotgun and Darcy in the back seat with the man she'd wounded. He hadn't stopped moaning since she'd stabbed him, and the noises he made totally unnerved her. Not a religious person, she nevertheless prayed the guy would survive. They set off on the bumpy road leading to ranch headquarters.

63

As they rumbled along, Brian turned over in his mind the events of the last couple of days. They were lucky to be alive. He wondered who all was still around. Chances were, DeRosa and Growney were long gone. Might be some employees. There was Mackie, the woman at the reception desk and the two guys he'd seen working on a fence, probably ranch hands. There was likely a horse wrangler and others involved with taking care of guests, but the guests were probably all gone, and maybe the employees were, too. Then there was Paola, DeRosa's housekeeper from back in Highland Park. He realized he hardly knew the woman. What was she doing here? And what about Barry Webb? Was he safe? Where had Growney gone in the van? Maybe the best course of action would be to get the hell out. But, to Brian, it all depended on what they'd find when they reached ranch headquarters.

It was fully dark now. The sky looked like an exhibit at the Adler planetarium, a twilight-blue inverted bowl of stars. Approaching the cluster of ranch buildings, Thorsten stopped the Jeep and he and Brian got out. They walked ahead on the road thirty yards, to a ledge affording a good view of the sprawling ranch compound about a hundred feet below and a football field's distance ahead. Bright security lights on tall poles illuminated the lodge and the space around it. They scanned the area for movement. Smoke curled from the brick chimney atop the lodge. The temperature had dropped rapidly since they'd left the warehouse. Brian wished he had a fleece to put on over his tee shirt. It was preternaturally quiet. A four-door Jeep Rubicon similar to the vehicle they'd just been aboard was parked out front. Thorsten's and James's vehicles remained where they'd left them. The dozen or so other vehicles that had been present during the Belcoe executive get-together had disappeared from the parking area. Party over.

They returned to the Jeep to find Darcy at the wheel. Pockmark reposed in the back seat, holding his stomach and moaning softly. As they got in, she said, "Anything?"

"Nothing much. Let's roll down there very slowly," Brian said.

Darcy modulated the brake pedal, coasting the vehicle ahead at a walking pace. The windows were down, and they listened and watched intently as they descended a curving incline toward the buildings. Darcy brought the Jeep to a stop just short of the parking area for the main lodge building. Still no signs of life.

"Okay, let's check out the honchos' houses," Brian said. He wondered if the Scotch-drinking double-crossing son-of-a bitch DeRosa would be there. And he was also curious as to whether Paola would be around.

Darcy drove toward the twin mansions nearby.

64

After leaving Brian, Darcy and Bill Thorsten lying unconscious and disarmed on the floor in the warehouse, DeRosa drove back to the main lodge. He and Paola were the only ones there. Joe Growney had taken the van with its load of MTR100s to the Clarkville airport. The two that everyone called Sumo and Pockmark were supposed to check in when they completed their mission at the warehouse. *If* they completed it, he thought. Mackie and the hand named Rick had one last task to complete before leaving the ranch for good. So he had to cool his heels, waiting for the loose ends to be tied up to his satisfaction before leaving to catch the plane.

"Would you like me to prepare you a whiskey?" Paola said.

DeRosa rubbed his face with his hands. "No, thanks."

"Will I have time to catch my flight to Chicago?" she asked.

"Oh, it depends on a few tasks I've got other people doing here. When that's all buttoned up, we'll leave. If you miss your flight you can take the next one."

DeRosa leaned back in the soft leather chair and closed his eyes, signaling the conversation was over. Paola went to the other side of the big room, sat on a couch and began to flip through a magazine.

DeRosa thought about the series of events that brought him to this current pivotal circumstance. That early Sunday morning two and a half weeks ago, he'd been unable to sleep, a not unusual occurrence. He'd gotten out of bed and logged onto the Belcoe network to see what might be new. He'd remotely accessed his own company desktop. Incredibly, someone was using it. He watched with alarm as the intruder opened a spreadsheet file DeRosa had received only the previous Friday afternoon, the file detailing his personal deal with the Syrian ministers. If that information got into the hands of anyone else, the deal would blow up and he'd be open to criminal charges. He remembered vividly tearing down the expressway to the Belcoe building, standing calmly at the security station and chatting with the guard as he always did.

Patting his pockets, he said to the night man, Harry, "Ah hell, I forgot my keycard. You know I'm me, though. Right?" Harry had smiled deferentially. "Sure, Mr. DeRosa." The guard waved him in and didn't even glance at the briefcase containing the Baby Browning .25. After he'd killed Matthew Growney and moved the body to the top floor, he'd breezed out as the lobby guard wished him a good morning. Neither the cops nor Brian McKay seemed to have connected him with the shooting.

Everybody from the FBI to McKay had found out about the accounting games Massey had been playing to pump up the financials and the stock price. Massey was a loose canon. His calling that analyst "asshole" during the earnings conference call had been the final straw. At that point, it was only a matter of time before the investigators dropped the hammer on the financial fraud as well as the illegal Belcoe sales to Syria. That was when he'd decided to implement his plan for escape. He'd triggered the final sale, the one where the proceeds would be paid to himself rather than the company. He'd destroyed the computer file containing the terms of his Syrian deal. Without that, it would be impossible for anyone to glom on to the deal until it was consummated. By then, he'd be long gone.

He'd hired Joe Growney away from his frustrating job as a policeman with an inferiority complex. As he'd told McKay, Joe was his new bodyguard. The man had failed in his role as sniper assigned to take out Barry Webb, but he'd demonstrated a willingness to take lethal action if directed to do so. And Joe had play-acted convincingly with Massey in the CFO's office for McKay's benefit. But today, he'd left the warehouse too soon in the van, forcing DeRosa to improvise, tripping the overhead gas spray himself and disarming the three occupants of the inventory cage.

So here he was, waiting and wondering. When Sumo and Pockmark showed up, he'd take care of them and call Mackie to set the fires. Then, it would be a dash for the Clarkville airport and the first leg of his flight. Paola would drive the rental Suburban to the Bozeman airport to catch her own flight to Chicago.

65

They reached the front door of Webb's house. Brian got out and was about to try the doorknob, when James's voice came from behind.

"He's dead."

"What?" Brian said.

"Somebody snapped his neck. I couldn't call it in, with no cell service and the landline dead."

"Who's still here?" Brian asked.

"Growney drove out toward the highway in a white van a while ago. Saw a jeep with two men in it headed up there where DeRosa took you guys. I was just going to drive to the warehouse to check on you. Haven't seen anyone else. They didn't come back through here. It's been totally quiet."

"Any sign of DeRosa?"

"No. He must be in the wind."

"We left one dead at the warehouse and we've got a wounded guy in that Jeep."

"A lot to report," Thorsten said. "We might as well head down toward Clarkville. We should be able to find a phone at a ranch in the valley somewhere."

"Darcy and I will grab my vehicle and stuff and meet you guys at the lodge," Brian said.

As Thorsten and James rolled away in their vehicles, Brian and Darcy walked to the cabin where he'd spent the previous night, grabbed his duffel and boarded the rental 4Runner. They returned to the parking area near the main lodge, where James and Thorsten sat waiting in their vehicles. Thorsten had transferred the wounded Pockmark to his Tahoe.

The black Suburban they'd seen in the lot earlier now sat empty at the side entrance of the lodge, its motor idling, headlights on. So somebody was still around, after all.

Suddenly, DeRosa heard vehicles pulling up outside. He peered out a window. Thorsten's Tahoe and an Escape were out there. As he watched, Brian's 4Runner pulled in to join them. No sign of the ranch employees, Sumo and Pockmark. They must have fucked up. In a way, he was relieved. He phoned Mackie and said, "Light 'em up."

"Come on, Paola. It's time to leave," he called.

As Brian watched, two people came out through the lodge side door. DeRosa gripped Paola's arm above the elbow, guiding her slowly toward the Suburban. Brian got out of his vehicle and ran toward them.

Brian guessed DeRosa had been waiting to make sure Sumo and Pockmark had taken care of the visitors before leaving for good. Perhaps he meant to surprise the two thugs, killing them as well. As DeRosa reached for the front passenger door, Brian shouted, "Hold it right there."

DeRosa muttered, "Fuck that."

The executive came around the vehicle, desperately clutching Paola about the waist and neck with his beefy arms. He was careful to keep her body between himself and Brian.

"Let her go, Lou," Brian said. "We need to talk, sort things out."

"I don't think so, Brian. You try to stop me, your little girlfriend here dies. Don't think I won't do it." Then, almost as if he were talking to himself, he said, "Too late to stop now."

DeRosa maneuvered Paola around to the driver's door. He kept a hand around her neck, pinning it tightly against his chest as he carefully tugged on the door handle. He backed into the Suburban driver's seat and shoved Paola to the ground as he wedged himself behind the wheel. With the door still open, he hit the gas and the bulky SUV shot forward. The truck roared past the open entry gate and continued on down the rough road below.

As Brian turned to check on Paola, Darcy's voice cut through the chaos: "There's a fire!" She pointed behind Brian toward the interior of the ranch. A cloud of gray smoke emerged from the direction of the Webb and DeRosa homes, and a tongue of orange flame rose above the treetops. The wind was brisk, and Brian figured it would be but a matter of minutes until the two residential buildings were beyond saving.

Brian detected movement coming from the direction of the blaze. An oversized white pickup came into view and moved swiftly toward them on the road, throwing up dirt and showing no sign of slowing down. A security light on a nearby pole illuminated the windshield as they approached. At the wheel, Mackie's face was set grimly in a rictus of adrenaline-induced tension. Another man occupied the driver's seat, a panicky look on his face.

Brian grabbed Paola by the shoulders and pulled her off the road, while Darcy removed herself from harm's way by diving in the other direction. At the edge of the road, Brian raised his pistol. As the truck neared, the driver suddenly cranked the wheel right, apparently aiming for Brian, but succeeding in sending the vehicle into a dusty skid onto the shoulder. He corrected back onto the road, but the unwieldy vehicle, not designed for hasty maneuvers, rocked precariously on its suspension. The tires on the passenger side rose several inches off the road surface. Then the truck crashed back down onto all four tires and began to fishtail back and forth. Finally, it settled into a course of relatively straight-line progress through the gate and down the outside road toward the highway.

A thunderous explosion came from behind them. Sounded like a fuel storage tank exploding. More flames were visible now, climbing high above the ranch buildings. The fire had grown quickly, whipped by a steady southwest wind and fed by the explosion and the flaming buildings. Brian figured the entire ranch was at risk. He hoped to God there was nobody else in there and that the horses and cows were able to get out through the fences. If the blaze wasn't checked by the remaining moisture in the ground, he feared it might well expand onto the neighboring public land.

"Let's get going!" Brian shouted.

Brian and Darcy and boarded the 4Runner. Paola stumbled over to James' vehicle and got in.

James yelled out the window, "The whole fuckin' place is on fire!"

Brian led the way down, with James behind him and Thorsten's Tahoe bringing up the rear. He knew it would be tough to catch the two vehicles that had just left. DeRosa had about a five-minute lead, the big white pickup slightly less. All the vehicles in the little procession were capable. The darkness and steep, twisting nature of the road would favor those most familiar with the route.

Brian pressed the 4Runner's accelerator down and they lurched forward. He moderated his foot on the throttle and quickly got the feel of the SUV's handling abilities as they descended smartly down the twisting route, high beams on. A glance at the rear-view informed him that the vehicles with the two FBI agents aboard were falling behind. He peered ahead and blinked. Where the hell was DeRosa's Suburban and the white truck? The lights of the two vehicles had disappeared, as if they'd dropped into the bowels of the Earth.

66

Brian slowed the vehicle and spoke in the darkness. "Darce, do me a favor and grab my pack from the back seat."

After reaching behind her and retrieving the small pack, she said, "Got it. What do you need?"

"Pair of weird black goggles."

"Man, these *are* weird. What's the camera lens thing on the front for?"

"Night vision. Here, let me have them."

Darcy handed the device to Brian, who took his eyes off the bumpy road for a brief moment, flicked on the power switch, and then lifted the ATN/PVS-7 night vision goggles to his head. Steering with one hand, he managed to push the headband down so it was resting above his ears. Finally, he fixed the flexible twin eyepieces over his eyes. He kept the vehicle rolling steadily and switched the headlights off. It took a moment, but his vision quickly adjusted to the glowing green tunnel-vision view of the road ahead. With the goggles and moonlight, it looked like an overcast day tinted green. Brian was able to make out movement on the road ahead. DeRosa's Suburban and the white pickup moved in tandem, lights out, down through the nightscape.

As they descended, Brian spotted a fork in the road that he hadn't noticed on the way up. DeRosa and his cohorts appeared to have taken the right fork and were on a wider, less steep route below. They had apparently gone off the main roadway in an attempt to elude their pursuers. The SUV and heavy pickup also seemed to have sped up quite a bit. Brian wondered where this route would lead them. In any case, he'd stay on their tail. He cranked the wheel right and headed down the ramp-like roadway. In the rearview, he could see James's headlights as he followed suit. Brian knew he'd never have seen the fork without the night-vision goggles.

The speedometer needle climbed from twenty to thirty as they continued the descent. In the far distance, lights of moving vehicles were visible on a main highway. Brian reckoned it was U.S. 89, the route he'd driven from the town of Clarkville up to the mountain road leading to the ranch. He pressed the accelerator down and they flirted with forty miles an hour. The 4Runner seemed to be gaining on the white pickup, which was almost on the rear bumper of DeRosa's vehicle. Five minutes later, they'd closed to within a hundred yards. Soon, they were approaching the rear end of the pickup. Brian switched on the headlights, revealing the blue Montana "Treasure State" license plate. The truck's dual rear tires kicked up a maelstrom of dirt and bits of rock. A pebble struck the 4Runner's windshield and a hairline crack materialized. Brian pushed on through the detritus, straight at the pickup, which was still running with lights off. The 4Runner's front bumper grazed the rear of the pickup, and then pushed into it with blunt force. Both vehicles began to slew back and forth.

Brian kept on the gas and steered straight on. The driver of the pickup hit the brakes and veered left. The truck careened over a basketball-sized boulder at the side of the road, rose up like a striking rattlesnake, crashed back down and flipped over. It left the road and slid to a stop on its roof on a sagebrush flat. Brian kept going. James came up behind him in the Jeep and continued as well, ignoring the pickup, which remained like a helpless upended turtle. It soon receded from view. Now it was *mano a mano* with DeRosa. Thorsten's headlights were about a half-mile up the road behind them.

The lights of traffic on 89 below were becoming more and more distinct. DeRosa would soon reach the highway. The question was which way would he turn—south toward Yellowstone National Park or north toward Clarkville.

Below, DeRosa switched on his headlights, hung a left and rocketed down the highway toward Clarkville. A few minutes later, Brian was behind him. Traffic was light. The needle of the 4Runner's speedometer worked its way above 100 miles per hour, and yet, he wasn't gaining on the Suburban. He wondered whether DeRosa knew he was after him. If the man checked his mirrors, he'd have to notice that only one vehicle was on his tail.

Brian checked his own rearview—no sign of James or Thorsten's vehicles. He guessed that they'd stopped to phone the Bureau as soon as they hit a rural residence with a landline to report the situation and request backup. Their cell phones had no doubt burned up at the ranch, so they were incommunicado for the time being. In any case, he felt the odds still favored him and Darcy in a matchup with DeRosa. Assuming the older executive didn't have reinforcements up ahead. He wondered where Joe Growney had gone in the commercial van.

67

Brian flew by a few cars and pickups. As he reached the outskirts of town, a McDonalds appeared on the right, along with a green and white sign indicating Billings via I-90. Brian followed in the wake of the Suburban as it bore off to the right and up the onramp to the Interstate. Both vehicles exceeded 100 again as they sped east. Five miles later, DeRosa slowed slightly and got off the Interstate. At the top of the off-ramp, he made a sharp right and lurched up a steep and narrow paved road. Brian noticed a sign reading MILLER FIELD as he followed.

He knew that Miller was the regional airport for the Clarkville area, located on a bench east of town in the shadow of Clarkville Peak. The airport was capable of handling the occasional commercial-sized jet, but, for the most part, the aircraft there were small private prop planes, helicopters and business jets. As he neared the top of the incline, he noticed in the moonlight a herd of pronghorns grazing like gray ghosts in a rancher's irrigated hayfield below the road. The animals eyed him warily as he rolled past, but kept on eating grass. After cresting the rise, the road flattened and curved to the left. Ahead, a small airfield with a modest redbrick terminal building lay on a sprawling parcel of land flat as a tabletop. Security lamps on poles surrounded the terminal, lending it the aspect of a guard station at a border crossing. There was a single paved and floodlight-lit runway about a mile long as well as a couple of smaller grassy ones. No sign of DeRosa's SUV. Brian slowed the 4Runner to a crawl. An ambush was possible.

"He must've pulled around behind the building," Darcy said.

A sleek white twin-engine business jet sat on the runway about fifty yards from the terminal, illuminated in the lights along the tarmac. Brian recognized it as a Gulfstream G500, capable of carrying a dozen passengers at nearly 600 miles per hour for six thousand miles. The purchase price of 45 million dollars limited its market to companies like Belcoe and super-rich individuals. A tall white Mercedes commercial van with no side windows was angled in almost touching the stairway leading to the plane's cabin. Joe Growney stood in the cargo area of the van, lifting cardboard boxes from the floor and handing them up to a man standing on the stairway to the plane. The men moved in a steady rhythm, as if they'd been at it for a while. As the McKays watched from their vehicle, Growney jumped down from the van and moved to the front, where he climbed in. He drove away from the plane a short distance and got out. Then he jogged to the jet and clambered up the stairs into the cabin.

Suddenly, Lou DeRosa came out of the terminal structure, towing a medium-sized black roll-aboard suitcase behind him. If he knew he was being watched, he gave no sign.

Brian and Darcy exited the 4Runner, leaving the doors open. As they neared the terminal building, DeRosa, caught sight of them, turned and gave them a double take, as if realizing for the first time that they'd caught up with him. He abruptly let go of the suitcase and pulled a Mac-10 machine pistol from his coat. He sprayed a quick burst of bullets in the general direction of the McKays, taking out a piece of the corner of the brick structure and sending a cloud of mortar dust onto Brian's and Darcy's heads. They stayed low behind the shelter of the building. Brian figured this was a tactic to pin them down rather than take them out. It worked.

DeRosa then jogged to the airstair, suitcase in one hand, pistol in the other. He was surprisingly dexterous considering his recent infirmity. He made it through the doorway and disappeared inside the cabin. Someone pulled up the airstair and slammed the clamshell door closed into the smooth convex fuselage.

Growney was pumped. He couldn't wait for the plane to get off the ground and on its way to Canada. He would be leaving the soul-crushing grind of a policeman's existence behind and moving on to a life that mopes like his late golden brother could never have imagined. DeRosa had outlined to Growney the details of the MTR100 electronic missile tracking devices the day before: each unit measured three inches square, so sixteen to a box. A unit would sell to the Syrians for 25,000 dollars so each box was worth 400,000 dollars. Three hundred boxes in the van's cargo area added up to a value of 120 million bucks. Growney's cut was to be ten percent, or twelve million. He'd been told that, no matter what, he was not to be stopped for speeding or to crash the van on the way to the airport. And if he got ideas of taking off with the precious cargo, don't bother. There were no markets on Earth that Joe Growney would be able to tap into on his own. And, if he tried, he'd only end up in prison or dead. Made sense to him. He'd managed to get all the boxes into the jet, and now it was show time at last. He wondered what DeRosa's plan was for the pilot. He would find out momentarily.

Brian dashed over to the plane with his Glock raised. He hoped to disable the craft somehow before it could leave the ground. As he drew close, the top of the clamshell door popped open, revealing Lou DeRosa holding a canister of some sort in his right hand. He fired a blast of spray toward Brian. The executive's aim was slightly off, but a fair amount of the vapor reached Brian's face, causing him to choke and close his eyes. He coughed and struggled to breathe as he staggered away from the aircraft and back to the safety of the terminal building. He kept low and half expected to hear another shot come his way from the plane. Instead, he heard the door slamming shut. Darcy raced to his side.

"Are you okay?" she yelled.

Brian rapidly blinked his eyes in an attempt to shed some of the stinging gas. "It's bear spray," he said. "I'm okay, but I hate to see those bastards get away." By that time, Brian's vision was already halfway back to normal. Luckily for him, the pepper spray, commonly used as a self-defense weapon against grizzly bears by hikers in Montana, hadn't fully inundated his eyes. He and Darcy went back to the terminal building as the jet's engines began to rev up.

A hulking olive-drab two-and-a-half-ton military truck with an enormous snow blower mounted on the front was parked nearby, presumably for clearing snow off the runways in winter. Brian raced to it, flung open the driver's door and climbed up behind the wheel. He remembered the starting sequence for the massive 7.8-liter inline six-cylinder diesel engine from his Army days: you had to heat the glow plugs by turning and holding the ignition key for a few seconds. Then you could turn the key farther to start the engine. He did this, and the motor sputtered but did not start. He tried a second time; after combusting intermittently, the engine finally cranked and roared to life.

Brian depressed the clutch and shifted the five-speed into first gear. The lumbering truck trundled forward on its burly tires. He steered it directly at the Gulfstream G500 and shifted into second as he mashed the accelerator to the floor. He caught a glimpse of Darcy cheering him on as he neared the plane's delicately pointed nose. There was a sickening screech of ripping metal as the ponderous truck's spiral-bladed steel snow blower contacted the front of the stationary luxury jet, crumpling the sleek nose on the left side.

Brian figured DeRosa had three choices at that point: Give it up and peacefully get down from the plane, pick up a gun and start shooting or try to somehow get away by using the G500 as a tool, possibly a battering ram in its own right. He was surprised though, at the executive's actual choice. Voices raised in argument came from the closed cabin. Then the sharp report of a handgun. Suddenly, the twin engines revved to a high ear-splitting pitch. Slowly, almost imperceptibly, the aircraft began to creep backward, as if the pilot were testing it to see whether it was ambulatory. It reversed steadily, gathering velocity. Soon, there was a gap of fifty feet, then a hundred. The plane began to move forward and executed a sharp turn to the east, so that it was facing away from the terminal.

"He doesn't really think he can fly that thing. He can't," Darcy said.

"I doubt it. And anyway, he's facing the wrong way, with the wind coming from the west. But he's desperate enough to use it as a weapon," Brian said.

"You're thinking small-scale 9/11?"

"Maybe. I'm not gonna wait to find out."

Brian raised the Glock and aimed it at the G500. The jet continued to lumber through a turn and began moving due east. He sighted carefully and pulled the trigger. The shot was on target. One of the four rear tires emitted a sharp popping noise and went flat as a pricked bladder. Brian aimed and fired a second time, but the round missed the mark. The G500 completed the turn and set off down the runway, picking up speed and bouncing a little as the flat tire revolved on its aluminum wheel. Clearly, DeRosa planned on continuing.

The plane rumbled on. Soon, it reached the end of the runway about a mile away and executed another awkward slow-motion turn so it was facing west, into the prevailing wind and back toward the terminal. Brian stopped in his tracks and watched with interest. The asphalt-paved runway was a little over a mile long, which seemed like barely enough takeoff distance for a plane that size and no flat tires. The jet's twin engines revved loudly in the thin mountain air. The machine began to roll down the runway, swiftly picking up speed.

Inside the cockpit, DeRosa grimaced as he gripped the high-tech digital side stick. He extended the leading edge slats and lowered the trailing edge flaps. He had never flown this particular plane, but he'd had his own small jet years before. Had to sell it to fund alimony payments. Joe Growney occupied the passenger seat next to him, his face an ashen mask. DeRosa raised engine speed near max to offset the drag of the smashed nose, which had slowed the plane significantly. Nothing to be done about the damage. And nothing to be done about the recalcitrant pilot, who now lolled unconscious on the floor behind him and Joe Growney. He'd had to shoot the pilot in the chest and maneuver him out of the control chair when the guy refused to attempt flying the wounded aircraft. The man was still breathing, but looked pretty bad. Unfortunate, but any high-stakes operation incurred collateral casualties.

DeRosa was running out of runway fast. He goosed the throttle to the absolute max and glanced at the gauges.

"You fuckin' trying to kill us?" Growney demanded.

Finally, the nose lifted off, followed by the rest of the craft, and they were airborne. DeRosa retracted the landing gear and put the jet into a gradual banking turn to the right, toward Interstate 90. The Absaroka Mountains loomed like frozen sentinels to the south, their rocky summits crusted with snowfields. The plane wasn't behaving normally, the aerodynamics trashed by the irregular surfaces of the crumpled sheet metal. He'd head south down the Yellowstone River valley, so that McKay and whoever else might be watching would be thrown off, possibly thinking they were en route to Jackson Hole. After a little while, he'd cut back to the north toward a small town just over the border in Canada.

There, another commercial van awaited them at the airport. Growney would offload the goods into the van, and then he would become expendable. DeRosa had arranged sale to Syrian operatives in Canada who would ship the devices to the deputy ministers of their home country, through the Caribbean and then on to Damascus. This was nothing new; it had been going on for weeks now. The big difference from prior sales was that now, payment would go directly to DeRosa instead of to Belcoe. The Syrians liked it because DeRosa offered them a 50% discount. There would be an immediate transfer of funds to one of his several personal accounts in the Caymans. He'd bought a villa on the Mediterranean coast of Morocco near Tangier, just across the Strait of Gibraltar from Spain, and planned on living there in un-extraditable luxury, with plenty of single malt Scotch to drink for the rest of his days on Earth. The Belcoe shrink, 'Doctor' Akbar, a Moroccan native, had come through with the real estate connection via his brother, a Tangier land agent. The flight plan had originally been: short hop to Coutts/Ross airport over the border in Alberta, then on to Montreal for re-fueling. Finally, nonstop to Tangier, a distance easily within the Gulfstream's range. With the wounded jet, the new reality was: get to Canada, transfer the goods, ditch the jet and find an alternative way to his new Moroccan digs.

DeRosa figured Brian and his niece were down there at the Clarkville airport, gazing up to track the plane's route. He felt a twinge of guilt. Brian had saved his life by rescuing him as he lay perilously close to death after being nearly broiled in his own sauna. Though he'd left Brian, Darcy and Thorsten in the locked warehouse cage and directed a pair of thugs try to kill them, he knew the captive trio were more resourceful and intelligent than the thugs. And he'd pepper-sprayed Brian just now, rather than shooting him. A bond had built up between the two men as they'd discussed Belcoe's business and drank whiskey over the past two-plus weeks. He sighed as he maneuvered the compromised craft.

Brian and Darcy craned their necks to follow the G500's progress. The plane shook with alarming vibration as it thundered by over their heads. It seemed to be in the grasp of a magnetic force pulling it down toward the ground. The engines screamed and the craft pointed upward, apparently struggling to gain altitude. As they watched the jet's running lights, they saw it tracking I-90 westward. But it was only about 300 feet above the busy roadway and battling to stay aloft. It abruptly veered to the left, gaining altitude. It was on a course now hugging the edge of the Absaroka Mountains and heading south. It looked as though the awkward aerodynamics of the plane were causing it to swerve toward the mountain walls. The question was: could it straighten out or climb enough to avoid those rocky precipices?

The answer came minutes later. The G500 was just beneath the summit of Clarkville Peak, when it seemed to falter and slow.

"He's gonna crash!" Darcy yelled.

A split-second later, the aircraft slammed into the mountainside. A sharp percussive crack was followed by a burst of flames. Fingers of orange fire immediately surged up from the wreck site, as pine bark beetle-killed lodgepole pines ignited and went up like tinder. Brian and Darcy observed the conflagration wordlessly.

"Guess we'd better call 911." Brian took his niece's arm and they walked into the deserted terminal building. He found a red telephone on a counter top inside, with a sign above it reading, "Emergency phone." After he'd called 911 and talked with the dispatcher in the Geyser County Sheriff's office, they found seats near the door and sat down to wait.

68

They followed a sheriff's deputy to the nondescript two-story City-County building in downtown Clarkville. The Geyser County Sheriff, Jim Reid, interviewed them in a drab gray-walled room within the building. Brian and Darcy knew Reid from the prior summer's adventure at the dinosaur dig. Reid, a young deputy, had taken over as acting sheriff from the murdered Sam Harrison and later been confirmed by the voters in a special election.

James showed up and was ushered in to join them. He reported that he'd called the Bureau on the way from the 606 ranch, as Brian had suspected. Bill Thorsten as well as a pair of Chicago FBI agents arrived shortly after James and commandeered the interview room.

The discussions continued the rest of the night. Responding to questions, Brian walked the agents through the events at the 606 Ranch, concluding with the fiery plane crash in the Yellowstone River valley. Darcy corroborated his account, starting with her arrival at the ranch with James. Food was delivered and a breakfast break was declared.

Brian asked about Paola and was told by an agent that she was being questioned at another location. Brian thought they might charge her as a co-conspirator, despite DeRosa's using her as a human shield. He wondered if she'd been involved in anything illegal, or whether she might have been simply a loyal employee, unaware of DeRosa's greedy and murderous schemes. Brian and Darcy were let go around ten a.m. and went to the venerable Masters Hotel in Clarkville to get some rest. When he went to check in, they told him they had him still in his room from two nights ago.

That afternoon, they awoke to learn that teams of both Federal Aviation Administration and National Transportation Safety Board investigators had descended on the scene of the DeRosa plane crash. A pair of NTSB agents met Brian and Darcy in the lobby of the Masters and guided them back upstairs to a room occupied by the agents. They interviewed the McKays as witnesses to the crash. Brian did most of the talking and confined his answers to the bare facts of what happened at the airport with DeRosa, followed by the crash. He asked about DeRosa and they told him his body, along with those of Joe Growney and the pilot, Max Camden, had been recovered from the mountainside and were being held in the county morgue, pending word from other authorities.

Afterward, they saw on local television news that a preliminary press release from the FAA indicated that the only known casualties of the crash were the three men on board. The on-air reporters said that the FAA labeled the cause of the accident as "structural instability of the aircraft," and that the investigation would continue. Fortunately, winds had been abnormally calm that night, and the fire from the plane crash had been limited to a few acres of forest near the wreck. Likewise, the arson fire at the 606 Ranch had been contained so that only a small area outside the ranch boundary had burned. The relatively snowy and moist ground of the unseasonable cool springtime was damp enough to have helped.

Sheriff Reid remarked to a TV reporter, "A couple of local hikers on the trail above the ranch, Doctor Phil Banham of Clarkville Healthcare and his buddy Jimmy Brownleaf, had seen the fires right away and raced to call 911, greatly limiting the damage." That part of the Custer Gallatin National forest had suffered a major fire incinerating twelve thousand acres in the summer of seven years before, and the mountainous ground was still in the infancy stage of recovery.

That evening, Brian delivered James to the Bozeman airport for his return flight to Chicago. Brian and Darcy had excellent late suppers of pan-seared sirloin steaks served with fries and a red wine bordelaise sauce in the Masters Hotel's restaurant. Carol Jensen and her nephew Jerry joined them, plying the McKays with questions about their recent adventures.

"I'm just glad you two are all right," Carol remarked over coffee. At that moment, her resemblance to her sister Laura struck Brian like an arrow. He touched her arm and said, "I'm glad you're glad."

Jerry shook his head in mock distaste, but his expression belied his affection for his aunt and the two visitors. Brian suspected the boy might have a crush on Darcy.

The next morning, with brilliant blue skies all around the Bozeman area, they flew to Chicago. As the plane reached cruising altitude, Brian looked out the window. The lofty Absaroka Mountains had a layer of white across the higher elevations. A flash of orange caught his eye near the top of a pointed summit to the east. He realized it was Clarkville Peak—the spot where DeRosa's checkered life had been snuffed out. He imagined the accident investigation going on far below: federal investigators within the orange crime scene markers picking through pieces of the doomed aircraft, cataloging them and storing them in zip-close bags for transport to a laboratory. They would, of course, account for the physical aspects of the crash and wreckage. No one would ever know what went through Lou DeRosa's mind during those last few seconds

69

Back in Chicago a few days later, Brian awoke in his apartment, grabbed a bagel and pulled up the Chicago Tribune on his iPad. The business section was dominated by a story on Belcoe Corporation. With the top executives, Barry Webb, Doug Spurgeon and Lou DeRosa dead, the remaining execs had squabbled and elbowed each other in an attempt to ascend to the top position, before a series of indictments against them had been handed down by a Cook County grand jury. Hamilton Massey, Nancy Northfield, Elizabeth Wheaton, Raymond Hunter and Oscar Gutman had been indicted for insider trading. Massey had also been indicted on charges of falsification of financial information. Additional financial crime charges were pending. Belcoe and certain of its executives had also been charged with selling defense articles illegally to hostile nations in violation of the Arms Export Control Act.

The Chicago FBI's White Collar Crime unit lead investigator, James St. Claire, told a Tribune reporter, "This is the most dishonest company and top management in Chicago FBI history."

The Belcoe Board of Directors had sought a "white knight" buyer for the business, but none had surfaced. Once the largest Chicago-based company, Belcoe was now in Chapter 11 bankruptcy. The stock had declined to a penny a share before the SEC stopped trading in it the previous week.

Brian had not received payment from Belcoe beyond the check he'd been handed by DeRosa in the man's luxurious office back at the beginning of the case. He mentally wrote off the unpaid time and richly deserved 'combat pay.' And he was grateful that he, Darcy, James and Bill Thorsten had escaped physically unharmed.

Brian had learned from James that they'd found no survivors and no bodies at the burnt-out 606 Ranch, other than the burned remains of Barry Webb. The two occupants of the white pickup that had flipped onto its roof during the chase down the road below the ranch, Mackie Jones and a ranch hand named Rick Proul, had been seriously injured, but survived. Neither had been wearing a seat belt. A sheriff's deputy noticed the two wore clothing that stunk of gasoline. Turned out, the smell came from the cans they'd emptied onto the houses they'd set aflame at the ranch. They'd been charged with arson and were being held in the Geyser County jail. Burning the ranch had been DeRosa's way of getting rid of the evidence of the murder of Barry Webb, attempted murder of Brian and his companions and DeRosa's theft of military missile systems units to be sold to certain Syrian deputy ministers.

The one mitigating factor for Mackie and Rick was that they had taken the time to open all the gates in the ranch fences, allowing the panicked horses and cows to escape to freedom. In Montana, that fact would serve them well when sentencing was handed down. The animals were later rounded up on Forest Service land by neighbors.

The FBI investigation in Chicago revealed evidence that Lou DeRosa had gunned down Matthew Growney in DeRosa's own office and directed Joe Growney to fire a long-distance shot at Barry Webb. DeRosa had kept the box of .25 caliber ammunition remaining after he loaded the gun he used to kill Matthew. Agents analyzed the chemical composition of the ammo and matched it with the slug removed from Matthew's head. They also viewed security video from the night of Matthew's murder from Sekurit. It showed Lou DeRosa passing through the Belcoe guard station without being required to put his electronic keycard into the card reader. When confronted with the video evidence, the guard on duty admitted that DeRosa told him he'd forgotten his card that night. The guard knew the older executive from many past encounters, so he waved him through and thought nothing more about it.

Joe Growney's apartment contained the Remington M24 rifle he'd employed to send a steel-jacketed bullet at Barry Webb in his 47th floor office from a vacant condo in the John Hancock Center nearly a half mile away. Ballistics testing found a match between the rifle and the bullet they'd extracted from the engineering manual in Webb's office. Spurgeon's death had been ruled a suicide by the Cook County Coroner. As for the accident on Lakeshore Drive involving a wheel flying off of Natalie Katz's car, Darcy told a local TV reporter on air that she was pretty sure it had been an attempt to stifle a woman who wouldn't be silenced. Brian was pretty sure she was right.

Barry Webb's remains had been salvaged from his burned-out house on the 606 Ranch and buried in a well-attended ceremony on the suburban North Shore. The Belcoe founder had been eulogized as a visionary. The business press had been less kind: Webb was seen as being dominated by DeRosa and his illegal machinations—Brian knew it was a lot more complicated, and he felt sorry that Webb had been so badly used and then murdered by his supposed friend and long-time business partner. A Montana-based filmmaker was working on a documentary about the business partnership and intertwined lives of Lou DeRosa and Barry Webb, culminating with the recent horrific events at the 606 Ranch and the nearby mountainside plane crash.

Darcy had returned to her studies at the University of Illinois more determined than ever to obtain perfect grades as a prelude to her senior year and planned graduate program in paleontology. She said she was now leaning toward Montana

State University for graduate school. Brian mused that Darcy would someday be nipping at the top dinosaur experts' heels.

Brian had not had contact with Paola Chavez or Mary Edwards since he'd returned from Montana. He and Michelle's romantic relationship seemed to be getting back on track.

One lovely May morning, his phone rang. He picked up and heard a familiar voice with the slight drawl of the Rocky Mountains. Carol Jensen in Clarkville, Montana. She'd been following the Belcoe story in the press. She remarked that, between Bone Mountain and the 606, the McKays had faced a cat's nine lives worth of danger in Montana. She said, "Jerry and I hope to see you out here again soon...without the usual drama."

"I'll be out, maybe this summer," he said.

After he hung up, he realized he had overdue personal matters to take care of. He decided to keep the beard he'd left unattended since departing for Montana. But maybe he'd break down and finally get a haircut. That would work well for his planned dinner with Michelle that evening.

That afternoon, a package arrived at Brian's apartment via UPS Ground, a cardboard box with no return address. He slit the tape and extracted a rectangular foam container. Inside, he found a bottle of Laphroaig 25-year-old Scotch whiskey. There was a small envelope. He read the hand-written message: "Brian, no matter what happens in the end, drink a toast to yourself." It was signed simply, "Lou."

Brian stripped the lead wrapper from the top of the bottle and tugged out the cork. He walked over to the kitchen sink and poured the amber liquid down the drain. He was not about to drink a stone cold murderer's liquor. But the idea of a toast appealed. He drew a glass of Chicago tap water and considered Lou DeRosa's final words for a moment. Then he raised the glass to his lips and drank it off. "Here's to a new life."

ACKNOWLEDGEMENTS

Dirty Money is a story that arose from my familiarity with American corporations both as an employee and as an outside contractor of financial services. My experience was greatly enhanced over the years by the lore and guidance provided by Raymond Powers, a top executive of a company for which he and I both once toiled. The support and wise counsel from nonfiction writer nonpareil Arthur Plotnik proved invaluable as I set out to tell this story of wacky fictitious events. The murders and other crimes in *Dirty Money* are made up.

Once again, I owe the highest degree of gratitude to my soul mate and reader of many drafts, Sally, who provided endless help in getting the manuscript of *Dirty Money* into proper form. Fellow writers and loyal supporters in the Livingston workshop writers group came through as always, reading, critiquing and improving *Dirty Money* with their special brand of expertise.

And heartfelt thanks to you for reading this second novel of the Brian and Darcy McKay series of thrillers. I hope you enjoyed *Dirty Money*. The third installment of the series is underway.

To learn more about Brian and Darcy McKay and other stories of mine, please stop by my website: robertdhughesauthor.com

ABOUT THE AUTHOR

Robert D. Hughes is the award-winning author of *Bone Mountain*, first in the series of thrillers starring Brian and Darcy McKay. His short stories of crime and mystery have appeared in numerous anthologies and magazines—see the anthologies published by Elm Books (elm-books.com): *Death and the Detective* and *Death and a Cup of Tea*. He earned an MBA from the University of Michigan. As a financial professional in Chicago, Bob investigated white-collar crime, bringing several embezzlers to justice. He has a special affinity for the works of Lee Child, Michael Connelly and John Sandford. An Active Member of the Mystery Writers of America, he lives in Livingston, Montana.

www.ingramcontent.com/pod-product-compliance
Lightning Source LLC
Chambersburg PA
CBHW031935110726
47902CB00001B/190